To Andrea

In Love, Light,
Laughter, Joy &
FUN

Jeanné

All That Matters

Channeled by
Jean Gerson-Greer
For Mind Lucius, I-O & Co.

...the Light that is shining through us...

BALBOA.
PRESS
A DIVISION OF HAY HOUSE

ISBN: 978-1-4525-5722-9 (sc)
ISBN: 978-1-4525-5723-6 (hc)
ISBN: 978-1-4525-5721-2 (e)

Library of Congress Control Number: 2012915133

Balboa Press books may be ordered through booksellers or by contacting:

Balboa Press
A Division of Hay House
1663 Liberty Drive
Bloomington, IN 47403
www.balboapress.com
1-(877) 407-4847

Because of the dynamic nature of the Internet, any web addresses or links contained in this book may have changed since publication and may no longer be valid. The views expressed in this work are solely those of the author and do not necessarily reflect the views of the publisher, and the publisher hereby disclaims any responsibility for them.

The author of this book does not dispense medical advice or prescribe the use of any technique as a form of treatment for physical, emotional, or medical problems without the advice of a physician, either directly or indirectly. The intent of the author is only to offer information of a general nature to help you in your quest for emotional and spiritual well-being. In the event you use any of the information in this book for yourself, which is your constitutional right, the author and the publisher assume no responsibility for your actions.

Any people depicted in stock imagery provided by Thinkstock are models, and such images are being used for illustrative purposes only.
Certain stock imagery © Thinkstock.

Printed in the United States of America

Balboa Press rev. date: 8/30/2012

This book is dedicated to all of livingness, everywhere. With special thanks to my wonderful editor, Marjorie Wheaton.

Contents

How It All Began

Once upon a time, many years ago, I remember hearing my parents say, "All that matters is that..." This expression took hold of me and became the watchwords of my life. All that matters is that she is healthy. All that matters is that no one gets hurt. All that matters is that you behave, use your common sense, and get good grades. All that matters is that you rest, relax, and have a good time. All that matters is that you finish school and make something of yourself. All that matters is that you take pride in what you are doing, what you have done, and what you are going to do. All that matters is that you find love and happiness in this cockeyed world.

I followed that "All that matters . . . " advice and achieved what I thought was right for me. I went to school and even continued my education receiving a PhD in Philosophy and one in Physical Science (not so opposing ideologies, by the way), studying at well-known and respected universities across our great country. I met and married the man of my dreams while in my very early thirties. He was also a respected scientist. Unfortunately, we never brought any children to term. Of course, this did depress us terribly, but I remembered, "All That Matters . . ." and we were then able to work through the depression of losses. We became so engrossed in our own work, traveling the length and breadth of the world as the needs arose, we pushed all thoughts of progeny aside to work for what our generation called, The Greater Whole.

We each became complete workaholics and tried, at the same time, to do the right things for our bodies as well as our minds and, we thought, for all of living-kind. "All That Matters . . ." became our united watch phrase. This went on for twenty-three years. Then everything changed.

I want to say he died, but in reality, only our relationship did that. The divorce was as most divorces are, ugly and terrible to live through, even though it was not difficult to divide our property. It was just the dredging up of long-buried times and events that were so horribly filled with shifting the blame as a constant. It was never a question of money, or even support. We both had earned well, and written well, with volumes sold scholastically and internationally. Prior to our divorce, I had been forced to not only observe, but hold the hands of many of our friends who had gone through the same thing, and when it was my turn, they welcomed me with open arms and I found comfort and solace in their company.

Before I realized it, I was an avid member of this clique of people, women, mostly, who had been dumped when their spouses reached that age of male menopause where they sought comfort, solace, and love from younger, more lithe people. What amazed many of us was that we too, were still lively and extremely active, running marathons, going to gyms, and keeping our forty-five to sixtyish appearances as young as humanly possible. We did all that while going through hormonal changes with real physiological symptoms very difficult not only to describe, as each person reacts differently, but devastating to our own emotional beings. Yet we never stopped seeking information, new ideas, and just plain old fun. And we all tried our damnedest not to let this take us over and ruin us and our relationships. But none of this was enough for the men we married or lived with for so long. Not even re-enacting the Kama Sutra satisfied their avid needs for the "younger set." We finally decided they wanted people who knew very little of the world in actuality, or in general. They wanted to begin again as though they too, were young and just starting out in their adult lives. They wanted to teach and mold, and chose only those so willing to be taught and molded. Once again, I thought "All That Matters . . ." is that I come out of this with some peace of mind, some sense of decency, and some of what was owed me for putting up with this stupidity at this time in my life.

Now, to be fair to you, I had better fill you in a little more. I am a Caucasian woman who could easily take early retirement from academia and the rest of this silliness, should she so desire, but I, Emma Epstein, by name (named after Emma Lazarus—my parents loved alliteration . . . or maybe it was for Emma Peel, as my Dad loved 'The Avengers'), am not like that. I do not like to retreat. I am a searcher, researcher and, in my own way a fighter. And speaking of fighting, I am not a featherweight either. More a cross between a welterweight and a middleweight even though I exercise, eat right, etc. I had often told my mother she birthed me at 110 pounds, since her side of the family

3

consisted of petite people. It was my father's family I took after: the Russian peasant stock side.

I tried for years to play the American game of looking "younger" dying my hair to hide the gray. Sometimes, I had blonde streaks, sometimes changed it all to the reddish-brown hues, but finally gave up because my travels and my work schedules often prevented me from going to my local salon, or any other, for that matter. I also found I liked my salt and pepper appearance. And he liked it too, at least for a while. But as I said, that all came to an end with the divorce.

After the ugliness had settled, I cut back the following semester on my classes, finished my latest book without my editor moving in with me and then took hold of myself once more. Leaving my hair out of it (since the dye never took for longer than a week around the face, and constant touch-ups were time consuming, costly, and boring) I began seriously working out every morning from 6:00 AM to 7:30 AM, seven days a week, walked everywhere I could, and cut out any kind of "bad" food. Okay, once in a while I cheated. Who doesn't! But I did lose the taste for ice cream and other overly sweet things, and switched to whole everything products, all the while reading labels as assiduously as I prepared my research and subsequent reports.

And before I go any further, I must tell you this is most definitely not a "women's" story or a philosophical book or an attempt at expiation. This is a story of the continuing survival of a human being—me, and through me, many, many others. This is a story about what can happen when one makes up one's mind to charge through all the muck and mire heaped not only personally on one, but on the entire world as well.

Exactly two years after the divorce, I knew I needed and deserved a vacation from work—all kinds of work, and luckily, a free one came my way. I did not hesitate to apply for a well-earned, year-long sabbatical which was unbelievably and immediately granted by the administration. I felt as though I was being watched over by a Guardian Angel for the first time in a very long time. I had been fortunate enough to have had three research assistants during my time in academia, and John, the only single one, jumped at the chance to take over where I had left off, not only in the research itself, but in traveling to prove the research. Now all I needed was to firm up this free offer lovingly provided to me by Harry Jonathan Spruce, one of the three divorced men in our clique who had become a stalwart and close compatriot to me when I was so desperately in need of companionship.

HJS, as I called him, had an old family place near the shores of Northern Maine, "not quite near anything and not far from anything," as he described it. It was mine for the asking for as long as I wanted to stay there. There was a caretaker and his wife who tended the place and did the lawn, chopped firewood, etc. HJS hadn't been up there in a few years as it reminded him of his spouse and yet, as this was family property and cousins were involved somewhere down the line, he couldn't sell it either. He described it as a place where I could find out who I was now, and work on what "All that matters . . ." really meant at this time in my life. Had it been a credible way to exist, or was it just a cop-out so one didn't have to investigate any further? I had big doubts about everything I could remember going through, and needed a place far away from everyone and everything in order to regroup, and this was just the ticket!

Accepting HJS's offer, I figured the simplest thing to do was to close up my apartment, buy a new laptop devoid of my scholastic work and anything else except email of course, pack everything I could think of in the way of clothes for all sorts of weather, as it was mid September, having spent much of the first month of my sabbatical going to theatre, concerts, and museums. And since I did intend a long stay, possibly even into the winter, I decided to leave all dressy things home—okay, except for one dressy outfit just in case—all I had to do was fill up the car and head north. All of this was accomplished in a moderately short time, and very early on a Thursday morning to avoid weekend travelers, I set out with great anticipation.

Having become a member of the gadget generation, I had a long term rental on a car equipped with the latest GPS finder and every other sort of equipment except a DVD screen. No children. Books had always been my favorite non-human friends, and I had packed quite a few of those and could always find others on-line or at a local library, even though HJS swore no place was very near or very far. Oh, and being the quirky but kindly sort of person he was, he had alerted the caretakers I would be arriving, and asked that the place be stocked with foodstuffs. He even provided a list of some of my favorite foods, and when I questioned him about a refrigerator with adequate freezer space, told me not to worry as there was even a separate freezer apart from the one attached to the fridge, because he always stocked up on coffee ice cream—once the bane of my existence.

He sort of led me to believe this place was slightly more advanced than a log cabin, but the more he talked about it, the more I understood it to be an advanced cottage with all the accoutrements required for modern living. What decided me on definitely going there was that I would not have to run to use an outhouse! I never was a great one for extreme camping sites for long-term use, and as long as there were logs I could build a fire against any chilly weather. And what was more enticing, HJS swore I would fall in love with the place and have the delightful peace and quiet I so longed for. But as I drove north, following the directions he had assiduously written out for me and that I programmed into my GPS, there was something about the way he said "peace and quiet" that gave me a strange feeling in my gut I could not quite identify.

As I said, he was a quirky person who had easily accepted his divorced style of living and seemed to need no one to take care of him or share his life in an intimate manner. We of our clique adored him but found him to be extremely odd in many ways, and could not put our collective fingers on what it was with him. He is a six foot tall, well built guy, who worked out assiduously, and was a workaholic, often being in his Wall Street office as early as six o'clock, and sometimes not leaving until ten o'clock at night, or so he said. He adored the company of women and loved teasing them, but stated without hesitation that he had sworn off sex and therefore serious dating. None of us believed him! There were too many times when he either reneged or wasn't available to meet us for an evening of fun and games, or dinner and the movies. We all felt he needed us to assure him that his masculinity and virility were still intact. But what was this strange feeling in my gut? Could Harry Jonathan Spruce really be trusted? Did he tell me the whole truth and nothing but the truth, or was there something he didn't tell me? Should I be prepared for the worst or the best? Well, I needed to ruminate and this did give me food for thought as I drove along the now quiet interstate, having left the heavy incoming city traffic far behind.

The Hounds Tooth Inn

The drive up was lovely. I stopped as needed and became a tourist, switching from the Interstate to US Route 1 and 1A, following the shoreline of New England with all the quaint and lovely spots where one could find marvelous food, easy parking, walk, shop, and even find a place to stay the night without any hassle. To hell with his directions! This was my time and I was already enjoying every minute. Before I realized it, I had spent nearly four days just enjoying myself, driving slowly throughout the region in a completely different capacity from any work-related issues and found, to my great delight, that New England was a marvelously magnificent part of this country not to be missed. It was one to be cherished as much as any other National Treasure, because so much of it had remained unchanged. The people had done everything possible, even in the more economically depressed areas, to keep their townships and historic sites clean and well-kempt, and their inns and motels in pristine order. And what was even more wonderful was the scenery! The Atlantic Ocean on one side, and the lush vegetation and gardens around homes and between towns lending their beautiful colors to the late September sky, still a brilliant blue with the sun blazing but not overly hot.

On the morning of the fifth day, after having veered away from the shoreline and back towards my initial destination, I awoke with a feeling of great agitation throughout my entire being. I was shaking so much I had trouble holding my toothbrush. After a quick call or two to find out if everyone was OK back home, I took a few very deep breaths, sat on the edge of the bed and began to cry and cry. The sobs racked me even further, but at least the shaking had stopped.

As I allowed this to pass through me, a light dawned in my brain. I had never cried after the divorce, even though it was two years ago now. I had never cried for me, for him, for our life together, for our joined families or for our joint work. I was a stalwart, and nothing penetrated, perhaps because I was not only used to being the stronger, but because I was too angry. I was still so God-damned angry, and over the ensuing years I had not even allowed myself to consider this. But now, I had no choice. Out came everything, pouring through me like Niagara Falls.

I was in a small hotel on Cape Ann, Massachusetts, with a room at the back where, thank God, no one could hear me, and after a hurried breakfast, wended my way back to Interstate 95, and drove hurriedly into Maine until the sun was almost ready to set. I had to switch from I-95 to Route 15 in order to reach the nearest larger town, Jonesport, before I collapsed. I had suddenly become very sleepy, cranky, and hungry all at the same time.

Maybe this was just a result of the morning's crying jag, or the fact that I'd been driving with only two short breaks for the past seven hours. I knew from HJS's directions that I had about forty-five minutes to an hour to go. He had shown me the shortcuts to reach Cutler, Maine, via a very circuitous route along the wonderfully craggy shoreline, that would lead me to my final destination.

I would love to tell you that for unknown reasons there was not a room to be had at any local inn, but that was not the case. It was almost as though I was expected at the quaint Hounds Tooth Inn, established circa 1850, where, as soon as I pulled in, a young man came out to the car, took the luggage I was reaching for, and almost carried all of us inside as the sun set with a brilliant pink and golden glow in the West.

Now, I have traveled near and far, and even though I am often impressed by my surroundings, I almost staggered when I entered this inn. Everything seemed to date from the mid to late 1800s. I half expected the innkeeper's wife or daughter to arrive at the desk in a long dress with a tight bodice and a cap on her head covering her hair, but allowing flirtatious ringlets to peak through around her peaches and cream complexion. Instead, as I approached the desk, I walked through a magnificently decorated early 1800s hallway full of beautifully carved wood, a settee, and five ornate but comfortable-looking chairs carved in what seemed to be ebony. With two crystal chandeliers with cups for candles providing light, I reached the beautifully carved desk that matched the chairs, and was greeted by two cats who leapt as one onto the desk. One was a large, barrel-chested shiny black male with what one could easily call a fox face, and the other a creamy latte-colored female with sable points on her ears and tail, similar to a Siamese, but not quite, as there were brilliant white boots and stockings going up all four legs and blending easily into the sable coloring with all colors blending into her

11

creamy main color. She also had an exquisitely shaped white bib and as I peered further, her underbelly too, was white. The three of us just looked at each other for what seemed like ages, none of us moving an inch. There was no way anyone could have mistaken the sex of each feline. Not only did their sizes differentiate their sexuality, their demeanors did too. The black male looked as though all he needed was a tool belt and the female kept tilting her head from side to side while she studied me. I didn't even dare put out a hand to see if they were friendly. We just held each other's stares as all time and space seemed to disappear.

"Excuse me, Miss, will you be staying long, and do you require a meal?" It was the young man who broke the spell, and all three of us turned to look in his direction.

"A meal would be lovely," I answered, "and I really only intend to stay the night. I am just traveling to the Cutler area, but I've been driving since early today."

"Not a problem, Miss. Please wait. I will get Mother and take your things upstairs." He whisked my belongings quickly away and just as he left the ornate hall area, a woman, seemingly in her mid forties or perhaps early to mid fifties (even though she didn't look a day over forty) appeared wearing, thank goodness, normal, modern dress. All the while the cats stayed on the counter, purring, and looking at me, longingly. Even before she spoke, I realized something was very strange here besides the cats. The young man did not have a Maine accent, and I knew she wouldn't either. In fact, he didn't have any sort of regionalism in his speech at all. Were they displaced people who got tired of big city life somewhere and relocated here? Possibly!

"Welcome to the Hounds Tooth Inn, Miss. Please sign our guest register even though your stay will not be long," she said. I just looked at her in amazement. "I've excellent hearing," she laughed, picking up on my dismay. "And yes, we are not originally from here." Could she read minds too? "But enough about us, you must be tired and hungry. Jess will show you to your room so you can freshen up. Your room is the last one on the right. And then please come back downstairs and go right through this entryway and join us all in the dining room. We will be delighted to wait for you, Miss....Ah, Dr. Epstein," she said turning the register towards her. Before I left, she added, "The felines have certainly taken a shine to you, Dr. Epstein. Usually they stay far away from newcomers! You must be someone very special," she added with a broad smile. "Oh, and you can call me Terry," she said. I responded with, "And please call me Emma, Terry, and thank you," I added hastily departing for my room and a quick wash and brush-up.

As I hurried after Jess down the long hall to the last door on the right, that strange feeling of unease crept back full force into my mind and body, so much that I didn't even pay attention to the hallway itself, or the number of doors, or the fact the two felines were following me. I was right behind him as he opened the door, nodded to me, and left me standing there, without waiting for me to give him a tip.

Just as I was about to step into a very spacious and airy looking room, I felt a tail on either side of each of my legs precede me into the room. That one action from these cats reminded me of the two Siamese from "Lady and the Tramp" but without any sinister connotations and

I began to giggle—always a wonderful tension reliever. A hurried look around showed me there was a full bathroom in this corner room and a look inside assured me it was private. Hurriedly, I freshened up, reapplied lipstick, and reentered the room. The cats had ensconced themselves on the bed and were curled up watching me. "Well, you two beauties, I've no idea if you're hungry or not, but I am. Are you going to stay or follow me?" I said reaching for my shoulder bag and heading towards the door. "Yeow!" was their joint response as I opened the door and stepped into the hallway. Just as I was about to close the door on them, the black one jumped from the bed almost to the door, nearly eight feet in length, flicked his tail high and marched down the hallway. The other slowly and with great elegance, followed suit allowing me to close and double lock the door. As I did so the scent of roasted chicken wafted up and without further hesitation, and still without looking carefully at the hallway, I went searching for the source of the aroma. All that mattered was that I be fed.

The dining room was a quick right off the entry hallway and like the hallway, it looked as though it had been transported from two and a half centuries earlier. It was neither garish nor overly plain, but exceedingly roomy and comfortably appealing, with two gaslight style chandeliers hanging equidistant from the middle of the room over a massive oak table. That looked as though it could easily seat twenty people and still allow for plenty of elbow room. The number of guests proved my supposition to a tee!

"Now, just you hurry up and sit down," Terry said, jumping up and ushering me to an empty chair on her right. "We saved the seat of honor for you tonight, Emma, and now that you're here," she continued assisting me into my seat as though I were a venerable individual, "We can all say Grace and begin eating." Obediently, everyone bowed their heads as Terry did the honors, followed by a series of "Amen's" as the door to the kitchen opened and two people came in with trays full of soup.

I gratefully accepted mine and after glancing at our hostess, dug right in to a creamy mushroom soup so fragrant it was obviously not from a can. Fresh scallions were gingerly sprinkled on top with a sprig of parsley floating in the middle. Half a bowl later, I stopped and, sated for the moment, looked around at the others gathered at the table. As I was formulating questions in my mind, Terry touched my wrist and introduced me. "Everyone, this is Emma. Emma, this is everyone. Of course you've met my son Jess, and these lovely folks are with a bus tour just stopping for the night as you are doing." I must have looked startled at the 17 other people sitting there because none of them seemed to be partnered with each other—a group of singles—I immediately thought, on some sort of outing throughout New England. But what confused me was there were not enough rooms for them all. "They are staying in the other wing," Jess chimed in gleefully seeing my look of amazement. "It's at the back of the house and can't be seen unless you walk 'round the place. We figured it was added on about the early 1900s and accommodates easily twenty people without having to share rooms. We think this was always some sort of hotel or seafarers' residence, it bein' right on the water," he added with just a twinge of the Down East accent in his voice.

"How interesting," was all I had the time to get out as the main course was being served and my stomach began to rumble again. The other guests had been talking quietly among themselves until the main course arrived. Then, they too, hungrily ate the succulent roasted chicken with four different sides of vegetables and a separate platter filled with seasoned boiled new potatoes prepared, I guessed for any vegans or vegetarians, and with seconds easily available, we all quieted down to fulfill our main desire, sustenance. When desert was brought out—home-made apple pies fresh from the oven and a choice of coffees and teas, the conversation again picked up and the two cats joined us, licking their lips as though they too, had just finished their dinners. Quite sated, the other guests all nodded and thanked Terry as they hurriedly made their way outside in what looked like one mass group tied together in ways unknown to the rest of us. I could not take my eyes off of this mass exodus and I guess my jaw dropped slightly.

"They are a strange bunch, is right, Emma. They come here every year at this time or at least the group leader does, as this has become a regular stop on their early fall trip," Terry whispered in my direction while Jess and the other staff members cleared the table. "We look forward to the business, but do find them rather odd."

"Are they American? They were so very quiet, I wasn't quite sure as I could only catch a small word or two and thought I heard some French phrases mixed in."

"You probably did. I believe they all hale from the northwest border region. They seem a close knit group, not very socially oriented," she added. "And what is more, they take their time and wend their way to Boston, stay for a few days and then return the same way they came, so we get them twice! But we do know in advance as to any dietary restrictions and food allergies among them. Better safe than sorry, is our motto here. Forgive me, I didn't even check those things out with you. I figured we had a goodly selection of foods and you could easily pick and choose." I nodded my thanks to this thoughtful woman, just as the two cats jumped in my lap at the same time and tried curling up to get comfortable. "Emma, I swear to you I've never seen them do that to anyone else. As I said before, they've really taken a liking to you and that is highly unusual."

"Where did you find these two, Terry?"

"They seemed to just come with the place. They must really be ancient as we've had the Inn on and off for ten years now and believe it or not, they do wander away for a time and always return. We were told by the veterinarian who gives them their yearly check-up and boosters that they are in remarkably great health."

"Did the vet have any idea of their age? Had he ever seen them before, or are there records of them anywhere in town?" Terry looked at me as though I were crazy, but I continued plugging away. "Did the previous owners tell you anything about them?"

"They appeared right after we arrived, and we got the place sight unseen except for pictures on the realtor's website. And don't worry, we did have them checked out then too, and were told they were in fine health and looked well taken care of. As a matter of fact, we posted 'Found' ads all around town, but no one claimed them, so they just became a fixture when they are here. But enough about them; what time do you plan to leave in the morning, Emma? I want you to leave on a full stomach!" She said with a chuckle.

"Oh, about nine-ish, I should think." "Well, breakfast will be ready for you any time when you come down. The tour bus leaves at seven in the morning, and I hope they do not disturb you," she added as she stood to take her leave. I thought there was something else she was not telling me about the felines but I let it drop. These two felines knew her and she knew them.

I stood also, but before I went upstairs, I wandered around outside to get a breath of clean, fresh air, and to take a good look at the place. Of course, I went around back and saw the addition which did look newer than the Hounds Tooth Inn itself, so I gathered that the information I had been fed about it was correct. In fact, it looked as though it had been transported from somewhere else and deposited right where it stood.

It was a two story building with two entrances and a covered walkway leading to the main building and did look spacious enough to house twenty people without overcrowding. Next to each regular-sized window, was a smaller one and I surmised each room also now had a private bathroom attached, or at least a bathroom shared only by one other person. After satisfying my curiosity, I continued my walk around the circumference of the Inn, went in the front door, and climbed the stairs to my assigned room through the hallway. Turn of the century sconces with electric lights in them were spaced evenly by each door. I hadn't noticed them before probably because I felt I had to rush to dinner. They were lovely and their light glowed against the burgundy colored walls white trim around each doorway.

I put the key in the lock, turned it twice to double unlock it, opened the door and to my shock, there were the cats, happily ensconced on the bed. "How did you two get in here? Did Terry let you in or can you walk through walls?" I asked them looking around to see if anything was disturbed besides the bed cover. Nothing was. All was as I had left it. Suitcase closed and locked, bathroom door ajar. The cats said nothing. Not even a meow. They just lifted their lovely heads, yawned as cats do, and looked right back at me. After finding my night shirt and clean underwear, getting things ready for an early start, setting the alarm on my watch and putting it on the nightstand, I put my other necessities in the bathroom. and went to the door. "Ok, you two. This is your last chance. You either leave now, so you can have your own creature comforts, or you are here for the night. Which is it going to be?" I said opening the door wide for them. Neither feline moved. I went to the bed, sat down on it and scratched them both on their lovely heads and necks reminding me of another reason why we had two hands. The purrs were thunderous but they stayed right in place. Even slight pushes did no good! "All right," I said, as I arose, closed, and locked the door, "Looks like we are going to be roommates for the night! I hope your people are used to this sort of behavior from you—or do you pay no attention to the hand that feeds you?" I said as I changed and then brushed my teeth and removed what little make up I had been wearing lately.

As I crawled onto the bed between my new roommates, a great weariness hit me straight between the eyes. I barely had the energy to find a comfortable position while trying not to disturb the felines, as they too, seemed to be drifting off into the Land of Nod. With a great sigh, I managed to put both legs under the covers, punch the pillows to suit me, and curl up. Sleep came instantly.

Mirror, Mirror On The Wall

I awoke with felines curled by my arms. The black one was on the right side and the latte-colored one on my left. Each had a paw resting gently on my arm as though holding on to me. Not really wanting to move, I turned on my side. They obliged me by shifting so that the Siamese type nestled against my back and the black one was resting along the length of my now outstretched arm.

I reached toward the night table with my outstretched arm feeling for my watch. I had set the alarm for 7:00 AM, but as it had not gone off, I thought it must have been much earlier. The watch was not there. Thinking the animals had knocked it to the floor during the night I pushed myself towards the edge of the bed, hung my arm down, and felt around the rug. Nothing was on the floor. Not even my slippers. Still full of sleep, I thought maybe I had the room reversed. After all, I had been spending my nights in a variety of hotels, motels, and inns, and maybe my sense memory had become confused, so I turned over, dislodging the other cat and repeated the exercise. Nothing was there. Figuring I was in the middle of a very bad dream, I shut my eyes again trying to regain sleep. It wouldn't come. After squirming around for a while, the only choice was to get up and find out what was going on.

"Okay, you two," I murmured throwing my legs over the side of the bed. "Let's see what's cooking!" I had one cat on each side of me as I groggily attempted to stand up. When I achieved this feat, they both jumped down and followed me as I went first towards the window. Drawing the sheer curtains aside, I looked out over a vast waterway. I had no memory of seeing water from the evening before, and I thought the curtains had been heavier, with the ability to block out the morning light. I dimly remembered the windows faced north and west. This one definitely faced east as the sun was rising.

"No. I must be mistaken, right, cats?"

They responded with chirrups.

"All right, what's happening? Where are my slippers for one thing and my watch? Did you knock them under the bed?" I said as I returned to the bed and on all fours, took a good long look under the mattress with the cats following my outstretched arms while playing with my hands as they too, crawled under the bed to play the game they thought I was playing.

As I righted myself, something struck me as stranger still. The underside of the bed had wires strung across it north to south and east to west. It was definitely not the box spring I noticed last night. And the mattress felt different too, as I used it to pull myself in an upright position. Grabbing the bed linens and pulling them back, the mattress was comprised of two flimsy thin ones; piled one atop the other and the stitching did not look as though any modern machine had made them.

I went to the door I remembered led to the bathroom. It was a water cabinet! Not the pristine bathroom I used the evening before. Hurriedly, I splashed water on my face from the ewer, ripped off my nightshirt and hurried into my clothes from the evening before.

My ever watchful companions seemed to have their eyes glued to my every move, and as I put my clothes on, each piece changed from what I'd worn yesterday to something from the turn of the century—and not the recent millennium century either! As I turned towards the door, a beautiful standing mirror drew me to look at myself carefully. My hair was gathered on top of my head and I had bangs and soft tendrils surrounding my face. The garment I was wearing was a middle-weight dress designed for horseback riding. A riding crop and pair of gloves were on a table by the exit door. Still shaking my head, I absently picked them up, opened the door, and, with my two feline companions, left the room.

The corridor was the same as the evening before, with the sconces in place and the walls a burgundy-hued color with white paint around each door frame. I didn't stop to see if it was paint or paper but I found the stairs and bounded down them as fast as I could in my current get-up. Once down, the entire entry way had become not a reception area, but a vast rectangular space with a beautiful, round, green marble table on which sat an Etruscan vase filled with large Calla Lilies. On the tabletop a small silver tray rested as though left there to receive announcements and mail. There were few chairs in evidence, but there was one long bench that looked as though a person was supposed to sit there and remove his or her boots or wet shoes. This bench was just to the right of the door and on the floor underneath it I could see a woven mat that seemed to have been rolled up for that purpose in order to save the beautifully maintained beige marble floors. On a closer look, a bootjack was placed to its far side out of the immediate sightline of anyone exiting the building.

Just as I was getting my bearings, I heard a disembodied voice from my not too distant past. I turned in its direction. There, standing before me, was Harry Jonathan Spruce, or rather a younger version of the very same, sporting sideburns, a moustache, and small beard around his chin. He was also dressed in the traditional riding habit of that day. "A very good day, and a top-o'-the mornin' to ya, dearest Emma. I do hope you slept well and have found everythin' to your likin'," he said with a strong Irish accent, as he came toward me from the hallway on the right. He walked right up to me, took my right hand in his, and began kissing it.

"I'm fine and thank you." I responded with very little enthusiasm, but a great deal of confusion. My brain felt like mush, and images kept going in and out with the two of us and the girls at our usual local haunts in the city, getting smashed, and the morning I was experiencing thus far. My confusion was added to by the sudden noisy rumbling of my stomach. After all, breakfast was long over due to my way of thinking, always having been an early riser.

"Did I miss Le Petit Dejeuner?" I asked, having no idea where either the French language or the French accent and intonation came from, as he adoringly held onto my hand, stroking it tenderly.

"Why, not at all, Emma. In fact I was awaitin' your arrival to partake meself, before headin' out for our mornin' ride!" He tucked my hand through his now bent

24

arm and led me down the hallway on my left towards where I remembered the dining room to be.

I allowed myself to be guided into the dining room which had not changed one iota, except that the table did seem slightly smaller, but I thought that was because there were only two place settings in evidence. There was a bevy of servants waiting to seat us and tend to what seemed to be our every whim. As I was assisted with my chair, Harry spoke to no one in particular. "Madam will have shirred eggs, toast with marmalade, and coffee. I will have my usual. Please see to it immediately!" He almost barked that last sentence, while I swallowed my bile. I detest marmalade and if that was the only spread available, I would rather eat my toast dry. Besides, I had a hankering for a Croissant, now that I was beginning to feel the full flavor of my being French in at least one part of my mind, and the thought that someone was ordering for me caused the bile to rise again in my empty stomach.

What was going on here! Where was I? Why was all this happening? These thoughts and more crossed my mind, but as soon as the eggs were put before me, I thought, all that matters is that I eat, and quickly, before I do become ill in public. So I set to the task before me and as a second cup of coffee was being poured, found myself slathering my toast with marmalade and loving it. Weird! Harry, meanwhile, had kippers, eggs, bacon, a few other items I did not recognize, and several cups of coffee. He gobbled them down without so much as a "how-de-do" to anyone, or even casting an eye in my direction.

As soon as the meal was over Harry stood up, came around the table to my chair, assisted me gently to my feet, and guided me back to the foyer. Another servant presented himself immediately, and opened the door for us. Two grooms could be seen holding two beautiful horses by the reins. One horse had a step-stool contraption on the left side of the animal and the saddle had a strange looking protuberance which I remembered was a leg hitch used for sidesaddle riding.

Without any conversation at all, Harry walked me to the step-stool and assisted me up as I put my leg over the leaping pommel and squared myself securely in my seat. He nodded to the groom and I was handed the reins. I was slightly taken aback at that, as I was sure this form of Harry would take the reins himself and lead me around like a child. But he did not, nor did I see the groom attach a tether to the bridle for that purpose.

I figured two could play this game, and as he was mounting and fiddling with his stirrups, I silently urged my mount forward with a tap of my heel and flick of the crop. Off we went at a brisk canter that I quickly forced into a hearty gallop. He was just picking up his reins as we flew like the wind.

I had no idea where I was going but it didn't seem to matter. The horse knew. Was this the usual morning game? I barely had time to think about it or even look at the scenery that flew by because I was really uncomfortable riding sidesaddle. In my work I had ridden through rough country many times but always either in an English or Western style saddle, and often bareback. This was completely new to me and my balance felt off. However, something was guiding me because I was able to hold on and still keep up the pace, and I even chanced to look back. Harry was nowhere in sight and something made me feel extremely delighted with this feat, so much so, I slowed us down to a trot and finally to a much more comfortable walk.

I finally had a chance to really look around me. We were not near the ocean, but I could hear it in the distance and smell salt air mixed with the sweet scent of new grass. I turned us around and began to follow the sound of rolling waves just to make sure I was still in the very same place I had driven to the evening before. I was. There in the distance was what I took to be The Hounds Tooth Inn, but this time it was definitely a private home of relatively palatial (to my way of thinking) proportions.

It had a lovely portico with the flavor of a southern plantation about it, as though the owner wanted everyone to know his or her importance in the community. The building itself was comprised of large stones, reminiscent of fieldstones and, although it was set back almost a half a mile from the ocean, I could understand the idea of these stones being used as a breakfront in case of extreme tidal surges.

What got me though, was when I went to mount my trusty steed, I did not remember hearing the ocean or smelling the salt air. Was I going in and out of dimensions and times and places? Had I inadvertently been injured? Was I hallucinating?

No answers came to me. It was then and there I decided to just allow whatever was going on to do its thing. I would no longer rebel in my mind. I would accept and go with the flow as the kids (my students) used to say.

A great sigh escaped me and I felt my body relaxing at last. The need to flee was gone. Curiosity took over.

I gave a gentle "cluck" to the horse, he fell into a canter, and, giving him his head, he took me home. Upon our arrival, two grooms approached, assisted me down, and led the horse away to be cooled down and watered. Still feeling like Alice in Wonderland, I went up the steps of the portico. The door opened instantly but no one was there except the two cats.

I started moving towards the stairs, but they herded me to the bench and in a matter of seconds a man appeared (obviously from behind the now closed door) helped remove my boots and slid my feet into the cutest shoes with small curved heels, that had buttons going up to the ankles. Then and only then did the felines move towards the stairs. I figured they were my current guides to this insane life, and as the man nodded his head and bowed to me, I followed the pair dutifully. When I reached the end of the hall, I reached for the last door on my right, but it wasn't there. Instead I was forced to take about twenty paces back as a door was opened by a young woman in a maid's uniform. Ok, I realized I was still not taking all of this too well, no matter what my recent resolve had been. I admit it. But what the hell! I could see this game through to whatever the finish was if I kept my wits about me.

I nodded to her, handed her my crop and gloves and strode purposely into the room, followed of course, by my companions. "I will bathe now, Marie and as we may have guests later, please put out my Nile green dress," I said upon entering.

"Oui, Madame," Marie responded as she helped me to undo my riding clothes. "When I have finished, I will want to speak with Master Harry. Please notify his man of this. We will meet in the drawing room." God! Was I bossy!

A warm bath was drawn for me full of bubbles and lovely scented soaps. And being slightly sore, I luxuriated in it for a while. After toweling off and exiting this bathroom, I was assisted into my underpinnings, the Nile green dress, more gown-like than dress-like and another pair of shoes with those cute heels, large matching bows but no buttons. I walked around the room for a while to get a feel for these clothes as I still felt as though jeans and a cotton tee shirt, and sneakers or flats, were more to my liking and my 'old' character. There was a fireplace on the wall opposite my canopy bed and a beautiful chaise longue positioned near the window so that one could rest and look outside.

While I was parading around the room, the felines were also busy bathing and grooming themselves, too. They then settled in the sun patches that streamed in through the very large oriel windows. They did not move as I sat to allow Marie to help me with my hair and accessories. She presented me with a large jewelry case from which I immediately extracted a magnificent emerald and seed pearl pendent on a finely made, but relatively heavy gold chain, and earrings to match. When the necklace was securely attached, I stood up, turned around, and there, off to my left side was the long oval mirror—the very same one that had been in my other room upon awakening. I arose, straightened myself out, and strode towards the mirror.

29

I could not take my eyes from the mirror. I was magnificent! Stately, statuesque exquisitely gowned and attired. I had never looked like this in my entire life! Not that I was dowdy by any means, but there is something a period dress does to one's physical form that really cannot be beat. I could not take my eyes from myself. I had never been one to dawdle in front of a mirror—okay, when I got married in full regalia, that was different. But this! This was incredible. As I stood there admiring me, I heard purrs coming from each side of my feet. I looked down and could have sworn the cats were giving their not-so-silent nods of approval to me and my appearance.

I jerked myself away from the mirror, stepped back, and made ready to leave the room. Marie, who had been delivering my message to Harry's man opened the door, curtseyed slightly, and told me Master Harry would meet me before tea.

Once again I entered the hallway and immediately looked around to see if it had changed again. Of course it had. The wall opposite my door was now full of windows with terraces looking out over a magnificently designed garden, which seemed to stretch endlessly north and south, but then, directly past the road that led to this manor house, I could see the shimmering sea. I walked over to the windows with the French doors and opened them. The sounds of children laughing could be heard from somewhere nearby. Stepping out onto the terrace I looked around to see if I could see them. Nothing. No one was in sight, yet the voices sounded directly in front and I thought, probably below me.

My curiosity aroused even more, I headed for the staircase. It was still in the same area, but on the right-hand wall was another mirror. This one was hexagonal in shape and seemed to be free-hanging. As I walked towards it, I saw myself change yet again. My hair was now flecked with grey and the dress had changed from Nile green to Lilac. The pendant was no longer emerald but a beautiful pear shaped eight-carat, African Amethyst with five mine-cut, two-carat diamonds surrounding it.

One part of me wanted to go downstairs to see what else was different or if anyone was there at all besides the cats and me, but the other part of me wanted only to retreat to my room, lock the door, crawl under the covers and put the pillow over my head. Just as I had decided to do the latter, I looked again and there I was, without any grey, and in the Nile green dress with the emerald pendant. Without waiting another second, I almost took the steps two at a time, although the dress did make that a rather difficult feat, so I ran down instead, just like a child on her first outing.

Thank goodness, everything downstairs was the same except for the flowers. The vase had changed to a Ming vase and the flowers were yellow and red roses instead of Calla Lilies. I hurried to the door, threw it open, and stood listening for the voices of children. Silence was the only thing that met my ears. Not even a bird or the hum of insects was in evidence. Shutting the door, I turned and went down the right hand corridor. The one from which Harry had entered that morning.

"Hello? Is anyone there," I called. There was no response. I even looked around for my faithful house companions, but they too, were gone. The corridor seemed to go on and on, but there were no doors to open. Quickly, I ran back the way I had come and there, on the right-hand wall of the entryway, was the same mirror I had seen by the upstairs landing. I was drawn to it again.

I crept stealthily to the mirror, crouching down low so as to approach it without its seeing me first. I don't know why I felt I had to do it this way. I just had very strong feelings I did not want it to see me coming. And I didn't want to see myself changing. I had done enough of that already. Ducking as low as I could in my present get-up (yes, the dress was still Nile green) I circumvented the direct gaze of the mirror. Coming right up to it, I slowly straightened my body to a full standing position and looked. I was as I had remembered myself to be and what was more; I was dressed in Levi's and a Nile green tunic length tee shirt. The Ming vase was still there but this time on the counter, not on a marble table and the flooring was again wood. Turning around hurriedly, I realized the bench and the bootjack were also gone as were the few chairs I had seen that morning. But there was something heavy in my hand. I didn't even look down to see what it was. With my heart pounding and perspiration beginning to soak through me, I hurled it at the mirror which shattered, and before I could understand what I was doing, my feet carried me upstairs to the fourth door on the right. I threw it open. There I was in the very same bedroom I had entered the night before and I was sleeping with the felines on either side of me. The only thing I remember was the scream. Darkness fell.

Reawakening

I slowly opened my eyes to see Terry and Jess standing over me. I felt a cold compress on my forehead and Terry was holding my wrist taking my pulse. There was no Marie present and the room looked orderly, utilitarian, and neat, but not turn-of-the-century comfortable. I began focusing. The felines were still on the bed but sitting up in that wonderfully regal Bast position, one on each side of my frozen feet. The black male even looked like a direct descendent of that regal Goddess. Realizing how cold my feet actually were, I began to shiver uncontrollably. The felines pressed themselves closer to my lower extremities and that did make me smile.

Looking in the faces of my hostess and her son, I noticed only worry and great consternation. Terry whispered something to Jess who left the room. She then pulled up the chair, and reaching for my hand again, sat next to me. She said nothing for a while, but busied herself changing the compress and having seen me shiver she went to the dresser, opened the bottom drawer brought out another blanket with which to cover me.

Quietly, she finally spoke as Jess returned with a steaming mug of hot chocolate. "Well, this is a fine way for you to begin the remainder of your trip, Emma. Do you know we found you slumped in the hallway all dressed and ready to go on with your adventure? And my goodness do you have powerful lungs! It's a good thing the group had already departed. Otherwise you may have scared them to death!" Terry said, not half as somberly as I expected. Jess handed her the mug and she, lifting my head off the pillows, cradled my head and neck so I could I could begin sipping. "I had Jess add extra sugar to the cocoa. Seems you went into shock. Do you have any idea what happened?"

As I sipped, I quickly stole a sly glance at her and noticed a strange look pass over her face. "Do you recall anything, Dr. Epstein?" Jess said suddenly, breaking my concentration. He spoke with such a grave sense of reverence, I looked at him wide-eyed. "Oh, forgive me, Doctor," he said in response to my look, "But last night I Googled you out of curiosity and, Wow! You blew me away! What haven't you done? All that travel. All those people! All those papers and books! And almost a Pulitzer!" he gushed.

Despite myself, I laughed. "Almost doesn't count, Jess. But all that is not really important. It is what was expected and what I wanted to do, and you too, can do the very same if you put your mind to it," I responded.

"Well, it's a good thing you found your voice, Emma. We were about to call the town Doctor to come to see you!" Terry said, also with a smile. "Now, can you tell us what happened?" Feeling warmer and with my blood sugar rising and strength returning to me, I sat up with Terry's help and held the cocoa myself, warming my hands on the large mug. I knew I needed to talk this out but wasn't quite sure I should do it with these folks. An unusual reticence over took me. "I'm not quite sure," I began slowly allowing my mind to sift through my experience so I would know what I could say and what I couldn't.

"Did you wake up and the room was different? And when you dressed, you were in different clothes from the ones you were traveling with? Is that it?" Jess said with an unsuppressed eagerness in his young voice.

"Why, yes. That's exactly what happened, Jess. How did you know?"

Terry placed her hand on her son's arm. "Emma, we want you to know you are not the first person who has experienced this phenomenon when using this room. It has happened two times before that we are aware of, and always seems to end this way—a horrendous scream and a guest in shock, passed out in the hallway." Terry, who had been speaking, put her wrist on my forehead to see if my temperature was returning to normal. It was. Even I could feel my body returning to normal, but my curiosity was peaked. "We have heard over the past two years the most interesting stories, and that started us thinking and researching this place in earnest, but we couldn't find out much more than I told you last night. Can you add anything? Could you start at the beginning, after Jess brings you some breakfast, of course, and you feel even stronger? Would you be willing to share your experience with us? And we would like to tape record it, if you don't mind too much."

I nodded as I pulled myself out of bed, petted the ever-present felines, and headed to the bathroom to put myself in order. I was still dressed in jeans and the Nile green tunic top according to my reflection in the bathroom mirror. I used the facilities, washed my face, brushed my gritty teeth and hair, and then bent over the bathtub. The towel hanging there was damp. It smelled of a soap laced with Lavender, not the soap now in the bathroom or the tub. I smelled both carefully. I knew this was from my "experience," and a new awareness dawned on me. This newly heightened awareness made me suddenly very wary again of my hostess and her son. Tape my recollections, indeed!

I had to leave the bathroom. There was no other means of escape. The window was too small and there were no other doors. With trepidation, I began to turn the door knob, but then stopped. What was I afraid of? Why didn't I feel I could trust Terry or Jess? After all, they looked as frightened as two people could look at the sight of a guest in great trouble. "You are just being silly and stupid." I muttered to myself as I continued my action and opened the door.

Everything was as I had left it. The same room, the same cup of cocoa on the bedside table, and the same two felines watching me exit the bathroom. As I entered the room, the black cat jumped off the bed and wound himself around my legs one time. Then he pressed himself gently against my left side and guided me toward the bed. The cream-colored and white one moved over so I could sit and lean back. She then gently stepped on my stomach, looking to see if I was objecting or in discomfort. When she realized I was fine, she curled up on my abdomen, purring wildly, and giving me the extra warmth I still needed. "Why, thank you two." I said stroking the cream-colored one as the black one jumped up to place himself beside me. Once again, the use of two hands became evident. Their purring and my petting lulled me into a comfortable state of warmth and safety.

"How silly of me to be afraid," I heard myself say from far away, as my hands continued their work, scratching behind their ears and gently rubbing the silky fur. I felt as though I was going to nod off and did not want that to happen again. So I stopped my hypnotic stroking, much to the disgruntlement of the felines, both of whom pressed closer to me if that was possible and butted me with their heads. "Oh, you two wily beasts!" I said to them laughing and forcing myself into a straight-backed sitting position.

"Are you two the cause of this 'experience' I've had? Are you witches in disguise? Is that why there seems to be no record of your existence at the vet's before you moved in here?" The thought of asking these questions made me giggle, and talking to the cats as I was doing made me giggle even more, but instead of being alarmed at my verbalized thoughts, I felt somewhat better. But I still needed to regain control of my entire being.

Taking a few deep breaths, I settled back, closed my eyes, and regulated my body and mind into a meditative state. I pictured a giant candle floating in front of me. As I breathed in and out, I saw the candle becoming smaller and smaller until it had only a miniscule flame. This flame, I placed gently in my heart and mind and opened my eyes. Just as I returned from my little trip, as I called such a meditation, there was a knock on the door.

"Come in," I said, and Terry entered with a bed tray full of juice, bacon and eggs, toast and coffee.

"I thought you would be ready for some sustenance," she said shooing the cats and placing the tray around my thighs. Helping to undo the napkin and pouring the coffee, she watched as I hungrily devoured as much as I could and washed everything down with a wonderful cup of now perfectly temperate coffee. When I finished, she removed the tray after placing a hand on my shoulder.

"I think you should still stay quiet for a little while longer, Emma. At least until the food digests. Your destination is really only a short distance away and you could be there before this evening, if you feel up to traveling, that is."

I didn't know how to answer her, so I said nothing. I merely nodded. "Now, if you feel stronger, do you think you could just tell me what went on? I have the tape recorder right here, just for posterity's sake?"

"Ok, Terry, but I'm curious. You said this had happened to a few guests before today. Did they tape record their experiences, too?"

"Yes, it did, Emma and yes, they agreed to tell what happened on tape." She paused and looked carefully at me for a few moments. "I feel you don't trust me, Emma. Am I right? Of course, we don't know each other and trust does come with knowing another person, so I do understand. But whatever you went through seemed to have been traumatic for you and sometimes, speaking it aloud can ease the stress, you know."

Instead of speaking, I pushed back the covers, put my feet on the floor, slipped into my shoes, and stood up. I walked over to my suitcase, made sure everything was in place, strode into the bathroom and collected my personal belongings, added them to my overnight case, zipped everything up and with it in hand, headed to the door. Before I opened it, I turned to her, saw my watch, put down the case, went to retrieve it, and put it in my pocket.

"I'm sorry, but I have no idea why you want this information. I do not speak on tape unless I am giving a lecture that will then be sent out as needed or used as needed, and you're right. I don't trust you. But that is not your fault. Trust is a difficult thing for me to build up today. I don't know why, but it is. Maybe it's because I feel uneasy about everything that has been going on here, whether it was the 'experience' or these cats or your group from last evening. I don't know. That's just the way I feel."

"Understood. I'll come downstairs with you," she said, putting the recorder back in her pocket and rising also.

"Thank you, Terry, for understanding. Maybe one day I will be able to write this down for you and, as I have the address, mail it to you for your collection." I said this with a big grin and she smiled also.

The four of us exited and went down the stairs without any further discussion. I stopped at the desk and drew out my credit card. "There is no charge, Emma," she said. "We, or rather, this place, gave you a hard enough time, so please accept your brief stay as 'on the house'."

I thanked her graciously, petted the cats, who, once again were sitting on the counter and walked out the door. I no sooner closed the door behind me when I heard a loud "thump" against it. I opened it up and both cats were staring at me, longingly. I bent down to pet them and again thank them for being with me, but they would have none of that. They avoided my hands and instead, they both came out, side by side and accompanied me to my car.

I opened the door to throw my purse inside and as I stowed my case in the trunk, I looked back at the door, which I had inadvertently left open. Terry was behind the counter and Jess was approaching the door. "What do I do now?" I called to them. "Could you please come and get these furry beasts?" I looked at them both smiling at me in my present predicament. I bent down again and reached for the animals, managing to grab each under the belly. Holding them as securely as I could, I headed back to the Inn. "You guys live here, and I'm just visiting the area," I said to them as we neared the door. "I am not set up to . . ." I was about to say, take care of you, when both of them began squirming and pushing against me with such force, but no claws, I was forced to let them go. Instead of heading into the Inn, they turned, swished their tails, and walked to my car.

"Looks like they adopted you, Dr. Epstein!" Jess called out as I went back to try to get them again. "Feel free. They are, so they can go wherever they want and if they want you, they're yours!"

Needing more than anything to get away, I opened the driver's side door and got in. So did the felines. They jumped into the back seat, sat like statues just for a moment, and then joined me in front. I had nothing for them, and I had mentally made a note to stop at a grocery on the way, just as Terry and Jess came out of the Inn carrying two large shopping bags and a litter pan. I popped the trunk so they could add these supplies to my suitcases, waited for everything to be put to rights back there and for the trunk to be closed, turned on the ignition and gave the car some food of its own.

I started down the drive away from The Hounds Tooth Inn, and signaled to make a left turn. The car stopped dead. For the next few minutes, I did everything possible to start it up again with the two felines just looking from me to the hood and back again. At last, fearing I had somehow flooded the engine, I just sat there, frustration building all around me, when I heard, "Somethin' wrong with the vehicle, Doctor?" I looked over my shoulder at Jess, who had a weird sort of grin on his face. "Maybe, you're out of juice!" he added coming forward and leaning in through my open window. "Nope. The gauge reads full. Wonder what it could be?" he mused more to himself than to me, as he walked around the car, opened the passenger side door, shooed the cats in the back and got in.

"Do ye' want me to give it a try?" he asked with his hand ready to assist with the ignition. "Maybe if ye' switch seats with me, I can get a feel of what's agoin' on with this here machine. I got a way with them, ye' know," he said proudly, his Down East accent becoming thicker with each word. "Sure," I said as I got out of the car and switched sides with him. No sooner had I entered the passenger side seat, he turned the key, gently pushed the gas pedal down and the car started. "Must'a' overflowed it, Doctor," he said as he exited the car and I slid over, thanking him profusely for his masculine prowess.

Keeping the pressure gently on the gas, I put the car in drive and continued for about a block, when the damn thing stalled again. The two felines, who had remained in the back seat, howled in what I thought was a protest to this entire procedure. And again, before I knew it, there was Jess standing by the driver's side of the car, shaking his head.

"Looks like yer not supposed to leave yet, Doctor, "he said, this time laughing out loud.

"What's going on here, Jess? Come on. Be straight with me," I said, looking him squarely between the eyes as I got out of the car.

"Cain't say, Doctor. Not unless I look under the hood. Meybe a loose wire or plug. But tell ye' what. You put it in reverse and I'll push it back up the drive so as I can look at it in the proper way. Okay?"

There being no alternative, I did as he suggested and with him pushing, backed up until we were at the beginning of the driveway. Then, wanting to gun the engine, and not caring if I ran him over, I put the car in drive while he pushed us up to the parking area.

"Pop the trunk, Doctor, and I'll take the stuff out, "he said.

"Why is that necessary, Jess, if you're only going to look under the hood? Do you think you can find the trouble or should I call for a tow?" I countered, wanting more than anything to be rid of the place.

"Well, I was thinkin' if ye do need a tow, it would be easier to take the stuff out now. That's all, Doctor, unless you think I should look first and then we decide from there."

"That's the more adult way to do it, Jess," I said getting out of the car after popping the hood and peering over his shoulder as he began fiddling with the wires and plugs. Little did he know I was not a novice in this area and had dealt with breakdowns in many out of the way places in this world. I let him play around for a few moments and then gently nudged him out of the way and with a quick twist of my wrist tightened the distributor cap and reseated the spark plugs. Everything was just slightly awry. I thanked him as I forcefully moved him away, closed

42

the hood, jumped in the car, and started it. It purred as I fed it gas, and I sped away. In my haste to get out of there, I had completely forgotten about the cats. I stopped for just a moment with the windows fully opened. They quickly and quietly jumped into the front seat with me, curled up, and went to sleep. As their breathing deepened my subconscious quieted too. Animals always react to whatever is going on around them and as these two, who chose me for the time being as their person, were showing me, we were free of whatever it was we had encountered.

The rest of the drive, all 45 minutes of it was uneventful and easy. I even stopped at a market along the way to buy some supplies including batteries, an LED wide-beam flashlight, extra coffee, and some cake. I had a great craving for sweets but I by-passed the wonderful array of cookies and candies and even ice cream. After having checked the bags in the trunk I also picked up some cat food. Only dried food had been given me and I thought a treat was in order. Besides as healthy as these two looked with their shining eyes and great coats, they were ever so slightly lean.

I took a few moments to memorize the rest of the directions HJS had given me from the market through the two little hamlets to his house. Upon pulling up to the driveway, I realized this was not just a house, but more like a Manor in the good old British tradition. Loads of grounds and a huge garden all well kept and manicured. The house itself, although not overly large was beautifully constructed. No mere summer place was this. It too, was not far from the Atlantic, and I was sure the surf could be heard on a windy day. The architecture was strictly Victorian and even had the perennial Widow's Walk. For a moment I felt as though I was about to play a part in "The Ghost and Mrs. Muir," one of my favorite books and films of my childhood. Yes, I even liked the television series being a pushover for real romances as my marriage had proven to me. Driving up to the house brought a unique sense of calm I hadn't felt before. It was as though the previous twenty-four hours had never existed except for the advent of my two traveling companions who still were curled up in the front seat, taking turns at napping so that one of them always had his or her eyes on me.

The French Blue House
With The White Trim

I had had pets growing up in the city. When I returned from college and moved out on my own, I decided not to get a dog and be tied down to walks in inclement weather or having to rush home to walk the animal before going out, or in between classes, etc. Instead I had opted for cats and had two lovely creatures until it was their time to pass over, which happened in the middle of my marriage. I think they really decided to leave because my husband barely tolerated them no matter what they did or did not do to please or displease him. Ah, if we would only listen to those we think are pets. They are really better judges of human nature than we, with our overbearing and mixed-up emotional systems. Listen to your pets and watch their reactions to your friends and sometimes even your family!

I parked right in front of the house, opened the passenger door and the cats, after stretching, and yawning for a few moments, got out, went to the front door and waited while I began emptying the trunk. Of course, they were most interested in the foodstuffs I had just purchased and kept stretching themselves up to look in the bags. Searching my overly big purse for the keys proved to be easy. For reasons that I could not figure out, they were right on top as though I was meant to get in without any further ado.

As soon as I opened the door, the felines made a mad dash inside as I lugged in the suitcases, my laptop case, and grocery bags and, leaving all but the suitcases by the front door, picked up the shopping bags and stood in awe looking over my new residence for the next few months. The entryway was warm and inviting and neat as a pin, as was the rest of the house. Hearing the scampering of feline feet I followed the sound. It brought me through a nice-sized dining area with great light and windows and a view into the well-appointed kitchen. Harry had been right. His family had done a bang-up job in redoing this area. Everything was spanking new. The refrigerator had been plugged in as he had promised, and was crammed with everything I could need. I grabbed the coffee, filled the electric pot, and pressed the starter switch. Then I searched for medium-sized bowls, filled one with water, the other with dried food, and left the third on the counter for their treat at a later time. By the time I had done this, the coffee was done, and I poured myself a mug and added milk which had been unopened and was properly dated. The cats were busy taking turns with the water and dried food as though they had been on a two-day journey without any sustenance at all, but they knew something else was going to be coming up, because between laps and mouthfuls, they each looked up longingly at the third bowl on the counter. Okay, I'm a pushover for a begging animal. I reached into the paper bag and extracted a can of wet cat food, opened it, and put it on the floor for them to take turns with.

Smiling, I took my mug and began wandering around the downstairs. My initial reaction was one of comfort with the eye-pleasing furniture in the living room/den (or substitute office, as there was even a small fax machine/copier/scanner) as well as bookcases filled with newly-dusted tomes. Combining these areas was smart. The office part only took up one corner of this large room. Sofas and chairs were all around the rest of the room and could be moved to suit one's needs and tastes making it the living room in my mind. It was spacious and filled not only with sofas and chairs but all placed so that the heat from the large, baronial fireplace would warm the cockles of anyone's heart and body, while the den or office area had a comfortable chair for working at the little desk. Each window had the drapes or appropriate curtains pulled back to let in the light and the first color changes in the trees and surrounding landscape. It looked as though there might be an early winter, if autumn were ready to descend. But then again, two or three days of temperatures back in the 80s would put this off for a while longer, and that was usually the way it worked in the Northeast. As it was going into the mid 70s today, I had no thoughts of a very early snow.

Taking a few steps back into the lovely entry way, I looked at it carefully. Was there a bench there with a hidden bootjack? Not at all. Not even a marble table; just a pegged coat rack on the right wall upon entering, and a side table on the left wall with a modular telephone on it. I took my mug back into the kitchen, leaned against the counter and looked out the windows as I finished the brew. I breathed a great sigh of relief and, noticing a door at the back end of the kitchen, went to open it.

It was exactly what I thought it was; a very large pantry, large enough to hold a freezer which I immediately opened. After all, HJS had promised me it would be stocked with everything from meat and chicken to ice cream, and I wanted to see if he was right. He was. No doubt about it. He had obviously phoned ahead and placed a lovely and large order with . . . now what was the caretaker's name? I know he had mentioned it and I must have noted it somewhere. I went to retrieve my purse which I had left by the door, placed it on the side table and began digging through it for my date book. There, attached by my old trusty paper clip to the front of my date book was the name, George Everett, caretaker. Wife, Maude—did cleaning and cooking if and when necessary. A telephone number followed. Following the protocol I had been taught, I picked up the phone and punched in the number. After five rings their answering machine went on and I introduced myself and notified them of my arrival, thanked them for everything, and mentioned that I had brought two houseguests with me who meowed. I didn't want anyone wandering in and being taken aback or even suffering an allergic reaction to these beasts.

That done, I took the heaviest of the suitcases which was on wheels and started upstairs. Instantly I found myself accompanied by the cats. "Are you two sated now?" I said as they rounded the corner to join me. "Did you find more places down here to investigate? I must show you the pantry. It was probably called a larder in the old days. You'll like it in there and I bet that's a good place to look for mice, you two." I realized at that point I had not only reached the landing but I had no idea what these two were named. Neither Terry nor Jess had mentioned it. I knew I couldn't go around calling them, "You two," or even worse, "Here, Puss," or even "Here Pussycats, or Kitties, or Felines," or even the shrill whistle so many people used to call their animals. Names gave one distinction, and these were very distinguished animals. "Let's find the nicest bedroom and then, while I unpack this case, the three of us will talk. How's that!" Their responses were curved tails that swished as they walked besides me.

Feeling a little like Goldilocks after a good meal, but before her disappearance, I headed straight for the door ahead of me. I figured this must be the master bedroom and was it ever. It ran the entire width of the house, had it's own bathroom, a dressing room, and two walk-in closets, and what's more, it faced West which would bring the setting sun and a wide and completely clear vista into the room. What a treat. A room with a real view! Something you paid dearly for in any big city.

Filled with glee I set about opening the suitcase and making piles on the bed. I no sooner had chosen what was to go where when the doorbell rang and a hearty voice floated up to me. "It's me, George!" a man's voice shouted up to me. "We got yer message, Missus, and I can bring up the rest of your bags if it's aright with yer."

"Yes, please do and thank you, George," I called down having come to the top of the landing. A tall, bulky, but well muscled man began to ascend the stairs carrying the remaining three bags as though they weighed nothing. As he approached the top of the stairs, he seemed to be in his fifties, but as his complexion was so very fair but weathered, and his face, unlined, it was hard to tell with his full head of grey hair. He was dressed in the clothes of his trade, overalls, and a checked shirt and was surprisingly clean shaven. "Come in, would you please," I added as he stopped at the bedroom door, "and just put them by the bed. It's okay," I added, seeing his questioning expression. He did so, stopped, and looked at the bed. His jaw dropped.

"Where did you two come from?" he said looking at the cats. "Why yer the spittin' image of Puss and Boots but they've been gone fer ages now." The cats only looked at him. I could have sworn they smiled.

"What do you mean, 'gone'," I asked him as he bent to stroke the cats.

"Oh, they was here years ago when the old Mr. and Mrs. Spruce was here, but when they died, the cats just up and disappeared! And what's more," he added looking at the Rya rug on the floor, "The Spruces didn't die here, ye know. They died in the city, and the day that happened, before Maude and me got the call, Puss and Boots vanished like they was never here a'tall!" We were both silent for a moment or two, staring off into space or at the rug, whichever took our fancy when the telephone snapped us out of our reveries. As I was the closest to it since there was an extension on the night table, I answered. "Hello?"

"Emma! Is that you! You finally arrived! You know I was getting worried but Maude just called me to let me know you were in one piece. HJS, here in case you couldn't figure that one out, dear girl!"

"I'm fine, Harry. It just took a little longer than I thought. Sightseeing and all that, and I guess the stresses just began to fall away, and I didn't feel like driving straight through the last hundred or so miles. I was going to call you, but George stopped by and just brought up the rest of my suitcases, so don't be angry. Okay?"

"Not a problem. Just as long as you're there. Oh, and before I forget, if you don't mind, I thought I'd come up and spend a long weekend just to acquaint you with things and to R&R somewhat myself, say, at the end of next week. Is that all right with you?"

"Why are you asking me, HJS? This is your house, after all, and before you begin your usual tirade about interrupting 'genius at work' I am not working. At least not for the immediate future, and I would be glad of your company. "Besides," I added, "Maude and George have stocked the place so beautifully, company is most definitely required in order to do all these wonderful foodstuffs justice!" Having been included in the conversation, by look as well as overhearing, George nodded his agreement as well, and being the kind of person I am, I told Harry we would all three be expecting him. I did not, however, tell him about the cats.

After disconnecting, I opened the remaining bags, continued making my piles, and, after finding places for everything, finished in record time. Meanwhile, George was still standing by the bed, vacillating between looking at and petting the cats. He made no excuses while I busied myself, nor did he comment on anything. It was as though he was suddenly in a different world altogether. Seeing he was somewhere off in space and not wanting to jar him, I gently touched his arm while saying his name. It did no good. He was so startled he almost jumped off the floor. As it was, he did a peculiar little hop, settled down, remembered where he was and what had been going on, and apologized to me for intruding on my privacy. I, on the other hand, told him not to worry about it at all, walked into the bathroom, turned on the tap, and taking the glass from the sink, filled it with water and brought it to him. "Drink this slowly, George. A sip at a time ought to do it," I said, still patting his arm. He turned to me and nodded. When he finished, he took the glass back to the bathroom, washed it thoroughly, and, still without speaking, nodded his farewell.

"Do you mind if I accompany you, George? I do so want to meet your wife and to take a quick look at the house from the outside and the beautiful garden."

"That would be fine, Missus," he answered at last, leading the way downstairs and allowing me the time to take the keys and a tissue from my bag. I was just about to head for the door, when he stopped me.

"Missus, I want to show ya something. Do you got a minute?" he asked politely leading me into the den/ living room area. He walked over to the mantelpiece and took a framed photograph down from it. This he placed gingerly in my hands. It was a picture of Harry's parents, looking as though they were in their mid-fifties, sitting in front of the fireplace on the divan that was still in evidence in the room. On their laps were two cats, the exact duplicates of the ones upstairs. Then he took the photo back, undid the back of the frame, and pulled it out for me to see. It was marked and dated: Mom and Dad with Puss and Boots, July 4, 1976 after the Bi-Centennial Regatta.

"Ya see the date Missus? They was in their late sixties, even though they al'ays looked younger, and the cats were getting up in years too. I think they was about four, and after fifteen more years, Mr. and Mrs. was gone and so was the cats! But those two upstairs, they are the spittin' image ain't they?" I nodded in complete agreement. A shiver ran up my spine. It was as though they had been cloned. Without another word, we both left the house.

As we walked down the path and to the left, a woman, who I gathered was Maude, approached. "Ah, there are the two of ya. I were beginning to worry, Georgie. Maybe things were not right, I says to meself, so here I come to take a look." She offered her hand as she spoke with an Irish lilt with rolling "R's," mixed in with the local brand of a Maine accent similar to George's.

"I am sorry we took so long to come meet you, Mrs. Everett, I mean, Maude, but I needed to unpack and your husband was kind enough to tote up the bags for me," I said apologetically. "I dawdled on my way up here and didn't realize how tired I really was."

"And yer won't believe whot she brought wif her," George interjected almost pushing me aside. "Puss and Boots! They's here like they's never left the place, all tucked in on the bed in the big bedroom just like they's use ter do!" Maude stood stock still. Her eyes widened and her jaw dropped. She looked as though she was about to faint as he put his arm around her waist and steadied her. I took the moment after realizing she was going to be fine to look away. I hadn't even noticed where we were standing or what was around me. When I looked at Maude again, she had steadied herself.

"This I must see, if it's a'right with you, Missus," she said making for the house. I nodded and they both went up the few steps and entered leaving me to my own devices.

Having had enough shocks for a while, I stood there and looked around me. The house, truly Victorian in every sense of the style, had been painted what designers were currently calling a French Blue. It was almost like the sky just as summer twilight descended with a daub of dark blue thrown in for good measure. It was crisp and inviting. All the trimming around the windows, the turrets, the Widow's Walk, were stark white in comparison. It was a house of distinction and beauty. Bushes were planted around the house, too, but not close enough to allow for ants and spiders to congregate and invade. They were backed by a foot high dark green fence on the far side that seemed to act like a moat of some sort making sure the bushes stayed away from the windows.

I turned slowly around so I was facing away from the house. The very large lawn area had been divided into three distinct gardens. The one on the left looked large enough to have had a maze in it at one time, but now it was full of what seemed to me to be apple and possibly cherry trees, a veritable orchard, while the garden on the right was filled with flowers, many still blooming in the late August warmth. Rose bushes dotted this part of the garden. And even though the center garden area was relatively devoid of flora, it had plenty of fauna and small trees. It had been designed after a rock garden with a distinctly Japanese flavor. I had never been involved in gardening, not even in my summers out of the city as a child, but I did know a Japanese Rock Garden when I saw it. Meditation and serenity was a big part of my previous life, but in actuality, I only knew about the few potted plants I had had during my lifetime . . . those plants necessary to keep the carbon dioxide in a closed environment to a minimum, but re-supplying the indoor air with needed oxygen. I was just thinking about taking a walk toward the back of the house, hoping there was some sort of vegetable garden, when Mr. and Mrs. Everett reappeared. She looked as shocked as he had been. She smiled at me, her face getting paler by the minute, waved gingerly, and went in the direction of their home.

"My Missus was very upset. She said to tell you if you need her call," George said shyly.

"Not a problem at all, George and if you want to follow her, go ahead. I'm just taking a look around, if that's all right."

"Yes, of course, Missus. When did Mr. Harry say he would be here? Next weekend, was it?" I nodded. "Well then, we had best make sure everything is in top running order and we do have the time to do it, too!"

"Not to worry about Mr. Harry, George. Just leave him to me. I've a funny feeling we will be very busy since he wants to show me around everything and every place, so you and Maude just relax. We have plenty of food and I love cooking, so there's nothing for you two to really do."

"Ah, but we needs to make sure the place is neat, Missus."

"Well, that's the only thing you will be responsible for. You two have worked hard enough to get this lovely old place ready for me!" I said as he nodded and started to leave. "Oh, by the way, is there a vegetable garden? I thought there must be since everything here is planted so beautifully."

"Yes, Missus. You have one by the kitchen door and we have a larger one by our kitchen door, too."

"Well, thank you kindly, George, now go on home. Maude needs you." He nodded, did not meet my eyes, and left me alone. I continued around the back of the house, located the vegetable garden, carefully chose two tomatoes to have with dinner, walked around the rest of the house, and finally reentered by the unlatched front door.

I had no sooner entered than the pounding of paws was heard upstairs and almost immediately the two cats galloped down the stairs and came to rest at my feet. I decided not to verbalize anything if I could help it, but only think my thoughts directly at them. Time to experiment! I knew so many members of the animal kingdom were intuitive once they relinquished themselves to be with humans and the telepathic exchanges were often quite rewarding, but my own intuitive senses had been very shaken up by George and Maude. I had to try anyway and re-center myself. Besides, I was still full of The Hounds Tooth Inn experience. I took a deep breath and let it out slowly. I did this again and again until I felt steadier.

Moving towards the kitchen with a tomato in each hand I thought, *'Okay, you two. I remember what I was going to do before George came in. I was going to try to find out your names. Can we do this now?'* I entered the kitchen with one of them on each side of me. As I finished the thought, they each brushed against the nearest leg and gave a slight "Brrp" sound. *'Shall I call you Puss and Boots?'* The response was a definite growl from each. *'Well then, how about . . . '* And I started with simple feline names, the names I had gathered in my travels and in the books I'd read. All were followed by growls with a few hisses interspersed until I came upon Napoleon for the black cat with Nappy as the shortened version, and Peaches for the cream and golden tan girl. Both of these names met with purrs and the two of them falling over and bearing their bellies for a rub.

'*Does this mean you can sense or whatever, all of my thoughts?*' They both purred louder in response. I knew then and there, I was in very big trouble. These two animals were so attuned to people, even relative strangers like me—although we had shared quite some experience the evening before, of this I was more than certain—I was forced to sit down hard and look them both squarely in their eyes while they looked adoringly at me!

'*Can you do the same thing with George or Maude?*' They hung their heads. '*What about Jess and Terry? Did you do this with them?*' They looked up slightly but then back down as I picked up, '*Only when they were sleepy.*' "Okay, you two," I verbalized, "We have to come to some sort of understanding here because something tells me none of this is really happening, and something else tells me to go with it and see where this leads. I have to get used to the two of you playing around in my head, so please do keep most of your thoughts to yourselves. After all," I heard myself say, "You are cats and cats are extremely independent and I expect you to remain as you are supposed to be without interfering with whatever work I'm doing. I don't need to know every little move you are going to make, or what you want me to make or do. That's not the way this should work, you know." As I spoke, both looked at me earnestly. "Each person is entitled to

his or her own thoughts most of the time, is that clear?"
I continued sitting back in my chair looking from one to
the other face to face to face. During my last sentence,
they had both jumped onto the kitchen table cocking
their lovely heads from side to side with their lips slightly
pulled up in what I assumed was a cat smile. Feeling there
was nothing more to say for the moment, I scratched
each cat around the head and ears, feeling their intense
purrs and went to wash the tomatoes, prepare a salad
for lunch, and decide what to make for dinner. I also
figured out it would be easier to take another look at the
foodstuffs, lay out meal plans for the next few days, plan
a surprise meal for HJS, and begin whatever preparation
was necessary during the days to come.

I had only just realized how I had missed being totally
domestic. I had always loved to cook and experiment
but in the last few years, had gotten clean away from
doing this sort of thing. Being single again and grabbing
bites to eat with our circle of like-minded, abandoned
people had really spoiled me. Like most new singles, I
still made the occasional hamburger or broiled chicken
or fish, but usually nothing more difficult. Now I craved
creating for the epicure in me and thought how lucky I
was to have brought my laptop because I had a whole
series of recipes I had collected over the course of my
travels on it. Taking the stairs two at a time, I ran into
my bedroom, grabbed my laptop from the bed, and
returned to the kitchen at breakneck speed. I did not
even stop to look around. I had a mission to perform.
That's all I considered.

I opened it up on the kitchen counter and went to my recipe section. As I scanned it, I felt the watchful eyes of the cats at the nape of my neck. They had jumped back on the table to have a better view, but I was blocking the screen. I moved to the coffee machine in order to pour another cup. As soon as I did this, they jumped on the counter and sat, one on either side of the laptop. Watching surreptitiously, I almost laughed out loud as each craned his and her neck to see what this machine and its screen were all about. With cup in hand I petted each of them and began explaining aloud what this contraption was and what it did. I guess I needed someone to talk to, and as I illustrated what I was looking for, both of them chirruped at me as though they understood. Of course, I knew they didn't, but it was a comfort having a response and one where I knew they were not probing my mind.

I found what I had been looking for; a recipe from Nigeria where you could control the spice (very hot peppers) depending upon your company. Harry loved spicy food and this Chicken with Peanuts was simple to make and what was more, we had everything except the peppers. But a quick trip to any market would solve that, because I could even substitute dried chilies, the kind used in any Pizza place I had ever been in. This, along with salad and a white wine and dried mustard dressing, with ice cream or sorbet for desert would do the trick. I had even seen wine as well as other alcoholic beverages stored in the larder, so not a problem there since I never used cooking wine for my salad dressings. Only the real thing would do.

That problem solved, I began foraging for my own dinner, found some frozen chopped sirloin in half pound packages (how very thoughtful), pulled one out, and searched for a bottle of tomato sauce and fresh garlic. Next step was to venture out back to see what was still in the vegetable garden. Lettuce, tomatoes, cucumbers, carrots, and green beans were still growing well, which was great as I needed more tomatoes for the Chicken with Peanuts! What a find! I finally took a deep breath as I harvested some green beans to go with my meat sauce and soon-to-be-pasta dish. Having solved the immediate food problems, I switched the laptop to standby and with coffee in hand decided to go into the living room cum den while the beans were air drying.

There on the table was the photo album George had pulled from the shelf. I picked it up and went to the recliner, put my cup gingerly on the end table next to it, as I did not have a coaster, and began to leaf through the pictures, taking out a few to see if dates were written on the backs. These pictures were dated mostly beginning in the 1940s and quite a few showed the house from many different angles. It still looked the same and as these were in black and white and the house showed up in a lighter grey, I assumed it was lighter in color sixty-six years ago. Even the gardens were similar and, I had assumed correctly, the one to the left had held a maze. In fact, there were quite a lot of pictures of the maze from various angles and even from the inside. Someone was very proud of their handiwork. The flowers in the flower garden changed as did the flora in the rock garden. I wasn't sure if it was seasonal or just to show off the prowess of the gardener. However, the one constant, other than the maze, was the house. Not one strip of wood seemed to have been added nor were the windows changed. In fact, the draperies in this room appeared to be exactly the same as could be seen in the photos. Since there were close-ups of the window treatments, the patterns were discernable and yes, to the naked eye, they seemed to be alike.

As I turned the pages of the album, there were Puss and Boots, in all their regal feline glory sitting tall by the front door and posing delightedly with their tails wrapped playfully around their legs. I looked long and hard at this one picture and agreed with George's assessment; the present cats looked exactly like the two in the photograph. Not wanting to go any further, I closed the album, took a drink of coffee, and pulled myself to my feet. Time to change my awareness. I had only had a cursory glimpse of the rest of the house, and decided it was time to get to know the entire place. I decided to start just where I was and looked carefully all around the room, feeling the patinas of the furniture and then going to the bookshelves and really looking at the library. I gently pulled a few books from the shelves just to see the pub dates and the condition of the books themselves. Everything was in a-one shape and the library was fabulous. Deciding to leave the books until I could investigate farther especially on the top shelves, for a rainy day, I walked out of the den.

I had noticed another door further past the office cum living room cum library cum dun and automatically headed to it. Since the door was closed, I tried the handle tentatively thinking it might be locked, but it turned without any problem. The room was humongous paralleling the size of the bedroom above it. It had floor to ceiling windows looking out over the expanse of the beautifully manicured back yard. And, it had a gazebo off to the right at the far end almost meeting the brush and forest area at what I thought must be the end of the property line. At first glance, I thought it could have been a medium-sized ballroom or music room in its early days. It did have a piano, a harp, and a few music stands, but seemed to be used as an area just for rest and relaxation. The room had been painted a very soft eggshell so as to catch the light and bring warmth into the room. As I looked up, the molding looked to be original, and the ceiling held a magnificent and large Austrian crystal chandelier, clean as a whistle, right in the exact center. I walked back towards the door and found a dimmer light switch, turned it on to see the effect, and then took a very deep and calm breath as a different sense of relaxation overtook me. There were comfortable looking sofas and easy chairs placed facing the windows, another magnificently hand-carved, large chaise longue with Chinese silk in a golden hue as its covering, a smattering of end tables, a card table and chairs in readiness for the usual evening game of bridge, and a beautifully equipped stereo system hidden in a full entertainment console. There was even a television, which did sort of take me aback as I had not seen one anywhere else in the house so far. In fact, come to think of it, I hadn't even seen a radio! But a retreat is a retreat, and the one thing most intelligent people wanted to get away from for a while was the negativity produced by the local and world news these past years. This added to the tensions of daily existence no matter what one's work was, and sometimes one required a complete withdrawal from the current time— but usually even if only for a few days. At least I knew I felt this way especially during my most reclusive times. I was tempted to turn on the TV but pushed myself out of this lovely room before I could follow through.

Still feeling a strong sense of newly found relaxation, I wandered over to the long sofa facing the windows. Of course the cats were there. Why hadn't I guessed it? I didn't even question how they had gotten in as the door I had entered through was closed as was the other door three quarters of a way down from my entry point.

"Are you Puss and Boots, or Nappy and Peaches," I asked slowly watching them intently for their reactions as I mentioned both sets of names. The reaction, a beating of tails, was to Nappy and Peaches, thank God! I smiled gratefully and looked around the room once more. I knew I would be taking full advantage of it. There was a small desk that would hold my laptop with ease and a comfortable chair that seemed just the right height for the table. Before I left, I moved both so I could look out on the beautiful expanse before me.

Dinner was going to be easy as I said, so I knew I had time to see what was on the second floor and even possibly the third and attic area, even though there were a few hunger pangs. I did not have to be a creature of habit and that alone was wonderful, so upstairs I went with my companions who had followed me out of the music room, as I had begun in my mind to call it. They stopped at the opened door to "my" bedroom, but I went past it to my right. There were two doors there and two more on the left side of the master bedroom. Opening each door revealed lovely bedrooms: one at the farthest end had a large double bed and a separate bathroom all decorated in peach and soft mauve in design with matching bed linens and bath ensemble. The other closer to "my" room had been done up in pastel greens and blues and had two long twin beds and a private bathroom as well. The third room, really the first to the left of the master bedroom was still designed as a nursery. It was large enough to hold two cribs and two single medium child-sized beds, while the fourth room, with a single full sized bed and separate bath adjoined the nursery through an interior door. Obviously this was for an au pair or nursemaid. I guessed the family did have small children and found that natural.

As I opened and closed the doors, my two companions waited patiently by the top of the staircase, without uttering one meow, but again reading my mind. The hunger pangs were growing and I wasn't sure whether they were mine or theirs. The tour over, we all went downstairs, through the dining room and into the kitchen. More of the dried food had disappeared but some of it has been crunched and dribbled about the floor a distinct sign of, 'We're not that pleased,' from the feline community. The one can of wet food had been eaten with such thoroughness it made the bowl look as though it had never been used.

"You know guys," I began as I opened two more cans and put the food in two different bowls, "There is one thing I did not think about when we came here to begin with, and that is where your litter pan should go. We really don't want it in the kitchen or in the pantry, not safe or sanitary, and there doesn't seem to be easy access to the back porch from here does there? I could put it in the upstairs master bathroom which would be easier if you guys stayed with me, but I've the feeling you two wander around a great deal especially at night. Right?" They just looked at me with their big eyes on the bowls of food. "Ok, you've one track minds. Not a problem. Here you are. Eat, be happy, I'll start my dinner and we'll take care of the litter problem later." I busied myself with my own fixings and when ready, ate with great abandon. Just as I finished, I heard a slapping noise behind me. I turned around to see Nappy standing by a well camouflaged flap right near the back door, but not in the door itself. Quickly I went and opened the door. There, to the far left of the door was the litter pan I had purchased filled with sand and showing signs of recent use. I had not put it there, nor had I known about the animal doorway. Shaking my head, I first thought George had done it, but he was with me until Maude joined him. Did he do this then? If so, why didn't he say anything the reticence of the New Englander not withstanding? Everything had been going along so well, with the exception of the duplication of the cats, I had almost forgotten about The Hounds Tooth Inn and all that it had entailed. In fact, I had really begun to relax at last.

I re-entered the kitchen, closed and double locked the back door did all the dishes, then went around to make certain the windows and front door were securely locked for the night, too. I returned to the kitchen, grabbed my laptop and a large empty glass for water and two pieces of fruit, and went to the bottom of the stairs. One last look around under great scrutiny told me there was no bootjack or wooden bench and that everything was as I had first seen it. The telephone was in its place and I know I had an extension upstairs by the bed but I turned on my cell phone just in case. I had put it in my pants pocket as I have always done, but had turned it off after my arrival here. Returning it to my pocket turned on and balancing everything else, I began the ascent with some trepidation. But when I entered the bedroom, all was as I had left it, including Nappy and Peaches curled into each other at the foot of the bed.

After I did all the necessary preparations for bed, I crawled into the most comfortable bed I had come across in years. Propping the pillows as I was wont to do, my hand inadvertently hit a button by the headboard because a panel slid aside and an entertainment console appeared on the opposite wall. I was not without contact to the outside world after all! Just to make sure I was still in the 21st Century, I opened the night stand drawer, found the remote control, and turned the TV on. A quick job of channel surfing led me to a re-run of "Law and Order," one of my all time favorites. I never cared how many times I saw an episode, but I was not one of those fans who could sit there and repeat word for word. I took each episode as brand new and priceless, never got bored and never thought ahead. I just got lost in it. Half way through this episode, where Lenny partners with Green for the first time, both animals jumped off of the bed, headed to the door, used another very well hidden cat door and after doing whatever it was they had to do, re-entered, and returned to their places at the bottom of the bed. I stayed awake until the end, switched the TV off, and turned over into a blissful sleep with two felines acting as angels guarding my feet.

I don't know how long I slept as I had yet to locate a clock, besides the one in the kitchen, and I hadn't pulled my watch from my pants pocket, but when I began to stir, there was a faint glow in the sky. I had purposely left the drapes open overlooking the back garden area and since the placement of the bed was between the two tall windows, sufficient light came through. I remembered removing my glasses and placing them on the night stand, I automatically reached for them before pulling my hand back with the memory of the last awakening from sleep I had experienced. However, I forced myself to reach for them, and there they were. Phew! One hurdle conquered! I took a deep breath and reached for my pants to get my watch. It said 5:40 and I guessed it was in the morning because the back garden area faced west and the glow seemed to be reaching only that point of pre-dawn sky. Putting on my glasses, I looked at the bottom of the bed. Yes, they were still there, but this time with their bellies up, their eyes open, their heads looking at me upside-down waiting for a scratch.

"Good morning, you two! Did you sleep well?" I ventured, as I put both hands to good use amid a flood of purrs and soft mewls assuring me they had. Stretching, I got out of bed, did some easy exercises, and went to make myself presentable to the day.

When I returned from the bathroom, neither animal was to be found. They might not have been there physically, but their thoughts sure were; hunger was doing them in. Obeying orders, I hurriedly dressed and headed for the kitchen, fed them, put the coffee on, in that order, and proceeded to pour orange juice and make some toast. With a mug of coffee in one hand and a piece of toast in the other, I headed back into the hall with the express purpose of stepping outside, only to stop so suddenly, I splashed the hot liquid over my hand and almost dropped the mug. There, on the wall over the telephone table was the mirror. My stomach turned instantly into a knot. I felt my legs begin to buckle underneath me but somehow managed to remain erect. I turned back into the dining room, place my mug and toast on the bare table, not caring at all about water rings, gathering my courage, and still holding my stomach, I turned to face the mirror.

I could not see myself in it. I guessed I was too far away. I thought about sidling up to the mirror and seeing if I could catch it off guard but decided to be an adult and strode towards it with purpose. My image still did not show itself. I went face to face with the glass. Still nothing was visible. Not even the dining room which should have been reflected in the glass.

I reached out to touch it and it was solid. This was no mere figment of my imagination. It was there, all right. It hadn't been the day before, but today was a new day and here was a mirror that showed nothing. It didn't even catch the sunlight glinting in from the window panels by the front door. My initial instinct was to reach for the phone and call George. I didn't want to be alone at that moment, but it was still early and I never liked disturbing anyone before a more reasonable hour. The kitchen clock had said it was only 6:25 A.M. when I entered to feed the cats, and even though common sense told me George and Maude would be up and about, I was not ready to disturb them. I even thought, but only for a moment, of calling the police, but what would I tell them? A mirror had followed me from The Hounds Tooth Inn just as the cats had done? Did I really want to spend the rest of my life institutionalized? Wasn't that what I was on a break from, an institution? I tried moving the damn thing, but it wouldn't budge. It was as though it had been nailed thoroughly to the wall, not hung with wire and a picture hook.

Maybe I was still hallucinating. Maybe this was a new altered state of awareness. Being without responsibilities tripped the synapse connections in my mind. But why? How? I could think of no rhyme or reason. This was just sheer stupidity. It wasn't even a case of "All that matters....." it was a case of being an overly stressed individual who had nothing else really planned. That was the problem. I had made no plans. None at all. I was just willing to take things as they came to me, and for the structured person I always was, this was just too weird, so my mind created something to titillate itself, put me in the starring role, and here I was, the proud servant of two telepathic cats (where were they anyway?), and a mirror reflecting nothing today, but two days ago had led me on a merry chase across a couple of hundred years and caused me to really doubt my sanity. Ooh, I could see myself trying to explain this to the police, to HJS, to George, to anyone who would listen as I was strapped down and given a good dose of a strong tranquilizer by the attending medics who had been called because I had really gone way over the edge.

All of this flitted through my mind in what was probably only a minute or two, when I walked back into the dining room to retrieve the mug and toast and again turned towards the mirror. This time I stood on tiptoe to see if I could see anything reflected in it. Maybe it had been my initial vantage point. No, nothing showed. "Nappy! Peaches! Where did you guys get to?" I called, just needing to hear some sound. No sooner were the words out of my mouth than I heard the cat flap slap against the wall and the patter of feet. They looked up at me expectantly, and I in turn pointed to the mirror. "Do either of you know how this got here?" I pointed at the offending obstacle and they, following my gaze, froze in their places. Growls began emanating from deep within each animal and the hair on their backs began to prickle upwards. They crept up so they were standing tightly by each of my legs not only still growling but now hissing with their teeth bared.

"Missus, are you there," George called out just as he knocked. I was so relieved at the sound of his voice preceding the knock; I mentally thanked him and went to open the door with my two companions still hugging my legs.

"Morning, George," I responded and then added, pointing to the wall, "Do you know anything about this mirror? I could swear it wasn't here yesterday, unless I was too tired to notice it," I added to cover my discomfort and fear.

"Eyup, Missus. It's been in the family for ages, too. Just like the kitties, and I got a note from Mr. Harry to hang it up for yer to use when yer put yer hat on so I did it early this morning when I saw the light in yer room!" I sort of breathed a sigh of relief, but said nothing about the mirror having been elsewhere too. "Funny thing, Missus, it just sort of stuck to where I put it so I didn't have to make much noise with the hammer or nothin'. Did yer want it moved or somethin'?"

"Well, I do think that would be a good idea, George. I mean, if it's possible," I said trying to remember what the downstairs rooms were like. "Maybe it should go in the room over there," I said pointing to the living room. "It would be lovely over the fireplace." I added trying to sell the idea to myself. "If I remember there was nothing over that fireplace at all." All I really did recall was that it was a tall one and the mirror would not be easily looked into from ground level.

Without another word, he walked to the mirror, grabbed it firmly, and lifted it up and away from the wall. It had been set in a brace of some sort and this too, he easily removed from the wall. We then formed a procession, George with the mirror and brace, me, and then the cats, all heading in a straight line for the living room.

"Well, Missus, I have to get the ladder to put it up there. It'll only take a little time, if that's OK." I responded positively and that I would wait right here for him. When he left the room, the cats and I went over to the mirror which he had put on the large coffee table and looked into it. All three of us were standing; the cats balancing on their hind legs with their front paws on the table.

I closed my eyes tightly and then slowly released the lids and looked down. There I was just as I had been when I got dressed earlier. The animals too, saw their reflections, sat down, swished their tails, and went about their businesses. I know I swallowed hard and tried to smile at my own stupidity and fear. Just as I was about to look into it again, George arrived with the ladder and other equipment and with a nod to me, went to work. I stayed until he was done, offered him a cup of coffee or tea, which he politely refused and returned to the kitchen for more coffee. As I was sitting there sipping the life-giving brew and nibbling on the second piece of now cold toast lathered with Apple Butter I had the sudden urge to re-explore the house outside and in. Nothing felt ominous, but I felt pushed to do this, so I hurriedly ate and drank up and began with the larder and pantry area. After opening cupboards, locating possibly necessary items and noting where they were, I was about to leave the larder but noticed a small recess around the side of the largest free-standing cupboard. There, almost hidden in the wall, was a door. It did not appear to be locked as it had a pull latch which I immediately tried. The door opened as easily as could be and on the wall was a light switch. This too, worked perfectly illuminating about fifteen steps going down. At the bottom of the staircase was another door with another pull-latch but the pull-latch looked to be the heavy duty kind telling me the door was very solid. As soon as I pulled it open an automatic light went on. The coolness that hit me smack in my face told me this was a wine cellar and an odor told me mushrooms were also grown somewhere in this space. Right by the inside of the door was a large door stopper. I put it under the door and began to investigate.

I really didn't think anyone was growing poisonous produce here but it wouldn't hurt to check to see what kind of mushrooms were being grown. A quick look at the wine bottles told me this was quite a collection indeed and I knew I would not take undue advantage of years of careful collecting. It even contained some very rare Rothchilds! I saw the climate control switch as well and wondered why the door was kept unlocked with all these precious vintages. But I couldn't locate the mushrooms. However, across from the wine cellar was a washing machine and dryer. What a find!

I spied another door at the far end of the wine cellar and it too, opened easily. There were the mushrooms and they too, proved to be quite a find. Shiitake's raised their lovely heads looking just about ready for harvesting. Funny though, that Shiitake's were the only ones growing here. There was enough room for at last half a dozen more varieties. I guessed this was one kind of mushroom relatively unheard of and unused in these parts by the locals.

Finished with this part of the tour, I retraced my steps and went from the larder to the back porch and walked to the large vegetable garden. Again, I explored in awe at the magnificent layout given this sustenance but wondered who would not only be harvesting them besides me, who would be canning, preserving, and freezing them for use during the winter. No sooner had this thought crossed my mind when I spied Maude pulling a cart behind her heading straight for their garden. We waved to each other and she went in the opposite direction towards the rows of tomato plants. Time for stewing, I guessed. I turned in the opposite direction and headed to the rear of the French Blue house with white trim.

It was easy to locate the music room, as I began to call it, with the master bedroom above it and the placement of the windows on each level gave this part of the house two eyes (upstairs) and a toothy grin (downstairs). Smiling at my own silliness, I continued around the north side to find a beautifully groomed and quiet arbor filled with flower beds and an outdoor lounge chair and table. The chairs were padded and there, curled up in two tight balls lying butt to butt, were my companions taking their mid-morning naps with the sun gently caressing their bodies. At the sound of my approach they both stretched out offering their bellies for the sun to warm and for me to scratch. Of course, I obliged and told them how lucky they were to have found such a lovely spot in the morning sun. Without any further ado, I joined them and put my feet up on the lounger. Before I knew it, they were both on top of me begging for further attention. While stroking them I felt my own eyes slowly close in the security of this lovely arbor.

The three of us must have slept for over an hour, for when I opened my eyes, the sun had risen further. Further than I had intended because I had also thought about exploring the surrounding area and whether on foot or by car made no difference to me. I wanted to know all about this haven, mirror not withstanding. Waking the cats was no problem. As soon as I stirred, they stretched languidly and jumped down to continue their ballet-like moves stretching backs and their hind legs one at a time. Stretching myself, I got up and continued around the rest of the house. The one thing that kept coming to mind was the color. The French Blue made it look like a gem of great value and it sparkled when the sunlight hit it as though the paint had spangles or tiny flecks of gold in it. The white trim also radiated with the same intensity. It looked as though it lived and breathed on its very own, but peacefully so. I breathed a great sigh of relief. Thankfully, no untoward anxiety bubbled up with these thoughts.

Feeling very pleased with myself I walked around again to the back door and reentered the kitchen as hunger pangs began to gnaw at me. With a hastily made tuna sandwich in hand I went back out to the arbor to sit and ruminate on the past seventy-two hours. I let my mind float free after half the sandwich was eaten, leaned back, and let thoughts flow in and out going where they wished. This was not a formal meditation. It was my way of letting in new information that often proved to be the key to difficult and untoward solutions. I had "floated free" as I called it ever since I was a child.

I felt my consciousness lifting out of my body and yet I was completely aware of my surroundings. I felt and sensed the animals returning to join me, I petted each of them and asked them to settle down for a while which they did without any hesitation. I let myself go higher and higher. and soon I was seeing the house, the gardens, and what felt like hundreds of miles from up in the air from where we actually were. I loved this out of body type of experience, but was fully aware and feeling safe and secure.

I was not prepared for what came next. Throughout my entire being on both levels I heard a strong but sensitive voice. It was not only in my mind, it was in my ears, and I know the animals heard it too, because they pushed closer to my legs and sat bolt upright.

"You are correct!" it said over and over. "You are correct! You are correct! You are correct!" The tone and intensity stayed the same. I felt no fear, just curiosity. In between this litany, I asked what I was correct about. I did this several times too, making it a litany of my own.

I was still floating freely, I waiting for an answer when there suddenly was silence. A kind of silence that was awesome. I had never experienced anything like it before. It was almost deafening, but still not fearful. Then I heard, "You know. You really do know, Emma. You are a catalyst to time and adventure. You will use this often from this moment on." I felt the response hit my deepest cellular structure and before I knew it, I was fully back in the arbor, the cats by my side and the uneaten half of sandwich on a plate on my lap. I wanted to move but I could not. Instead I felt my eyes shutting and my breathing become gentle as though I was falling into a deep sleep.

I stayed like this for only a few minutes, but it was enough time to put me completely back together again. The cats, too, had settled down again but what surprised me most was they had not even paid any attention to the tuna sandwich! It was still in pristine condition, so I took a big bite, suddenly being hungry again and scooped some out for each animal. They refused it. Then I remembered they hadn't even begged last night at dinner either. It seemed they preferred their own kind of food, canned, with some dried food left out for nibbles. Well, time would tell.

We all stretched and got up at the same time and wended our way back towards the house, when I was struck with another sensation, one of unfinished exploration, and did a complete turnabout. I headed past the back of the house and into the grassy knoll behind the house.

As quickly as I could I headed towards the bushes and trees in back. My route was very direct. It was as though I knew where I was going. Nappy and Peaches were gamboling beside me as though they too, knew what was ahead. Every once in a while I looked in back of me just to make sure the house was still behind us. I also checked the sky but it seemed as though the sun had not moved much at all. That correlated with my watch and I thought how slowly time can move up here away from the city as only a half an hour had past since I made the sandwich.

Without hesitation, my feet made a bee-line for what turned out to be a hidden path. This area looked as though it had once been well trodden. Even the overhanging branches seemed to have been thinned for easier access. At this point Nappy let out a loud yowl as he and Peaches dashed ahead of me. Mentally I heard, "Hurry up, Emma. Hurry up!" in a plaintive and urging voice. I picked up my pace and right around a bend in the path was a wrought iron fence with a gate surrounding what must be the family graveyard. The grave stones looked to be very old indeed. Before even thinking of entering, I peered over the fence and the closest stone. The name on the marker was Harris Jonathan Spruce. It was dated 1707 – 1757. Right next to it was a small grave and head stone at which the cats were sitting. I opened the gate which did not creak or squeak at all, went right to that small grave and looked at the marker. "Puss and Boots, Faithful Friends for Life" was etched into the stone. The date read: "Departed In 1925." Below the date a smaller etched area read: "Departed In 1945", and below that it read, "Departed In 1965", and still below that it read: "Departed in 1985."

Amazing as it was, these animals died every twenty years or so and seemed to come back, or maybe, others were named for the original two and all seemed to live about the same amount of time but did resemble each other, at least according to George and the photographs. I shook my head to clear it and looked at my feline companions. "Does anyone want to comment on this?" I asked. Both lowered their heads as if in prayer but conveyed nothing to my mind.

Without looking around any further but promising myself to come back tomorrow, I left the cemetery and headed back to the house as quickly as I could. The day had proven to be one of confusion from its not so glorious beginning until now, and I needed to get away.

As I exited the bushes I took a good long look at the house. I wanted to make sure it was the same one I had left, not an earlier version of it. I was in no mood for any time changes today no matter what I had been told in my meditative sleep state. I wasn't ready for anything. It seemed to be fine, with the position of the windows on both floors in the rear glistening with their "smile."

Starting my approach, I again noticed the turret and the Widow's Walk surrounding it. As I looked up there seemed to be a faint movement along the Walk, but as I had not gone all the way upstairs to investigate it, I assumed it was just the sun glistening from the Widow's Walk path and continued on my way. "Probably made up of some sort of stone with Mica in it," I said aloud. Stopping, I looked up again. Nothing was apparent. But just as I resumed a step, something peripherally caught my vision over on the far right side of the Walk. Again I stopped and looked up. Nothing was visible. I turned to look back at the bushes. There were Nappy and Peaches, or rather Puss and Boots IV, as I decided to call them for the moment, also staring up. Determined not to be enticed by any of these shenanigans, I made a bee-line for the French Blue House with the White Trim, threw open the kitchen door and proceeded to make a fresh pot of my favorite beverage.

Having left the cats nibbling and with steaming mug in hand, I began making my way upstairs determined to see the turret room. A quarter of the way up, I remembered I had looked into all the rooms and had found no other set of stairs. Therefore, the entry had to be from the first level of the house or even possibly the cellar. Maybe it had been used as a servant's room and redesigned with a different set of stairs for easy access to the kitchen. I returned to the kitchen. There were no hidden doors at all. I had investigated pretty thoroughly already. So without any further hesitation I headed through the pantry and down the cellar steps. After all, I had only opened the door to the wine cellar as it was the most evident. Maybe there was another entry way.

Thirty minutes of a more careful search of the entire cellar and then the kitchen just to make sure I had not missed anything, yielded nothing. There was only one more area to check. I had never looked around the staircase and many old houses, following European designs had hidden doors and areas there used for storage or other access. Gritting my teeth, and determined to find access, I walked slowly around the staircase. Nothing was apparent.

I began tapping, pushing and fingering the wood paneling. Finally, yes, there was a very well hidden door that opened with a slight push. It was located at the back of the main staircase on the kitchen side, of course, for easy access. Before entering, I checked to make sure there was a pull latch on the interior side and a light switch of some kind. Feeling around on the left side of the door I did locate a modern light switch but when I flipped it to the "on" position, nothing happened. I marked where the door was by counting 12 panels from the rear of the main staircase and ran back into the kitchen to search for a flashlight and a light bulb.

The flashlight was easily accessible, but I did have to hunt for another light bulb which took me a little more time than I wished. I returned to the staircase to find both felines sitting in front of the correct panel waiting for me with great anticipation made evident by the swishing of their tails. As soon as I opened the door and turned on the flashlight searching for the nearest light socket, the cats were off and running up the stairs. Oh, how I envied their ability to see in the dark!

One socket was easily found and easy to change. I did this quickly and turned the switch on again. Let there be light and there was — at least for the first series of steps. Using the flashlight to guide me the rest of the way, I hurried after my two companions. It seemed as though I was going around and around for ages until I came to the top of this circular staircase. Peaches was pawing at the door at the top and Nappy, being able to reach the handle, was stretching himself at an attempt to turn it. "Ok, ok, you guys. I'm here now. Let me give it a try," I thought in their direction. They moved away and sat on their haunches allowing me access. I turned the knob. It moved, but the door didn't. It was probably warped so I put my shoulder and ample hip into it and it began to budge. Two more times proved successful. The door opened out onto the Widow's Walk. The sun was waning. "Be careful, you two," I verbalized to the cats who wove themselves through my legs to get out on it. "Don't stick your heads over through the railing, you could fall!" I called after them and then proceeded to follow at a much slower pace. The door had opened up on the left hand side of the turret pointing towards the center of that railing.

I took two steps forward but suddenly felt I was walking through a thick pea soup fog even though the weather was still clear. I had estimated I had about forty-five minutes before the sun would actually begin setting. I knew we were up high, but not high enough to change the atmosphere. There was something else here. In fact, quite a few things felt as if they were there, not just one something else. It was like walking through a miasma of energy, but each had to be gently pushed aside so that I could continue. I slowly continued around to the back of the house, stopping often at the railings, standing at the center of each in turn and looked out over the expanse before me. The views were startlingly magnificent. I felt I could see for miles and miles in any direction and with the changing light and the slowly deepening shadows, I had a wonderful feeling of the beauty that surrounded this house and me. As I experienced this feeling, the miasma began pressing in on me again. When I reached the railing in the front of the house, something made me hold on tightly with both hands. A strange sensation wafted over me. I began to feel I should climb on to the railing and let gravity takes its course. Just as I felt my body being lifted slightly off the walkway, the cats were by my side butting the air around my feet and legs. I had always known animals sense thing we humans cannot see, but this was the first time I actually experienced it. They were butting and then pawing the air adding hisses and spits to their activity as though they were fighting for my life. Suddenly the spell lifted.

"Missus! What in the Lord's business are ye doin' up thar! Stay where ya are. Don't move! I'm acomin' up to get ya!"

"No, no, George," I shouted down to him as his words broke the remainder of the spell. "Everything's fine. I was just taking a good look around. Why don't you come in and I'll be right down. OK?" He didn't respond verbally but entered the house, slamming the front door with quite a bang. I made it back to the door as quickly as I could, called to the cats, thanking them for their help, and began descending the stairs, flashlight still in hand and still turned on. I was so thankful to see the last flight lit by the bulb I had replaced, with the burned out one still on the rung, I could have cried. Things were just the same. There had been no time change and my mind had not taken off in any extravagant flight of fancy.

Just as I was about to push on the door, George flung it open for us. Normalcy reigned, but he was glowering at me. "Missus, no one has been up thar for years and years and those old rails are probably not steady at all. Ya could a falled, ya know!" He was so unnerved his body and voice were shaking and his forehead was beaded with perspiration.

"Thank you for worrying so, George, and for caring, but I'm all right. And the cats were with me."

"Yeah, I did see them, but they were batting at something that were not thar, wasn't they! I seen that much, I did." He stormed off towards the kitchen and after turning of the hidden staircase light, I followed. He handed me a large glass of water and had one for himself, drinking it all in one gulp before he continued lambasting me.

"Ya see, Missus, I promised young Master Harry we'd look after ya because this is a very, very old house even though it don't appear to be and strange things have a'happened here over the years and years and sometimes . . . " He faltered, hanging his head.

"Don't worry, George, I understand completely. Each house comes with its own history and events and sometimes terrible things occurred in these old houses. But I'm not afraid of them at all. In fact, call Maude and if she's not busy and hasn't begun cooking, ask her to come up here for dinner. I'll cook, and I'll also tell you two what happened at The Hounds Tooth Inn where the cats came from. He looked at me strangely for just a moment and then went to phone his wife while I went to the freezer, took out a chicken and started to thaw it in the microwave. I took out two lemons, retrieve garlic and onions and some white wine for a sauce, and got to work.

"She says tha's very good of yer and wants me to come clean up first," he said, looking at me sternly. "Please, Missus, don't go lookin' for any thing else today, ya promise? We'll be here in a hour." I nodded and he took his leave this time closing the front door quietly.

I too, washed up and changed after making sure everything was cooking and the table had been set. My guests arrived exactly one hour later and as we sat down to dinner, with two bottles of wine on the table. The story of the French Blue House with the White Trim began to unfold with George as the principal story teller and Maude nodding her head at certain intervals. I didn't even get a chance to tell them about The Hounds Tooth Inn but I was so pleased I had thought to put out two bottles of Chablis because all the information I received to begin with as we ate our way through everything on the table was basically a reiteration of what George, Maude and HJS had told me. As more wine was poured, George's tongue began to loosen considerably and Maude followed suit.

The house had always been in the Spruce family. In fact almost all the land around had once been owed by them. That much was known because the first Mr. Spruce, as he grew richer, gave the land to those who had settled on it. However, George did say that when the family was still living in England, one of their ancestors had killed someone and was hanged for it, so the old story went, but no one ever mentioned it. It was just a story passed down from generation to generation from Maude's family primarily. I was sure that there was probably more than one bad seed in the family history, because human nature is what it is. But it seemed no one else took anyone else's life here in the New World, and if they did, there had never been any public record of it.

The family was a mixture of farmers and seafarers, therefore the wide expanse of the land and the Widow's Walk, which, from the front rail did still capture a glimpse of the sea, although over time, the flora had grown full and luxuriant preventing a straight-on view of the ocean. I was sure centuries ago only a telescope was needed to see any incoming vessels more clearly and that much of the original farmland led closer to what is still the main road and the sea.

When the history of the place began to lapse, I served coffee and liqueurs and confessed that I found the graveyard past the back yard. Before I could continue along that line and ask about the felines, both George and Maude had a slight coughing fit probably due to their shock of my discovery. But before they calmed down or decided to leave, I explained I really only looked at the first grave of the clan founder, Harris Jonathan Spruce and the small grave for the felines with all the different dates etched in. As I spoke of this, I poured double brandies for both of them and a short one for me. Anything to keep the conversation going!

"Oh, that's an easy one, Missus. Ever since Master Harry's dad was growing up, they always had two kitties and for some reason, each kitty looked just like the ones who are here now, as I a said a' for, and come to think of it, Master Harry's great granddad also always had two cats, so we was told. It was just since no one was living here any more permanent-like, the cats disappeared."

"Why were they all buried in the same grave, do you know that?"

"Well, Missus, after all they's small creatures and the grave yard was not so big even though the family did grow and move away and they wanted to hold spaces in case anyone wanted to come home to be buried the way so many do up here. Besides, their bodies were not boxed, just placed there." Throughout all of this, Maude kept nodding her head up and down in agreement.

"But these cats all looked alike. Do you know if their parents were the ones who previously died? Or did they just appear, George."

George looked at Maude who just looked back at him. He was on his own now with me prodding him on and pouring more brandy for both of them. I was wondering though, if she had had enough. Her glance at him was the look of someone about to be permanently stewed.

"No one ever said, Missus. We only recognized Puss and Boots each time they showed up."

"Did they come fully grown, George?"

"No Maam." Maude finally added spoke up. "They was always little uns, and I had to keep them separate from the house much of the time so they didn't mess things up. I'd let them come in only when I was there to keep an eye on 'em so's they wouldn't scratch the furniture, but they was always fast learners and it seemed like soon as they was six months old, they knew what to do and what not to do. Better 'en most children, I can assure yur!"

"Did you see them being born, Maude?"

"I surely did, Maam. They was always born in the barn out yonder and in the hayloft by our place. Mama and Papa made a nice nesting place before they was to come, and both Mama and Papa stayed there until it was all over!" With that, George looked at her as though she was totally insane. Obviously he had no idea what his wife did when he wasn't there. "Now don't you go lookin at me like that, Old Man. I seen what I seen! I can tell yer that! So don't go on at me. And yer know somethin else? As soon as they was six months, the Mama and the Papa passed!" She gave her head one final, definitive nod, placed her napkin on the table and made ready to clear it of the cups and glasses.

"No, no, Maude. You were my welcome guests and it's my job to clear and clean up. In fact it's not a job at all, it has been a pleasure!" I said, hoping she would sit down again and we could continue. But there seemed to be no hope of that since George rose as well. "Before you go, I do have one more question about the cats," I added hastily as they headed toward the door. "When was the last time you saw these two, do you recollect at all?"

"Why, when Master Harry and the others were here for the summer quite some time ago now. He was still a youngster," Maude responded while George nodded his head. "When they left, the cats did too. We thought they'd crawled into the cars and went with them! How was we to know they ran away waitin' for you to come! Now, are yer sure you don't want any help? George, yer got to get up early and go to town with the shoppin' list." Maude's voice had a hint of something different in it so I agreed, said I was rather tired, and would truly appreciate her capable help. George thanked me heartily for a good dinner, pumping my hand, looked searchingly at his wife, yawned, and went out of the door.

After we loaded the dishwasher and stored the very few leftovers, Maude put her hand on my shoulder and guided me to the kitchen table. "Maam, I surely want you to know somethin' else about this place." Her voice took on a very hushed quality and even seemed a bit shaky. "At certain times of the day and the night, when the light is right, I seen things no human should see. Why, I'd say this place has its ghosts. Does that surprise ya?" I shook my head and said most very old places had something of the sort going on since so many people died at home and left something of themselves behind, especially if their passing was full of pain or anger, or unexpected. "Well, I'm sure glad to hear ya say that 'cause there were many who died here and one who jumped off the Widder's Walk or so the story goes."

"Did she do that after finding out her husband was lost at sea?"

"Oh, never, Maam. No Spruce was ever lost at sea! They was too good sailors and captains for that, and the sea was always kind to this family. No, she jumped when her husband found out she was sleepin' with someone else when he was at sea so as he wouldn't have ter kill her, or so the story goes."

"Well, if he was at sea, did someone in the family tell him? Or a friend? Were they seen together?"

"Oh, no, nothin' likes that. We was always told she had a lover and maybe a babe on the way and she knowd her husband would be able to count the months he was gone from the last time he was here and figure it out because the baby was newly born just before he was ter come home! But no one ever saw the babe or heard about its being born, so we was told and my parents was told. What a shocker it must 'a' been, I tell you!"

"I can agree with that, Maude. Do you know when this happened?"

"Middle of the 1800s as I was told, during the War Between the States as they called it then."

"Who spilled the beans, do you know?" She didn't reply but continued: "Why, my family was born and bred here too, Maam. We been here since the beginning. I was always told we came on a big boat that sailed for many months across that ocean out thar. George's family too, but they came from Down East and weren't here as long as my kin." Maude spoke with the pride of the first settlers built into her very fabric and instinctively I hugged her and beamed my feelings of pride for her as well.

"Ya know, Maam, I saw ya on the Widder's Walk today and called George to get ya down, ya know. It's not safe there late afternoon or really any time. Last time I went up there to sweep the leaves almost a year ago now, I felt all sorts of strange things around me and told George he could go do it from now on come autumn. Goodness!" she suddenly exclaimed, "Just look at that time!" It was just past 9:30. "Have to make sure he's okay and set the alarm clock. Ya know, I need it, but he never does," she said with a big grin on her face as we gave each another quick hug. "Just one more thing, Maude," I said and she stopped cold. "Please call me, Emma. Not Maam. Okay?" She smiled and nodded and we hugged again. I walked her to the door, turned the dishwasher on and then went upstairs. I knew I had made a special friend.

Time And Tide Wait . . .

All that matters, is that time and tide wait for no one. But that seems not to be the case with me. I went into my bedroom, readied myself for sleep but it just wouldn't come. Every time I looked at my watch, it seemed to say the same time—midnight, yet I knew it was either earlier than that or later. I had come upstairs directly after Maude left and I locked up and that was just before 10:30, and I never loll around when getting ready to sleep. I was so exhilarated by the events of the day, I couldn't get comfortable, and they, in turn, kept tumbling through my mind. Nothing I could do would still my mind from its wild ride — not deep breathing, not meditating, not even gentle exercise, or reading. Besides, when reading, I found my eyes going over the same paragraph several times over before the gist entered my frazzled consciousness. At that point, in a state of complete frustration, I heatedly tossed the book across the room.

I hauled myself out of bed and went to my cosmetic case to see if I had any aspirin or cold medicine. As I am rarely ill, I doubted it. I even searched my handbag dumping everything on the bed to make sure one lone pill was not hiding in the bottom. It was only then I noticed I was alone. Neither cat had joined me. Maybe that's why I couldn't sleep! I had grown so used to them already; they were indigenous to my current existence.

I called to them but got nothing in return. Not a meow or a thought. Maybe they were outside. Cats did hunt and the weather was certainly still good for that from the feline point of view. Stepping into my soft clogs which doubled as bedroom slippers, I headed downstairs not only to look for them but to make some warm milk. Maybe the calcium would quiet me down. After all, it was an age-old recipe for insomnia. My eyes felt so heavy as I made my way downstairs, I held on not only to the banister but went down one step at a time as though I had an injured foot or ankle.

When I reached the bottom, I turned on the light in the dining room and went into the kitchen, opened the back door and looked out. Neither animal was in sight. I called to them softly both verbally and mentally but again got nothing. Suddenly I was gripped with an enormous feeling of anxiety. Were these guys old? Was it their time to pass on? Did they go back to the graveyard to do this? But Maude hadn't said anything about newly born kittens.

I had to sit down. Everything was whirling around and around in my brain. I took several deep breaths, long and slow, forcing my diaphragm in and out trying to relax it and my stomach at the same time. When I felt steadier, I began making coffee, not warm milk, and when it was ready, poured a mug full and sat there sipping it while trying to put my now completely addled thoughts into some sort of order. How did the day begin? I couldn't remember anything except waking up, dressing and coming down to make breakfast for the three of us. The next thought that penetrated was walking around the outside of the house, lounging in the garden with the cats while eating a sandwich, napping.....no, not napping... meditating. I had heard something and went somewhere but I couldn't pull it together. I let that go and continued my sluggish recall. Yes, going through the foliage in the back of the house and finding the family graveyard, investigating somewhat, being intrigued by the number of times the small grave had been used for the same named felines over decades and then the Widow's Walk! The feeling of being up there! That flew freshly into my mind as though it just happened. Draining the mug I opened the drawer where I had replaced the flashlight, grabbed it and hurried to the secret stairs, pushed open the door, turned on the light and ran up the stairs to the top.

I put my ear to the door and listened hard. I've extremely keen hearing but all I heard was silence. My anxiety and overactive imagination, spurred on by the age of this house and probable ghosts made me think I would surely hear someone sobbing. Opening the door as quietly as I could and hooking it back against the turret I stepped quietly out and made a quick tour of the walk. No one but me was there.

As I went down the stairs, I wondered why I thought about ghosts when the synapses finally began connecting. My initial experience at The Hounds Tooth Inn would have set me up for this, as well as Maude's warning about the Widow's Walk, and HJS's joking about the age of the place all penetrated my mind for a ride I was not sure I really wanted to take. As I reached the bottom, turned out the light and reentered the hallway, my feet pointed me in the direction of the living room and seemed to move me there of their own accord.

The mirror was there over the fireplace right where George had hung it and on either side was a cat staring into the mirror as though transfixed. Not wanting to startle them, I sent mental messages, but neither responded. I tiptoed up to the mantle gratefully remembering I couldn't see into that thing as it was too high, reached up, and patted each cat on the rump. All I received was a flick of the tail. They were totally immersed in whatever they saw, or thought they saw.

What the hell was going on here! I felt as though I was reliving reading "Harry Potter and the Sorcerer's Stone" and all the works of Henry James, together. What were these animals seeing? I wanted to find out but knew, the coffee not withstanding, I should most definitely not try. Whatever they were seeing was their own business and besides, if I looked in it I would probably see something quite different. But when I looked in it at the Inn, the cats were right beside me and I thought we all saw the same time period, but who am I to judge what another being sees — be it feline or human.

"Ok, you guys," I said aloud. "Now that I know where you are and what you are into, I'm going to bed and that's all there is to it. You can either stay down here or come and join me. Your choice," I said walking to the doorway and sneaking a peek back at them. They were still staring into the mirror but their tails had begun twitching in 'tail talk'. I went into the kitchen, rinsed out the coffee cup, put it in the drainer, and headed towards the stairs.

Just as I was about to go up, the most excruciating yowl flowed out of the living room. Now, as I have said before, I hadn't had pets for quite some time in my adult life and was not used to things like this. It sounded like what I imagined a death knell would sound like from felines. Without any hesitation at all I ran towards the sound.

Nappy was standing up, looking intently into the mirror, but his back was arched, and the fur on his tail was standing straight up as was the fur all along his back. Peaches was just sitting there looking between him and the mirror, back and forth and forth and back as though she thought he was crazy. Suddenly, she just got up, looked in the mirror again and at her companion, and turned her back on the entire situation with her rump facing the mirror and her tail batting heatedly at it.

Now my curiosity was most definitely peaked. Throwing all caution into the proverbial wind, I ran into the kitchen, grabbed the four rung step ladder I had seen yesterday and ran back into the living room. Neither cat was on the mantelpiece. Both were curled up together on one of the fireside chairs watching me intently as I set the step stool up and readied myself to climb up. My eyes told me this small ladder would make me just tall enough to peer into the mirror. Without even taking a deep breath, I scurried to the top rung, holding on to the mantelpiece to balance and brace myself and looked into the mirror. All I saw was the room as it was except for the mantle and the fireplace of course. No time changed seemed to be involved at all. I was there as I was, hair disheveled, in my night clothes with eyes staring wide at the reflection.

Climbing back down with great relief and folding the ladder up, I walked hastily out of the living room telling the cats they were on their own and if they wanted to scare themselves silly thinking their image in the mirror was an enemy that was fine by me.

I didn't even replace the ladder in the kitchen. I left it near the dining room door and made it upstairs and into bed just before my entire body went into a state of collapse due to extreme exhaustion. As soon as my head hit the pillow, dreams overtook me. Dreams I knew. Places I had been in my life as well as all the eras I had experienced since The Hounds Tooth Inn. What I found most interesting was that I was standing above all of the images, which did not blend together but kept themselves separated by some trick of the imagination. I even saw myself sprawled out comfortably in the lounge chair with the tuna sandwich near me. As I watched this part intently, there was one part I could not recall. It kept slipping away from me. I saw myself lying there with a long silver cord stretching from my heart and weaving its way upward and upward. Then I spied a gauze-like version of me following the cord upwards until it finally came to rest on what seemed like a cloud. Then I heard, "You are correct!" it said over and over. "You are correct! You are correct! You are correct!" This was followed by, "You know. You really do know, Emma. You are a catalyst to time and adventure. You will use this often from this moment on."

I expected this 'dream' to end there but it did not. Instead the voice, soft but strong and very soothing, continued. "You think everything you have experienced is something different. But you have forgotten: not only were you as you are now, but you saw yourself as you have been in different times. And your dear friend was also with you as the need arose in different guises. He

95

also had the same characteristics you have always known to be a deep part of his emotional being." At this juncture, all the images came flooding back in perfect sequence, concluding with my very last run up to the door of the turret. However, there was something new here. Something I had not heard then. Someone was sobbing wildly.

I know I was tossing, turning, and moaning in my sleep because my companions, who had deigned to join me, were pushing against each side of me. In this 'dream state', I even felt myself shaking so hard I felt as though this very solid bed was moving. What was more, I felt as though sweat was pouring off of me, but I could not wake up. No matter what I tried, I could not wake up, nor could I suddenly move. I felt hot, but frozen in time and space. I wanted to scream, but before I could do so, a soft warm breeze covered me from stem to stern and I was comforted. Way back in the very far recesses of my mind, I felt, rather than heard the Lullaby from Humperdinck's, "Hansel and Gretel," and drifted off into a deep refreshing sleep.

I had no idea of the time when I was gently awakened, again by the felines, and the soft warm breeze, but I felt completely refreshed. "You are correct, Emma," the voice from my out of body experience at lunchtime whispered. "You and Harry are connected and have always been. That is why he was always calling you once the two of you met again. You are no longer like ships passing in the night. Your bonds have been reconnected. That is why he is joining you so soon. You two will experience much together but he does need the tutelage you will be giving it to him in your own inimitable way.

"You have come here to find out more about your lives together and apart—especially his. You have seen and experienced glimpses of them and there is much more to see and experience." I sighed deeply and turned on my side. "There are wrongs to be righted. You will succeed," the breeze whispered in my soul. With this, the felines, stretched out languidly on either side of me and a blessed, deep, serene sleep washed over my entire body.

One would think after a night such as the one I had experienced, that the day would dawn bright and sparkling. Just the opposite was true. What really returned me to my present reality was a series of booms caused by thunder and flashes of lightning with rain teeming down in torrents. My eyes opened wide as the sounds of the storm fully penetrated my consciousness, but my two companions did not move. When I attempted to sit up, I found I was pinioned down tightly. Each animal was still pressed firmly against my sides holding the blanket close to my body. I tried to move and Nappy opened his eyes, pushed harder against me, and went back to sleep. Peaches did not react at all. Strictly female, was my only thought as I too, closed my eyes and slept a while longer.

At long last, I felt my body could move freely and like my two felines, I stretched long and languidly, wriggling everything from my toes through to my head. The rain was still falling heavily, but I didn't care. After a long hot shower I hurriedly dressed and headed to the kitchen. There, the two cats were sitting by their food bowls waiting patiently for their morning victuals. Of course, being a dutiful slave, I attended to their needs, while at the same time brewing my favorite drink and, quite unusual for me, pulled out a frying pan, then the eggs, bacon, and bread for toast.

After all of us were satisfied, the cats headed to the back porch and I, not really feeling as though I was fully ensconced in my body even after the stretches, hot shower and a good meal, just sat at the table staring through the torrential goings on with a completely vapid and vacant mind.

I have no idea how long I sat there, but it felt as though it were days and days. When I finally focused on my current reality again, I did glance at the kitchen clock and noticed that only five minutes had passed since the cats had gone out and I had sat down with my mug of coffee. I then glanced into the dining room and the doorway leading to the main hall. There, propped against the door jam was the ladder, just as I had left it the night before. However, as I had walked towards the kitchen earlier, I had no memory of seeing it. "Maybe I was just not all together then," I said aloud rising with mug in hand and automatically heading to the ladder, picking it up, and taking it back into the living room.

Once more, I positioned it in front of the oversized fireplace, and still holding the mug gingerly, climbed up to the fourth and final rung, and closed my eyes. Standing there, pressing the tops of my thighs against the mantle piece I slowly opened my eyes holding the mug so it could be seen. It had lilacs all over it, but when I looked at it through the mirror, it was festooned with roses.

For No Man Or Woman

I raised my eyes from the cup to the surroundings in the mirror. They were all the same. Then I focused in on me. I too, looked the same, right down to the clothing I had put on this morning. Then I peered again at the mug. The roses were gone and the lilacs were there.

"Okay, not so terribly shocking," I said aloud. My verbalization must have been the cue the cats had been waiting for as they immediately jumped to the mantelpiece and also looked into the mirror. They spent the next few moments looking from the mirror to me and then from me to the mirror. I was watching them and the mug almost at the same time and noticed the lilacs disappeared again and the roses reappeared. "Who likes roses do either of you two know?"

"I do. I think they are the most beautiful flower nature ever created."

"Harry! Oh, my goodness! I didn't even hear the door open!" I said in amazement turning on the ladder while holding onto the mantle, but still clutching the mug. "You weren't supposed to be here for another week but how wonderful you are here now!!!"

"Well, how could you hear anything through the torrents outside, my dear Emma? Now let me help you," he said as his very wet body came close and he reached for my waist in order to help me down. "I missed you and only after almost a week and a half!"

After a soaking wet hug, I pulled him into the kitchen and gave him a steaming cup of coffee, topping mine off at the same time. I then went upstairs and grabbed a blanket from the foot of the bed and, returning to the kitchen, threw it over his shoulders. Knowing Harry as I did, I set about making him the same breakfast I had made for myself and joined him with another piece of buttered toast and three strips of bacon – a very unhealthy but favorite sandwich of mine.

It was very strange, but throughout this time we didn't say one word to each other. It was almost as if we both knew what had gone on the night before and words were not needed since the sharing had already taken place.

As he mopped up the remainder of his yolk with his toast and washed it down with a gulp of coffee, his eyes met mine and after only a swift moment, he grinned from ear to ear. "Well, that was wonderful, Emma. I could always count on you to know me like a book, and boy, was I starved. The rains started coming down just as I crossed the state line and I knew it would be stupid to stop for anything. Just knew it was best to get here as fast as I could before any roads flooded.

"Now tell me all about you and your brief time here and where did those two come from?" he asked pointing at the floor where both cats had seated themselves like dogs waiting for crumbs to fall. Absolutely polite, they were sensing this was the person they had to impress.

Pouring us both more coffee I related the entire saga beginning with The Hounds Tooth Inn, the cats, the mirror, coming here, George and Maude's reaction to the felines, finding the private graveyard and the twenty year lifespan for these animals. Throughout my entire discourse, Harry just nodded and smiled. When I finished, slightly breathlessly, he said, "And what was going on last night, may I ask?"

"Why?"

"I had the strangest dream when I pulled over for a quick nap on the way up. Something pushed me to get here lickety-split and I've no idea why. I knew you were fine. That much I did know, but it was something in your voice, I think, when I spoke with you. Don't quite know what it was. Maybe the trips through the looking glass, right Emma, or should I call you Alice?"

Laughing at his inane sense of humor, I just said, "I've no idea Harry. None at all, but I am certainly glad you are here. George even went into town with a long list of supplies as I intend to spoil you rotten with my cooking," I responded with just a hint of irony in my voice to match his.

"Silly woman, I'm only here for a long weekend, and there are some wonderful restaurants hidden around these parts and besides, you came here for R&R, not to play chief cook and bottle washer for me, ya' know. And besides, I don't think Gertrude or McDuff would appreciate you staying around all the time, am I right you two?" Upon formal, verbal recognition, the cats jumped easily onto the table and stared harshly at him. "Did I say something I shouldn't have said," Harry continued as Nappy hissed at him while Peaches turned, showed him her rear end, and thumped her lush tail heatedly on his wrist.

"I think proper introductions are needed. Harry, meet Napoleon, or Nappy, and his friend, Peaches," I said pointing to each animal as I made the introductions. "They seemed to like those names and somehow, neither Gertrude nor McDuff ever entered my mind when we were communicating about it."

"Communicating? You mean they spoke to you, really? I guess you are in need of solitude and R&R after all, Em!" Harry only called me "Em" when he was upset, so I knew I had to fill him in gently without upsetting his equilibrium any further. After all, he had driven almost straight through from the city and I knew he must be tired. And what was more he even came up earlier than he said he would! Now, why did he do that, I wondered!

"Well," I said, standing and walking over to the sink with his dishes, "I kept asking each one if one name after another was suitable to his or her taste, and when I hit on Napoleon, he jumped into my lap and began purring like there was no tomorrow. The same happened with Peaches, but only after I told her it related to her coloring."

"Oh, you had me scared there for a minute, Emma. I thought you had lost it completely!" He said beginning to giggle. The giggle turned into a big guffaw and I knew we were again on an even keel. "You are such a tease, Emma! But they do remind me of the two cats who lived here while I was growing up. But they were called something else. Now what were their names?"

"How about Puss and Boots, Harry," I said, returning to the table. "The Everett's recognized them immediately and George even showed me the family album with pictures of almost the very same cats."

"That's right! That's right! I remember now," he exclaimed standing to pull the blanket tighter around him. "There were always two cats around that resembled these two and for some reason, they were always named Puss and Boots. Guess Dad and Granddad loved those names."

"And what's even stranger, dear," I interjected, "is that the animals lived for twenty years and died after giving birth to two more that looked like them. At least that's what Maude told me, and believe it or not, they are all buried in your family grave yard! A whole bunch of them! When the rain lets up and the ground is dry, I'll take you there and you can see for yourself. And if you remember what I just told you, I found them at The Hounds Tooth Inn and they decided to join me. I just didn't pick them up and carry them off. Terry, the woman who runs the Inn told me she had no idea how they got there, but they'd been there for quite some time and no one in the village had ever seen them before. Not even the veterinarian! Now, I think that's weird. But enough for now, Harry. Just look at yourself. Your eyes are beginning to go around in circles so upstairs you go. You need a good long nap, and you are still damp," I said, helping him stand and navigate towards the stairs. "Oh, I took the master bedroom, but if you want it, it's yours. I will only take a few moments to move some things out of there so you will be comfortable, dear."

"No, no. I sleep in the Blue and Green room. Always have, always will." He bent to pick up his duffle and attempted to sling it over his shoulder, but he was really flagging, so I took it from him and guided him up the stairs and into the room of his childhood.

As soon as we entered, he gave a sigh of relief, kicked off his still wet shoes and almost fell on the bed. It took every ounce of mustering I had to convince him to get out of his damp clothes while I opened his bag and threw a robe at him. Once he had changed, he fell on to the bed and was snoring almost before his head hit the pillow. I picked up his clothes and shoes and gently shutting the door, headed downstairs to the washing machine.

Three hours later, with the rain finally having become a fine mist, and George having stopped over to check up on things, remove Harry's luggage from the trunk of the car, and leave the groceries, Harry was again sitting sleepily in the kitchen with another mug of fresh coffee in his hand. "Wish I felt more refreshed, Emma. Don't know what it is, but forgive me because this is one of the reasons I don't come here and stay."

"What do you mean, Harry? I'm not following you." I said as I finished folding his now clean and dry clothing.

"Weell, ever since I was a small one, I started out with great energy and then I seemed to have to force myself to play with the others and to stay awake as long as I was in this house. Outside was different. My energy seemed to return then. It seemed I do remember mother remarking that I never fought about taking an afternoon nap when I was very young and I also remember dad saying that was because I was playing so hard, but that wasn't the case at all. I just wanted to curl up into a small ball and not be seen or bothered by anyone. Of course it was different when we went visiting. Then I fought about napping like mad just as any kid would. God forbid I would miss something!

"Don't know why this place affects me so, but I'm feeling it all over again. And you know I completely forgot the extent of this feeling! Amazing, isn't it, Emma!"

"Well, dear, you did drive just about straight through, and the air pressure from the storm does weigh heavily on one's body." I responded trying to soothe him as his brow furrows deepened in even more consternation.

"Nope, that's not it at all! It was in the back of my mind on the way up and believe it or not, if you weren't here, I would have just turned around! You see, Emma, I've always felt there was something weird here and I guess the only way to avoid it was to sleep as much as possible even though I didn't want to do that! Funny, but it's all coming back to me now! "I guess I got used to it all after a while because this was my home. And maybe my parents were fighting. I really don't remember those early years too well, but when parents do fight or pay little attention to their kids, the kids just seem to fold into themselves, which is what I did. And to tell the truth, my parents were very into themselves and as I started to grow up, they paid less and less attention to me. I guess sleep was my only escape."

He stood up heavily but began pacing back and forth as he continued. "I remember one time in particular when everyone was heading to the ocean for the day and my family had the hardest time trying to get me up and fed and ready, and I was only five at the time and loved to dig in the sand and let the waves touch my toes, but this time, I didn't want to leave at all."

105

I waited for him to continue, but he had stopped cold physically and verbally. His eyes had that glazed look one gets when one is remembering something from the far distant past. He wrapped his hands around the mug he was still holding and slowly lifted it to his lips. Without taking a sip, he put it down on the table, reached for his clothes and headed upstairs. His eyes still glazed over.

Feeling slightly uneasy myself, I followed discreetly after him. His door was closed, so I positioned myself in my room with the door open waiting for him. After 20 or so minutes had passed, I knocked gently on his door. There was no answer. Slowly, I opened it and saw what I knew I would see. The great HJS curled up in the fetal position on his bed. The clothes were thrown haphazardly on the floor beside it and he was snoring like there was no tomorrow.

I knew there was an answer to this and I also knew where I would find it, but I loathed doing so. However, since this was in the best interest of a dear friend I went back to the kitchen, grabbed the ladder, and headed toward the living room and the mirror. Of course I wasn't alone. Both animals were already in position on the mantelpiece, but not facing the mirror. Instead, they were facing the doorway their eyes watching my every movement. As soon as I placed the ladder in front of the fireplace, they each moved to the farther sides of the mirror leaving more than enough room for me. When I reached the top rung, they came closer to fill in the gap between me, the mirror, and the ledge of the mantel, as though to protect and be with me. My own trepidations lessened greatly and after thanking them and patting each one, I turned to look into the mirror. "Mirror, mirror on the wall," I heard myself say and then I began to giggle so hard I had to clutch the ledge to steady myself. I guess the cats didn't like my sense of humor born of fear because each one slapped my arm with their tails. Getting a grip on why I there and what this was for, I peered into the glass.

The living room was nowhere to be seen. Instead I was looking at the Widow's Walk, watching a young woman pacing back and forth and wringing her hands. I know I made a face because this was an idealized scene from any and all period mysteries involving similar structures and I couldn't really buy this one as truth. Of course I remembered Maude's tale from the evening before, but even so, this was almost too much to be believed.

I was just about to climb down the ladder when lightning and thunder was heard again just outside while I was still looking at the mirror. The lightning and thunder seemed to shake the tower and in a matter of moments, when the skies opened, the young woman was completely soaked. She opened her mouth to scream and at the very same time, lightning flashed and thunder roared in stereo.

I held on to the mantelpiece for dear life as the scene shifted to the door which was violently thrown open. A man emerged. "Well, of course he would," I said to the cats who were as transfixed as I had become. "And I'll bet you anything it is Harry!" The felines seemed to be in agreement as both of their tails twitched mightily. The sound effects started again full strength and as the man stepped close to the woman, the flash of lightning lit up his face. It was most definitely not Harry.

Not wanting to miss a moment, but needing a reality check, I hurriedly glanced down at myself. I was still dressed in the clothes I had put on earlier, and a fast turn showed me the living room was the same. I quickly glanced back at the mirror wondering what this was all about, remembering how, at The Hounds Tooth Inn, I had been changed and moved into the same time and space I had been viewing in the mirror. Yet, here I was still in the present. Looking back at the mirror, I noticed the action had stopped. Was it waiting for me?

I had no sooner concentrated on the fact that the man was not my Harry in any way, shape, or form—my Harry was about six feet tall, robust, with brown hair, graying at the temples and piercing blue eyes. Then he grabbed the young woman by her upper arms and began shaking her violently and yelling at her. He appeared to be much older then she was by at least twenty years, but I could have been mistaken about that. Once again the skies boomed in both places and the rain came down in torrents but still he continued to lambaste and brutalize her. Her mouth was open as though she was screaming. I was so angry I didn't care what I did or what, if any, consequences there would be.

I backed down the ladder and ran to the hidden door, flipped on the light but nothing happened. I ran to the kitchen, grabbed the flashlight, and again headed to the secret stairs. I made it half way up with the flashlight in hand when everything changed: I was carrying a hurricane lamp and wearing a long dress and buttoned shoes of the mid1800s. I ran as quickly as I could to the top of the stairs and found the door standing wide open. The man was still shaking the young woman, but her head was lolling all over the place as though she could not hold it up. Without any further warning, and right on cue with the booming skies, her body went completely limp. He let her drop. As I exited the stairwell, my physical demeanor changed again. This time I was male. I rushed the older man, pushed him aside, and knelt down by the woman. Placing my hand on her heart, I felt nothing. Through the raging of the storm, I put my face close to hers to see if I could feel the breath of life. Nothing.

In a complete rage, I flew at his ankles and toppled him over pounding my own strong fists into him until he too, collapsed. Not caring about him, and crying myself, I bent to pick up the woman and carried her out and back down the stairs. Reaching the living room, I put her on the divan soaking wet as we both were and, with the fire in the fireplace going full blast, tried reviving her as best I could even blowing air from my mouth into hers and pressing down on her chest.

I have no idea how long I did this. I was totally oblivious to any other sounds or movements, even though the house did shake every once in a while from this terrible Nor'easter. She had to live. She just had to!

I remember standing for a moment and looking wildly around the room. On the wall just opposite the fireplace was a mirror. I was staring back at Harry. Harry from another time and place. Harry who loved too well, but it seemed not wisely. I knew where I was and I thought I knew who these people were. Harry was the lover, I thought to myself, the older man, his father, her husband. "Harry, Harry, Harry!" I said aloud in my own voice as though I was splitting from the Harry I had become. "It seems to me everyone is to blame, but there is no sense trying to sleep off the guilt from a time so long ago!"

As I uttered this, I heard footsteps coming down the circular stairs and the older man, who sort of resembled Harry entered the living room. His face was swollen from my fists and one eye was terribly blackened and almost completely shut. I turned to face him, rage and hatred filling me, but before I could act upon it, the scene changed and I was in my present time, standing up on the ladder peering into the mirror with the cats in their same position.

Okay. Okay. So I was role playing now. And it seemed to be safe even though I was not in control. I wanted to get down but couldn't yet there was no fear with this at all. I knew what was happening and what had beset HJS in his youth. After all, children are always more open than we adults. We begin to shut out what is commonly called the "psychic" elements of our existences when we are about six or seven because it is no longer accepted in our "polite" society by the adults who surround us. And Harry, it seems, immediately tapped into the horrible killing of the young woman by this probable ancestor of his who, in his lack of understanding, caused the current Harry the full guilt trip and its consequences to Harry's psyche, but without the knowledge to go along with it or the understanding to work with it.

I knew I had to get Harry up and explain things to him. This was going to be the only way to help him through this. But I still didn't feel as though I could move. Was I being held there or was this by my own choice? To this day I don't know. Neither I nor the felines seemed to be upset by this turn of events. And what was more, they seemed to be smiling at me.

"Emma! Emma! Where are you?" Harry called galumphing down the stairs.

"In the living room, Harry, and don't be alarmed. I'm standing on a ladder looking into a mirror," I responded.

"What the hell are you doing up there, woman? How stupid can you be? You know you are not the steadiest person in the world, and the very last thing you should do is to tempt fate and break something," he said coming up behind me and grabbing my legs. "You are here for a vacation, not to recuperate from a broken body!"

Now, as I have said previously I knew HJS pretty well, but I had never heard that tone of voice from him. Maybe it was because ninety-nine percent of our time together was in company with the rest of the "gang" but tonally, his voice was just like the one I had seen and heard through the mirror. After all, social situations are very different from one-on-ones. This upset me, but I did not lash out in response. It was as though something or someone had put a hand over my mouth.

I let him ease me down the steps, still holding my mug. I quietly thanked him, patted him on the shoulder, and smiled. I hoped this would let him know I was not afraid of heights or steps. I allowed him to lead me gently to the sofa, and there, once we were both seated, I began to tell him about this mirror and all of the experiences I had encountered with it. I mean, really tell him! Way over an hour later, when I had finished, with both felines sitting on either side of him, I got up, went to get him a cup of coffee, and upon returning, found him standing on the ladder, glued to the mirror.

"Oh, my God!" he said when he heard me coming, "I see my parents and, and grandparents! This is unbelievable!" He backed down the ladder and almost snatched the mug from my hand. "What is this, some kind of joke? You've really honed that gift of yours, Em. That power of projection stuff you were always titillating us with! It's really power of suggestion! Is this the Disney mirror or is this one of your own brilliant concoctions? A microchip in back honing in on a person's desires? Something like that? Is this something out of "Harry Potter?" He began to shake so hard, coffee spilled onto the rug. "For someone of your background," his voice began filling with rage, "I'm sure you could have rigged this!"

"Harry, Harry," I said quietly, sitting down and reaching for his hand. "George told me it was you who sent this mirror, and I just told you it is the exact same one that was at The Hounds Tooth Inn. In fact, I think I even said it before to you when you arrived wet and exhausted. I'm not sure any more, because so much has happened since you arrived!" I reached for his hand and gently pulled him down beside me. "And there is one more instance I didn't tell you about. Yesterday afternoon, I took a sandwich out to the garden where the patio lounges are and . . . "

I proceeded to relate, my out-of-body experience in depth and I also included my night's dreams. He just sat there with his eyes wide, staring at me. His breath came slowly, but his forehead was beading with perspiration as though he had run a ten mile race in five minutes! He started to hyperventilate so I forced his head between his knees for a few moments until his control returned.

I got up and started to walk around the room. I had to move. I just couldn't stay still any longer. Too many ideas were bombarding my mind and brain. "I know just how you feel, Harry," I said, "but I don't think this is dangerous; at least not the way we usually think of danger. And, before I go on," I said, taking a very deep breath while watching him carefully, "I've a question for you."

"What is it," he responded sullenly..

"Why did you come up so soon? After all, I've been here less than a week, and gone from the city for only about a week and a half, and it was you who said I needed time, space, and peace and quiet." I knew I had hurt him, so I added, "It's not as though you and I have been having a physical affair, dear. We are just very good friends and I did tell you I rarely get lonely, remember?" He looked a little less upset. "So, please HJS, please think what brought you here so soon? Oh, yes I did hear you loudly and clearly when you called. I even planned out a few wonderful recipes and George already went into the village to get a few special items not stocked here, but why, Harry? Why? And don't misunderstand; I am happy to see you. Very happy indeed, even. But why, Harry, why!"

There was no verbal response. I hurried back to his side, as he arose from the sofa, placing his mug on the nearest table, and going toward the mantelpiece. Instead of climbing the ladder he checked out the room and headed for a small secretary against the far wall. He took the chair from its side carried it over to the fireplace, placed it next to the ladder, and stood on it. The chair and his own height enabled him to easily view the mirror.

"Come over and join me, Emma," he said, his voice sounding calmer than I knew he actually was. "I think this thing can give us the answer to your question if we both look in it at the same time. Maybe I'm wrong, but it's worth a try, because I've no idea what propelled, and yes, I mean, propelled me to fly to you ASAP! Something pushed me all the way here, and I was right in the middle of another project, too! Oh, do we say, the good old, 'Mirror, mirror, on the wall' stuff?" First he giggled, and then he turned almost glaring at me. "You should have heard Sam Edison, you know him, my editor, when I called and said I had to postpone and would hopefully make the next issue!"

"You lied to Sam, your best friend? How could you! You adore that man and the topics he ferrets out for you to investigate. What did you tell him exactly?" Harry stood there, still facing me, and placed his elbows on the mantle.

"I told him my other dearest friend was ill and needed me immediately. I didn't even wait for his response. Just hung up the phone, grabbed some things, threw them in my bag and left. I'm not even sure I double locked the door! But I do know the stove was turned off because without you and the gals around, there was no reason to do any cooking whatsoever, other then the morning coffee, so now that I'm feeling steadier, please come and join me, Emma, and forgive my reaction a few minutes ago."

I just stood there unmoving, looking at him. I think my mouth even fell slightly open; my shock at his transition was so great! He knew something. I was sure of it, but I also knew he would not tell me. I felt as though this was one of his experimental exercises and I was the dupe!

You see, I was the only one of us who really knew what and who Harry Jonathan Spruce did for a living. He worked under a variety of pseudonyms for a syndicated esoteric magazine conglomerate that published under a wide variety of titles. Everyone else thought he wrote for small group of newspapers spread across the country. Oh no, Harry was as weird in his thinking as I was, and if our mutual friends knew this, they would have dropped him like a hot potato, just as quickly as they would me, if they really knew what I had been involved in during my many lifetimes, my PhD's not withstanding. After all, legitimate credentials were essential to me and my own personal research — as essential as they were to Harry! And I know what I said about myself at the beginning, but now it is time to delve further into the 'real' me and admit that although I've been involved in what was so commonly called the esoteric or the occult back in the early twentieth century, I was really taken aback by what was shown to me in that mirror, because it pulled me right into it. And my name is most definitely not Alice, and what is more, I do believe in this reality no matter what it has in store for me or for anyone else!

One question kept coming to the forefront of my mind: Did I really trust Harry? Was he 'stronger' than I was, or were we equals? Still standing there and looking at him looking at me, I got real quiet and began to breathe deeply. Just as I was doing this, both felines appeared and rubbed against my legs. As they did so, I heard that voice from a trillion miles away telling me all would be fine.

I nodded to Harry and walked over to the ladder. He turned and offered me his hand, but I just smiled at him, nodded my thanks, and climbed the steps myself without any effort. With that accomplished, I nodded to the cats and they also sprang up. Nappy on my right side, Peaches on Harry's left side. Each animal sat on its haunches, tails twitching lazily. Then, before I realized it, Harry and I were touching elbow to elbow.

"Why did I come here?" Harry asked at the same time I said, "Why did you come here?" We both then gazed into the mirror. All we saw were our own reflections with the felines still beside us. We both stood there for what felt like hours, but in actuality, was really only a few minutes, staring in the mirror, searching for an answer. Then without warning, our elbows separated and the mirror became a split screen.

I looked straight ahead and saw only a blank space. Looking at Harry's side, I saw a complete repeat of the scene I had been embroiled in from the turret and Widow's Walk right back to the sofa with the injured man. It was all exactly as I had told him. Not one thing differed. Turning my head and looking at Harry, it seemed to me that he was seeing the very same thing, but then he turned his head and looked at my half of this split screen.

"I don't believe one fucking thing!" He shouted. That's not me! But it is me in a way—it's my grandfather and his father, but who the hell is that woman? She's most definitely not my grandmother!"

"It's exactly what I saw, Harry. What I just told you all about. You recognize yourself and your dad! But you've no idea who she is?"

"None!"

"Are you sure? It's not some distant relative of yours? Do you have a photo album besides the one in the music room where I saw your family and these same two cats?"

He pushed himself away from the mantle with a great effort and while holding onto it with one hand, began to step down from the chair. "Photo album! You found a photo album?" He turned and looked up at me, his eyes glaring! "Where!" The voice emanating from him sounded exactly like the older man in the vision. It was full of hate and violence, but it didn't upset me one bit. I stood right where I was and, holding on to the mantelpiece for all it was worth, stared into the mirror, noticing through my peripheral vision that the felines had now moved closer to me and flailed their tails on my back.

"You know where it is, Harry! Go find it yourself and while you're at it, pull yourself together, because that's something you must do for you. It's not something I can do for you. You are on your own here. After all, this is your home, not mine," I said softly as though I was dealing with a recalcitrant three-year old and felt my voice, or what there was of it, full of love even though the words seemed to be more in my head than actually vocal. I glanced quickly in the mirror and saw my lips move as my vision was still intent on the blank side of the mirror which was now showing me the room as it was in my current time.

He stood there, his hands becoming fists held so tightly his knuckles turned white. I felt no fear as he raised his

117

arm to strike me. I knew what would happen and it did. He fell to his knees, unclenched his fists, and covered his face with his hands.

"We are in this together, whatever it is, dear," I said, "But there are things we must each do for ourselves." My voice was still soft, almost a whisper, and I turned to look at him. He slowly got to his feet, looked up at me, as a tremor run through his body.

"Sorry about that, old girl," he too spoke softly, and walked down the hallway that led to the music room.

Many hours later, long after the cats and I had climbed down from the mirror, I had made two sandwiches, gone out for a breath of fresh air and eaten mine outside after calling down the hallway that vittles were on the kitchen table in case he was hungry, I found myself back in the living room sitting at the small desk having moved the chair back to it. I had brought with me my drink of choice as well as pen and paper and began to write down everything that had transpired since I left home. I was looking for parallels especially in the time warps as well as with the people involved in those time warps besides Harry.

I visualized the faces of all involved, including those travelers from The Hounds Tooth Inn who seemed to vanish so suddenly the following morning without a sound of cars or buses. I was so intent on my purpose, I even began sketching not only what I remembered of their faces, but of all the rooms in all the time frames involved. I also numbered each page as I did this so that I could not only keep them in order, but shift them around if push came to shove. I knew somewhere way down deep inside me that all the clues were there, but I couldn't fathom them as yet. As so many mystery book writers have their heroes say, "There's something floating in my mind that I can't pinpoint that would solve the mystery, but what it is . . ." Even though the reader may have had an inkling, the hero or heroine could not grasp what it was. And that's exactly how I felt.

I remember getting up to refill my mug and seeing Harry's food untouched, knowing I had planned a wonderfully sumptuous meal before this past event occurred, but all that would have to wait. I thanked the Powers that Be that nothing I had asked George to purchase would spoil if not immediately used, and this made me more adamant about finding out what the hell was really going on—from the beginning to the present.

Needing a break, I went to the kitchen, picked up the lone sandwich and went to the music room. It was devoid of any human. However, books and albums were scattered on each and every surface, and Nappy and Peaches were spread out on the middle of the floor in full stretch cat mode, their heads pointing towards the long windows facing the back of the house. Their tails twitched ever so slightly upon my entrance but no other recognition was granted me. Their eyes never wavered from those windows.

Ah-ha, I thought, so, that's where he went—out the back way and probably to the old graveyard. Just as I was about to head towards the French Doors, I head the front door slam and the stamping of feet head towards the kitchen. "Okay, who ate my lunch," Harry's deep voice echoed throughout the house. "Coming! Coming!"

I shouted back and headed for the kitchen. I quickly glanced to see what the felines were doing. Neither of them moved an inch.

As I neared the kitchen, I tiptoed to see what shape he was in. He was sitting in his chair, elbows on the table, one hand holding a napkin, ready to dig in. "Here it is, HJS," I said putting the plate in front of him. "I went to bring it to you in the music room, but you must have gone to the bathroom." I did not let on where I thought he went. "Only the cats were there. Would you like tea, coffee or something else to go with it?"

"You can make me another just like this one and yes, some pickles and olives would be wonderful. I'm starved! Oh, and a big glass of water will do fine. Not been drinking enough of it lately," he said with a big grin on his slightly gritty face. As I said before, I'd known him for quite some time now, but never knew him to be a big water drinker. Coffee, yes, tea, sometimes, and alcohol when the group got together, but water!!!!!!! He started to eat as though he had been without food for ages. The first sandwich disappeared in a matter of minutes and then as I placed the second one before him, he blithely asked for the jars of mayo, catsup, and mustard, and a knife. He began slathering these on the next sandwich not only on the bread but in the middle of it too. Now, I had never heard of adding catsup to tuna fish, but I figured with all the weirdness going on, to each his own!

When he finished, something else odd happened. Usually when we were together, I played my part perfectly and took the dishes to the sink. Whether I washed them or not was another thing, but I always took them from his place. This time, he got up, took his dishes to the sink, rinsed them, put them in the dishwasher, and then returned the jars of everything he had used to the refrigerator. His last feat was to refill his water glass before he turned to me. "There! All done and thank you for a lovely repast, dear Emma. You always make the best tuna salad I know. Now how about joining me for a walk while the weather is still sort of balmy?"

I know my mouth fell open at that kind of back-handed compliment but I girded my loins, thanked him, and said, "I would love to Harry, but how about giving me another half-hour? Before you came in for lunch I was working on something, and I really wanted to take another look at it before enjoying the great outdoors." Without comment, he smiled, nodded, and left the room. I just stood there, dumbfounded. This was all so unlike the Harry I knew and had grown to adore.

I hastily returned to the living room, went through my notes and drawings again and was just about to give up, go upstairs and get my walking shoes when I looked again at the group sketch of the visitors sitting around the dinner table. The man who had nodded at me when I entered and who had passed me the veggies looked very familiar. His nose and forehead drew my attention. I looked closer, and suddenly realized he had a familial resemblance to George Everett. Not that he was a twin, by no means; he looked to be a brother or possibly a cousin. Just as I had come to this realization, there was a knock on the front door, and I heard the now familiar, "Hello, Missus? May I come in?" Instantly I arose, ran to the door, and opened it for George.

"We was gettin' worried about you 'cause we'd not seen you all day —only Mr. Harry wandering around like a lost soul. Is everything okay here?" he said with deep concern in his voice."

"Of course, George, I've just been busying myself with my work today. Nothing to worry about if you don't see me," I said smiling at him while I carefully looking at his features and mentally comparing them to the visitor. I really saw the resemblance this time without a doubt. "Are you and Maude okay?"

"Er, yes we are both fine and dandy but got a little worried about you, that's all. So since nothin' is wrong, I'll be goin' now. I'm headed back into town so if there is anything you need . . . "

"No, we're well stocked but thank you again for all you do and have done for me and for Harry," I said smiling up at him and patting his arm. He smiled back and gently closed the door behind him. With his face so fresh in my vision, I ran back to the small desk and looked at the sketch of the visitor again. There was no doubt about it. There was a great resemblance here and I did not think this was one of those doppelganger occasions. I knew I had to find time to ask my new girl friend, Maude, about their family, especially since they and their parents and grandparents had been living on this property almost forever. Things were becoming stranger and stranger from one point of view, but also there was a new clarity forming in my now, less addled mind.

Something had drawn all of us here together. Whatever it is or was, was now active and becoming more alive not only in my mind, but in everything that had transpired. Realizing I had some time left before Harry would be calling to go for the walk he so wanted me to join him in, I went back to the fireplace and climbed the ladder. I had no sooner done so, when both cats joined me. They had disappeared while Harry was eating. So with my 'protection', as I had begun to think of them, I peered into the mirror.

It was no longer a split screen but one solid piece showing me the dining room at The Hounds Tooth Inn. Without asking anything, like a scene in a movie, it zeroed in on the face of the man in question. It was George, but not George. The differences were subtle—the shape of the ears and chin were extremely different, as were the hairline and hair color. This man's was brown with grey sideburns, while George's hair had much more gray in it. But their noses, foreheads and now, upon closer inspection, the eyes were similar in shape. Only the color was different: George's eyes were hazel and this man's eyes were a very deep brown. I knew I had to get down quickly, so I petted each animal on its flank and backed myself down the ladder steps. They joined me without any complaint and when I bent down to thank them, it seemed as though they were smiling at me.

My next step was to put everything in a safe place where only I knew about it and then get ready. A quick look around showed me the only safe place would probably be under my mattress, so without waiting any longer, I almost ran upstairs, hid my drawings, put on my sturdy walking shoes grabbed a sweater, scarf, and jacket, and went back downstairs to find my friend standing by the door ready and waiting for me.

The sun was past its zenith but the air was still relatively warm even though it did have a hint of crispness in it. I breathed deeply a few times and then took his hand. I thought it wise to let him lead me to whatever it was he wanted me to see, since he seemed to be such a different person than the good old Harry I knew back in the city and even the afternoon before.

We walked around the grounds and finally took the hidden path towards the graveyard. But as we neared it, he veered off to the left pulling me along behind, but being the gentleman he always was, held the branches that had covered over this old, overgrown area.

We plowed through this for what seemed like miles. It was hard going due to the undergrowth, but suddenly a path appeared almost out of nowhere and down it we went. Harry was still silent, but he turned to me and smiled such a radiant smile, I found myself joining him in his enthusiasm. The ground only mildly sloped so I had no idea we were really going down a hill until we came to the end of the path. There, in plain sight was a small hut-like structure.

"Come on, Emma. I want you to see this. It's where I really existed. It's more important to me than the house."

"Ah, every child has a secret hide-a-way," I called after him as he ran to the door, "And this was yours!"

"You got that one right, old girl, now hurry! Everything has been left as it was because no one remembered it was here. My great-grandfather had built it and had long forgotten it so neither my grandparents nor my parents knew about it to begin with." As I approached, he threw the door open (it opened inward) and beckoned me to follow him inside. The smile on his face belied the shaking his body was going through, or maybe he was shaking

124

because he was so very excited and could not control his eagerness.

I slowly stepped in the hut. The first thing I noticed was that the walls were painted almost the same shade of French Blue, but about three shades lighter so that light would reflect more easily in this space. There were also four windows, one on each side. The glass was thick, very old, but unbroken. The wooden floor was still highly polished and contained a series of small rugs of various descriptions. It looked as though these rugs were part of larger pieces which probably had been in the house at one time or another, but each was finished with a strong binding so as not to unravel and the colors from one piece to another clashed. However, I was certain this was something no child would notice or care about.

In the middle of this structure was a small wood or coal burning stove with its pipe going upwards and through chimney so small it was not evident from the outside. No youngster would freeze in here, I told to myself, still taking in everything from an ancient rocking horse to all sorts of toys and building blocks scattered around. Against the far wall was a small series of two-tiered shelves each containing books and what looked to be a chess set and other board games of the period. But what period was this? I had to find out. Without asking permission, I walked quickly to the shelves and reached for the first book in my vision.

"Stop that right now!" a different voice screamed. "No one told you you could go and take something from the shelf. It's mine. IT'S MINE! Get away from there, NOW!!!!!!!!!" I was suddenly grabbed around my waist and pulled backwards by an individual I did not know with an unbelievable strength. I wrenched away from him and turned sharply; there was a youngster about nine years old now in front of me. Oh, it was Harry, alright! There was no question of that even though his adult features were far from being there and his clothes were at least 40 years out of date: that made me look down at myself. I was wearing the same shoes I had put on for our walk and the same pants and shirt, but something was different! I was the same height as he!

What in anyone's name was this changing dimensions all about! I was beginning to think I was going mad. Then, without warning, we two were as we were in our present time. Harry looked at me, his eyes wide open and full of awe.

"I . . . I . . . Sorry, Emma. Don't know what came over me and did you see us? I was only about eight or nine then and that little girl . . . oh, I remember it quite well, was visiting with her parents and I brought her here to get away from the adults who were talking amongst themselves and paying absolutely no attention to us. We needed to be kids! Only," he continued, and then stopped for a long intense moment, "I can't remember her name. Wait . . . wait . . . it's on the tip of my tongue." He sat down cross-legged in a way I'd been jealous of for the past few years since no amount of Yoga would allow my knees to do that any more, and he stared out into space.

Without any warning, he jumped up exclaiming, "Terry! Her name was Terry, and her parents had just moved into the area and were looking for property to buy. I remember hearing them ask Dad about a place that would be good for a B&B! Oh, and she was about two years younger than me, and I scared her so, she began crying. Boy, did I have a time quieting her down. I knew no one would hear us, but I didn't want to go back to the house with her and a tear-stained face. Oh, God! She's the same Terry who owns the Inn! I never realized it until just now!"

He stopped abruptly again and went over to the shelf and grabbed the same book I had been going for. "Why this is even the same book she was after! 'National Velvet' and the only way I could get her to calm down was to take it from her and start to read it to her. Then, after she was OK, I remember helping her to get on the rocking horse and watching her carefully, helped her to rock gently back and forth while I continued telling her the story since I knew it already by heart! What an afternoon that was!! And then we became friends and she was often here!"

While he was telling this to me, my mind flew back to The Hounds Tooth Inn and I pictured Terry, the proprietress. "Right on!" I said to myself. Terry was just about the right age. It could easily have been her no matter what she'd told me during my stopover there and that's where all of this trouble, this shifting of time and dimensions, began. And the mirror was there too! How could I have not remembered that first? But I didn't want to bring that up at this moment, so instead I said while entwining my arm through his, "Show me around your secret place, HJS. Which toys did you like best? What did you do here when you were all alone?"

Harry began walking around the playhouse and pointing at the tin soldiers, the building blocks, the rocking horse, and then went over to the shelves. He ran his hands lovingly over the books and then turned to me. "The one that drove me most insane, Emma, was the chess set. That's why I never learned to play. They tried to teach me at the house, but for reasons that still defy me; I could never get the hang of it. But checkers were a different thing altogether. That's why I still love to play it, and . . . Ooh, Parcheesi! That was another game I loved! Monopoly, was okay, but you needed at least three people for that and since that was played at the house, the adults became as kids and it was never much fun, since they knew more about the economy and how to do things than I did. I just loved to roll the dice and move the car—I always got the car—around the board. What did I care about buildings and hotels and get out of jail free cards. I only wanted the fun of going around and around."

"Do you still feel that way, Harry? I'm asking because I feel we're going around and around and around and have been since you arrived—at least in our conversations and the truthfulness behind them," I countered.

He just looked at me with his head tilted to the side. "You're right! We have been." He took a deep breath and sat in one of the child size chairs that surrounded a small table. "It's just that I don't know why I rushed up here. I knew you needed your time alone, and . . . "

"I think you were called here, my friend," I said. "I think we've something to do that is going to make big changes here, and after all, isn't that what we've both done all our lives?" I said softly and joined him at the table.

"Yeah, I guess so, but I'm just God damned tired of making changes!"

I smiled quizzically at him because I understood completely. I too, was tired, hence this "vacation," but something inside my heart would not allow me to let him get away with that as an excuse. "Ah-ha!" I said. "So that's one of the reasons you hung around us girls, huh? Well, I came up here to get away from changes also, but as I'm finding out, we can never get away from them."

Harry stood up so suddenly his chair tipped over and crashed to the floor. "Don't you dare start in on that Destiny stuff with me Emma Epstein! It's in all of your books and that's where it should stay," he yelled.

"Well, if that's so, Harry Jonathan Spruce, why are you here. What made you follow me? Think about it and stay here as long as you like. I'm going back to the house now with or without you and your temper tantrums. It's time for me to think too!" I know I sounded haughty and slipped into my all knowing teaching voice—but that's the way it came out, so I stood, opened the door and left. Following my instincts has always been my way of doing things, and I was suddenly fed up with him. Fed up to the hilt!

I know what I know and I do what I do because of it. I'm never ashamed of my actions and I rarely apologize for being who I am. It has taken me more than fifty years to know and realize my own I AM and if people don't like it, so be it. They don't have to deal with me. Therefore walking out on Harry was not something I would allow to upset me.

Feeling as I did, it took me half the time to get back to the house. No sooner had I entered, when Nappy and Peaches both jumped into my arms and began caressing my face with theirs. Ah, the psychic ability of the so-called lower animals never ceases to amaze me!

I hugged them back and carried them into the kitchen, put them on the floor and made myself a cup of coffee, adding a heaping spoonful of cinnamon to it. I felt I needed the calming effect of that spice as well as its aromatic benefits just then. Since I was treating myself, it was only right to treat the felines and when they finished theirs, I went upstairs and took the notes and drawings from underneath my mattress. I quickly looked at Terry's drawing and saw I was right. It had been her. I knew it in my core being even though I had no photograph . . . wait a minute! Photos!!!!!!!

I flew down the stairs and into the music room. I looked for the albums on the shelves, on the piano, on the table, even under the settees, but they were gone! Had Harry taken them? Had he secreted them in his room as I had done with my stuff? Ooh, did I want to look, but I knew I shouldn't. He could return at any moment, and I didn't want to incur any more temper tantrums, so, just out of curiosity, I checked the living room. Nothing there either. Only one avenue was left. Grabbing my jacket which I had left in the kitchen, I went out the side door, my companions following me, and headed to the Everett's house.

Something directed my feet towards their vegetable garden in the back of the house. Besides, this way I would not be seen if Harry had decided to appear. And I was right. My guidance was with me. There was Maude with two large baskets full of the last of the summer tomatoes and beets. I knew she was going to can them. It just would have been the right thing to do. "Yoo-hoo, Maude!" I called out not wanting to scare the living daylights out of this lovely soul since she was so intent on her work.

"Well, Emma, m'dear! How nice of you to visit!" she exclaimed as she turned to see me approaching her. "Would you like some of these," she said pointing to the vegetables. "I'm getting ready to can them for winter but we've more than enough fer the two of us."

"No, we've enough," I said bending over and picking up two ripe tomatoes. "Well, just these two for tonight, if that's okay with you," I said with a feeling of chagrin, as my first reaction had been a negative one.

"Take what you need, m'dear. It's no problem fur us. Now tell me what brings ya out here. You've a puzzled look in your eyes," she said in her soft Maine lilt. She put her strong arms around me, then bent down and picked up the baskets without allowing me to assist and guided me into the house. After offering me tea or coffee which I refused and asked only for a glass of water, she proceeded to get two glasses, fill them with cold water from the refrigerator and then sat down at the kitchen table with me. This gave me time to take in the well-used and well-worn kitchen which exuded much love of life and living and cooking, and even though some of the pots which were hanging were worn, it didn't matter one iota. All of the necessary ingredients for canning were spread out along the counter and about 20 jars were in the middle of the table at which I sat but what was even more amazing, the kitchen was spotless. It would have survived even the most audaciously stringent white glove treatment!

"Now, Emma, what is troubling you? And take as long as you like since m'dear George went into town to see to our truck which was makin' what he called eerie noises, and you know well what men are like with their automobiles of any kind," she said with a very broad grin on her face. "After all, we two is friends, right? We can tell each other whatever we want to tell, so out wi' it, girl!"

"I really just have a few questions, Maude. That's all. Nothing dire, I promise you." She put her elbows on the table letting her hands cup her chin and cheeks and leaned closer to me from the cattycorner position we were in. Her eyes seemed to penetrate mine as though she was panning for gold, so I began. "I know from what you said the other night that the two of you and your families have been on this property for generations, or did I get it wrong?"

"Not at all; now continue if ya don't mind. Ya see, I've a very good memory and can help in any way. !n fact, mine's better than my ole man's!"

"Thank you Maude. It's just that I don't understand what's happening to Harry. He took me along an unused path through some very thick foliage and . . ."

"And ya found that ole confounded playhouse and he went . . ."

"Ballistic, is what he went, Maude! I've never seen anything like it! A grown man suddenly becoming a spoiled brat, not like an adult, but . . ."

"But like the child he once was. It's nothing new, Emma. Not really. It seems almost every time he comes back here now since his folks are gone, somethin' strange besets him. An' that's why George keeps on a checkin' up on you. We was worried, acause we never know what's goin' on in his mind when he gets that way." She took a long slow sip of water, reminding me how thirsty I'd suddenly become and I followed suit. Maude stood, went to the refrigerator and brought out the pitcher and poured more water in each of our glasses, speaking as she did so. "He usually comes back to his right self in due time, and we've both seen him thrash around sort of like a madman, but he never has hurt anything or anyone. At least not that I can remember, and George would've told me if Mr. Harry had done somethin' not quite right, acause I would a called for the doc immediately!"

I sat back and took a deep breath, letting it out slowly so as to steady myself as this information was being filed away in my brain. "I think he was a very lonely child, Maude, with almost no one to play with and when he comes back here, those memories flood this consciousness. But that's not the only thing that I find troubling. It seems that everyone around, even those I met so hastily at The Hounds Tooth Inn, seem to be related not only to here but to George and possibly you, and Terry, who runs the place now, may just have been one of Harry's playmates. Am I right or not? That's all I really want to know for now." I looked deep into her eyes before I sat back in my chair and pushed my legs out in front me not only to achieve a more comfortable position, but to try to put her at ease as well.

Maude took her hands away from her face, slowly stood up and began preparing coffee. Ah, I thought, we were now going to get into the nitty-gritty of this entire mess. Well, it was really more of a conundrum than a mess, and I was really upset at seeing Harry suffer so, or at least it seemed to me as though he was suffering and from what Maude had just said, she thought so too.

She did not speak one word while making the coffee which gave me nothing to do but to look around again. I hadn't noticed the walls of their kitchen. They were painted a light cream color so that the sun, when it shone in, was easily reflected off the walls casting a loving glow throughout the room. On the walls, various trivets and other kitchen knickknacks were hanging, including a Kitchen Witch to cast off any evil spirits that might find their way in. I turned in my chair and looked at the kitchen door. There, unusual as it was, was a very large Kitchen Witch that appeared handmade. It was on the very top of the door, and right below it were two hooks, probably for coats. To the right of the door was a solid rubber mat probably used for wet boots and shoes. I pictured George coming in out of the rain, closing the door, and holding on to the handle, slipping out of his boots and hanging his raincoat on one of the hooks. Altogether, a neat, efficient setup, so that all he then had to do was to go to the sink, wash up and then sit down for his meal. I became so engrossed in my ruminations I was not fully aware that a steaming cup of coffee had been placed before me until the scent of it reached my nostrils. And on a tray on the table, there was a creamer, sugar bowl, and plate of homemade cookies. She had silently moved the canning equipment to the other end, away from where we were both seated.

"I've been thinkin' about this, Emma, and I guess the best way to explain everything to ya is to tell ya we are all related 'round here and that includes the group you must have met at the Inn because George's third cousin is the tour leader and takes folks, a lot of 'em from Canada around to see the sights, especially the old villages where whaling was the industry. Did ya know there are many small museum type places set up in most of the General Stores in those villages? Oh, there is stuff for the tourists to buy, but there is also a lot of stuff they can only look at and it's usually kept under glass at separate counters. And Missus Terry, yeah, she was a frequent visitor here when Mr. Harry was a youngster and I even dare say he liked her a lot as they were growing up, but then he went away to school and the university and her family had suddenly moved out west because a land deal for the Inn property with Mr. Spruce fell through, I guess, and there she met and married and that was that."

"Thank you, Maude, that sort of answers my questions, but how come your folks stayed here for so long? It must be at least three or four generations at least!"

"Oh longer than that, Emma. My family came first and then George's to settle almost right on top of them. We was only separated by about two miles of land between our two farms and before the town started growing and the church, my folks were home schooled. But in my time, George and me went to the local school in town which, long ago when we was growing up, was very small—not like it is now 'cause there are so many more people living around here and raising their kids and then the schools got better and . . ."

"Understood Maude. That seems to happen just about everywhere these days, but how come your folks stayed here? What did they do—just farm? If so, why is it so easy for Harry and for me to go into different times?" I was waiting for a response, even though I thought I already knew the answer—what with the Kitchen Witches, but she said nothing for quite some time.

"Oh, that's easy to understand. Whatever we planted grew and was always ready for harvesting, and the men in our families took truckloads to the various towns, and we made money—and that was besides the sugar from the maple trees. Why did you know corn grew fine here and strawberries too? Also for All Hallows Eve, pumpkins!"

"Wow!" I said. "I'd no idea corn grew successfully here but I do remember seeing in a specialty store, those small, potently sweet strawberries once in a while, and some grapes too, if I'm not mistaken."

"Why yes, and many, many different kinds of vegetables. Farming kept our families busy and George's great-great-grand uncle had a forest of maples trees! And we all went there yearly to tap them for harvesting their sap. In fact, these cookies are made with our very own family-run maple sugar business. But I think you mean something else, am I right, Emma?" she asked, pouring us each another half cup of coffee. "I think you think there's been strange goings on here besides the lady atop Mr. Harry's house."

"That's exactly what I do mean, Maude. And I know you know what's been going on here too. I bet your family told stories to all the kids as they were growing up about certain areas that they could not go into because of ghosts and goblins, right? I bet these stories have been passed down through the generations, and what's more, there is some truth in them, yes?"

Maude stood up and glared at me. "Never. Everything here is fine and has always been. We've no such stuff here at all, Emma!" she said through clenched teeth, her face turning red with anger.

"Maude, Maude, whenever somebody gets so heated up over something like you're doing now, there is some truth in it. I really didn't mean to upset you. It's just that the playhouse is in an area that seems to have been kept off limits for quite a few years, because the undergrowth is so very dense, and I bet it has a magic all it's own. And, before you go on, please sit down and take a long deep breath. I'm not accusing you or George or your families of anything." She did so and I continued. "I've traveled a great deal in my lifetime to places other people never went. It was always for my research and my work, and I found many places where there were no explanations for what went on. It was just something the people grew used to and prayed about and told stories about.

"There are things on this planet that are greater than we, who live here know anything about. We just accept it because it's what we've been born into. It's what we've grown up with. Why even in New York City, there are places, where, if someone is sensitive to them, they can walk into different time zones for a moment or two, or at least think they've done so. And this has happened to many people I've known even if the old buildings had been leveled and new, modern ones erected in their place! It's nothing to be ashamed of, Maude, because it just is!"

Maude grew quieter and her breathing slowed. "I'd no idea ya was one of them, Emma! No wonder George has been so careful of you being here and watching in all the time to see if you are OK. And his talks to me are mostly about you!" She began to giggle and hid her face in her hands, but just for a brief moment before she looked me directly in my eyes. "I was becoming a little jealous of you, ya know. I thought he had the hots fer you and now I understand why. And those cats! Oh, my goodness! I think I've gone back a good fifteen or more years in my own mind: but let me tell ya some stuff, OK?" I sat back, relaxed, and nodded.

Before she began to speak again, Maude stood up, walked around the kitchen, opened the refrigerator, and took out a large stew pot, obviously getting things ready for dinner. "Now, we've not much time as you can see by the light, but here goes: Both of our families have been here forever and both families have worked on and off for the Spruces, who have also been around on and off forever. It seems we cannot escape one another. When the Spruces moved to Boston for a few years after Mr. Henry went away to school, our parents were put in charge of the property and all the farm lands and even, early on, in charge of those farmers who worked the lands. As time changed, some of us did travel elsewhere, met mates, had families, but always returned here, and when the Spruces started selling off the farm lands, our families were still in charge of all the dealings and goings on. That's how much our parents and grandparents were trusted. It was an honor, so we was told, but as far back as we and our parents could remember, strange goings on happened. Not only the lady on the Widder's Walk, but oftentimes, even going through one field to another, or through the woods brought us all into strangeness. Sounds no animal ever made; colors or trees and flowers that were not natural to here; there were even times when the snow piled up by our houses but not in some of the woods! Not even one flake was spotted on the trees in those woods. The old tales told over and over was that this land was special. We weren't to be afrightened of anything. We was safe because we lived here and were protected by the land because we took good care of it. Even when the old man killed the lady—the gal who walks still—we were safe. No one even came to accuse our families of anything. Oh, sure, they asked questions, but that was only once or twice, so we were told, and then they went back to the main house. We even took the cats to be matter of factly!

"Nothing seemed strange to us except when George and I went to the school in town. But you know how kids are . . . yeah, we talked about the strange forest, and by then that little house had been built up there, and when we went inside, things had been moved around not just from the day before, but when we went outside to toss a ball and went back in to put the ball away—everything was changed! Don't remember who said about it first, George or me, 'cause we sort a grew up together, our houses only being so near one t' t'other and we both walked to school and home together almost all the time, unless one of us was sick or sumptin', then one of our parents would take us or even one of the farmhands. George and I is both the only children in our families, strange as that was to our parents, acause our kinfolk always had two or more kids each. And I know my parents tried for more kids, but none were born and it was the same with George's parents. But both our parents knew to accept what was given them and let it be.

It was our loneliness that brought us together for our lifetime and as ya see, we don't have kids either. Strange as that is 'cause we tried and tried and tried! I know our parents were disappointed but that was just the way it was and there weren't anythin' we could do about it, even though we went to the doctor in town. Ah, well." At this point she looked on the verge of tears, but only for a moment or two. Then she pulled herself together and continued.

"We even asked the preacher if he had any ideas, but that was that, and we've grown used to it bein' this way. Although the last preacher we asked about fifteen years ago did know about the strangeness of the land and said sumptin' about the land bein' in charge and that maybe we was to be the last on the land. By that time, it seemed that everyone in town knew about the house and about our families. But, don't you worry none, Emma. I'm gettin' to the point. Many of our kinfolk roamed up north into Canada and had families there and they still come by twice a year not only to say "Hello," but to stay at The Hounds Tooth Inn and then go on to Boston and then back. It's traditional. Don't know why they do it, but they do, year in and year out and when one dies off, one of their kids takes his or her place." She grew very quiet for quite some time, her face wrinkled in thought. "Maybe they is watchin' over us and the land. Maybe that was part of the bargain they made when they went away. Who knows! But it is nice to see kinfolk once in a while even if they only stop by for an hour or so!"

"True, Maude. I sort of understand that part but where does Harry fit in? And do you know about the mirror George hung in the living room? The one that just appeared on the second morning I was here?" I decided I had to ask everything I could as the sun was now way past its zenith and not only did she have to get things ready for their supper, but so did I. However, it was not to be. We heard the truck coming down the gravel road, and I knew we were done for the day. I also knew I had to sneak out because if George found out what we'd been talking about, he just might not have been a happy man. I put up my hand to stop her speaking, rose quickly, took, my cup to the sink, washed it out quickly, went back to her, gave her a quick hug and ran through their house and out the front door where I knew I wouldn't be seen due to the tall hedges surrounding it.

The new day dawned with brilliant sunshine and much warmer temperatures. My two sleeping companions were so anxious to get out and play, they awoke me at second light, mewing softly in each of my ears. They barely allowed me to stretch and do any of my morning exercises and were so impatient, I opened my door and let them out so I could bathe and get ready for the day.

By the time I got downstairs, they were not to be seen! It wasn't until I had the coffee ready and was on my first cup that they marched back inside, looked at their empty bowls with baleful eyes and tails thumping and little whines. I laughed so hard at their antics as I began to put their breakfast out for them, tears began running down my cheeks. They hurled themselves at their food, gobbled it up, and then threw themselves on their backs, stretching for all they were worth, purring loudly before they both sat up and began to wash their faces. While they were performing the rest of their post feeding routine, I unloaded the dishwasher and took out juice, eggs, and bacon and began breakfast for me and Harry, should he ever wake up and join us.

I guess the smell of the bacon frying wafted through his closed bedroom door because as soon as everything was ready, he appeared, still full of sleep on his face and in his eyes. I quickly handed him his juice and coffee and led the poor sleepy man to his seat at the table, placing the rest of his breakfast before him. Not one word was said until his plate was empty. Ah, the memories this brought back to me. Three years into my marriage this same pattern had begun. Men and their empty stomachs! Even when my ex and I woke up together, whether we made love or not in the morning, the very same thing occurred. No talk at table until he was sated. God! Was I well trained! It only took a quick glance at Harry to see where his mind was—food and satiety! Well, such is life, I thought to myself, shrugged my shoulders mentally, smiled at him, and said a soft "Good morning" to him, rubbing my hand through his already messed up hair while clearing the plates in front of him. He smiled warmly at me, echoed my greeting, and said he was going to get ready to face the rest of the day. With that, he stood, stretched, and charged up the stairs. All that was missing from the scene was a bugle in his hand and his voice yelling, "Charge!"

Forty minutes later, he came bounding back down the stairs but just as he arrived at the last five steps, slowed his pace, held on to the banister and ambled down like a gentleman, not like a three year old child. As soon as he saw me (I was on my second cup or maybe it was my third) a wide grin appeared on his face.

"Well, good morning again, my dear, dear Emma. Thank you for such a lovely repast. I was really hungry, although I can't imagine why after the fantastic dinner you prepared last night and that reminds me, tonight it's my turn to cook for you. After all, you're the one on vacation! And that also reminds me, I'm going into town to do some shopping for our evening meal. Is there anything you need or would you like to come with me? It's completely up to you!" The old HJS seemed to be back in full swing. The gleam in his eyes told me that much as well as his tone of voice.

"Not this time, Harry. Next time for sure. Today, I just want to wander around and see what else is on this wonderful properly of yours. But don't worry. I won't be alone. Take your car and have a blast and stay away as long as you like!" I said matching the gleam in his eyes. "But if you're coming back for lunch I really would like to know."

"I think I'll have lunch in the village. There's a delightful little shop— a deli of sorts, and I've not been there for ages. And as far as food is concerned, you take it easy and leave room for a sumptuous feast full of calories, okay?" I smiled at him, nodded, stood up and gave him a big hug which he reciprocated before he turned, took his car keys from the table in the foyer and left. I went over to the kitchen window and watched him as he got into the car, started it up and drove leisurely away.

"Okay kids," I said to the felines, "It's just the three of us today. I'm leaving it up to you as to where we'll go. I'll be right down in a few!" As if they understood me completely, the both sat down on their haunches. I could feel their eyes on me as I went upstairs.

. . . Or Feline

No sooner had I opened the door than all three of us bounded out, with me slamming it behind us. It was as though something during our sleep states had programmed us to just go and do, but I had no idea where. I followed my leaders who went straight down the path that led in from the main roadway. Just as we were about to reach it, they both veered right, with Nappy calling out to me to hurry with his Siamese like yowl, while Peaches looked back to see if I was keeping up.

We went on in that direction for about a quarter of a mile, finally leaving the manicured lawn and heading into another forest. This one was much less dense than the ones leading to the playhouse or to the cemetery. Now as I've intimated before, this property was really vast. I would even call it a good old fashioned estate—the kind that is rare to see anywhere any more, with land and taxes being what they are. There seemed to be many nooks and crannies in and around the well-cared-for lawns and gardens, some with stone steps leading off in different directions and through wooded areas. I was hoping to see an arbor along the way as we easily traversed the path the cats had taken, but no such luck. There was only one set of stone steps which were wide and easy to run down without even thinking of tripping since there was no handrail of any sort.

On and on we went for what seemed to me to be at least a mile when suddenly the cats veered off again, looking back at me as this time they went left. Were we going around in circles? Did they think I needed a good run? I thanked my lucky stars that I was in fairly decent shape and could keep up with them. As suddenly as we had started out, they stopped dead in their tracks waiting for me to come up behind them. There, right through the trees I could see a shack. It looked as though it had not been used or remembered in a hundred years. The wood was well worn as though the elements had had their way with it for centuries.

Slowly, oh, so slowly did the felines crawl on their bellies closer and closer to this monument of time. Then I noticed their ears were flattened against their heads and their tails bushed out quite dramatically, the way cats behave when they are frightened or even possibly stalking their prey. I, of course, did not follow suit. I just strode quietly behind them until we grew closer and closer. Nappy began a deep throated growl and Peaches matched his sound throwing all caution of her female behavior to the wind. As I drew nearer, my nose began to pick up a strange odor. It didn't smell like severe mold or even like death. It was an odor I couldn't recall having experienced before. It was worse than the poorest street person back in the city.

As they crept closer, still growling with ears flattened and tails puffed out, I took the proverbial bull by the horns and went to the door. Having been properly brought up, I knocked on it, softly at first and then when there was no response, I rapped louder.

145

"Who the hell is it and wha' do yer want!" A thundering voice responded with heated anger. "If those dang smart cats brought yer here, get 'em the hell away and go too, a' fore I come out and do some real hard kickin'! I don' hold wif no strangers and I know there is one livin' up at the house an' if you be she, go fuck yerself and get out now!"

Suddenly I began to laugh. Oh, this individual sounded very nasty indeed, but I felt in the pit of my stomach this was not the case. I continued laughing so hard tears again began to roll down my cheeks, and that seemed to do the trick! Within a split second the door was pulled open. Then I recognized the odor. Fish: dead, decayed fish. It had been many years since I had smelled that odor, and then only in the very poorest fishing villages during my travels and research.

A tall, extremely scruffy man, about six foot two inches with a long, dirty beard and hair to match, all streaked with gray and grease, stepped over the threshold. He was wearing a torn, faded long sleeved shirt, filthy overalls, and a baseball cap on his head. His feet were bare and filthy, and he stank to high heaven. He began to approach me, thinking, I'm sure that I'd step far away from him. I didn't move. Neither did my feline companions. "What's your name, sir?" I asked in a soft voice. He didn't respond. He just kept coming closer to me in an attempt to menace me. The felines growled louder.

"SHUT UP!" He yelled at them. "No more fish fer you if'n you don'! I told yer not to bring her to see me! I don' need anyone but me! Nappy and Peaches immediately stopped their noise and sat up on their rear ends with their heads hanging down.

"You know, sir," I continued, I've always found that animals know better than humans what's needed and I think they come to visit you not for the fish, but to be friendly even though they made a game of it getting me here to introduce myself to you. My name is Emma. Will you tell me yours?"

Like the cats, he hung his head and quietly said, "Dave."

"Dave?" I responded with a gentle smile. Somehow you don't look like a 'Dave.'" Completely taken aback, he just looked at me carefully. His eyes became clear and focused.

"What are yer, some sort a mind reader?"

"Not at all. It's your accent. So, what is your real name? I always prefer calling people by their given names—not the ones they think others will take to."

"Eben," he said still giving me a look of questioning disapproval.

"Thank you, Eben." I replied. "You just don't look like a 'Dave' to me at all. In fact, you look to be a native of this area and from the way you are dressed, and the odor coming from your home, I gather you are a fisherman or at least you fish to keep yourself alive." There was no response from him at all, so I decided to continue with the questions that were building up in my mind whether he liked them or not. "I gather this is still the Spruce's property because I don't think I came that far from the main house. Does anyone know you are living here? And living like this? I know there are many strange things about this land and the house, and the people who once lived here long ago, and have seen the woman on the Widow's Walk; the strange things in the playhouse;

the graveyard. Need I go on?" I stopped long enough to not only catch my breath as the odor kept hitting me, but also to see if I was getting any reaction from him.

"Arrrgh!!!!!!!" was all he said as right before my eyes, he and the hut disappeared.

"What the hell is happening here?" I said turning to where I last saw my feline companions. They were still sitting there like statues and I swear they were smiling at me! "Well you two! What are you trying to tell me? That this place is full of ghosts and goblins as well as strange events? Is this past, present or future? What do you want me to do now?" They both looked at me and took off like bolts of lightning returning the same way we came. I followed as quickly as I could but it seemed to me that hours and hours had passed before I was clear of the wooded area and back on the main grounds of the house.

Something was pulling me inside and I knew it was not the need for coffee. Maybe I'd overdone that this morning and my mind was playing tricks on me, but somehow I knew that was most definitely not the case. My mind's eye kept seeing that blasted mirror and that was the last thing I wanted to look at especially now. I hadn't been frightened at all with Eben's closeness or even when he vanished. It all just seemed to be a part of everything else that was strange about this place, and what was more; I wanted to see if Maude was available and alone to continue our conversation from yesterday, as that still haunted my waking thoughts. But it was not to be.

With great trepidation I headed for the front door, opened it, and tried to go into the dining room to get to the kitchen. The cats were right in back of me pushing me toward the living room. I tried, as we passed the staircase to grab the banister and go upwards. Suddenly, they both took hold of my pants legs and pulled me away. "But I have to go to the bathroom!" I heard myself whining at them like a child. It made no difference. They pulled and pushed me until I was before the mantelpiece. I looked up suddenly and the mirror was hanging right over the fireplace within easy visual contact. They propelled me to it and it seemed to adjust to my visual height. I had nothing to hold on to. I was just forced to look into it. I felt my breath coming is small fearful gasps while my mind said this was insane. I'd encountered the mirror before at my own height and dealt with what I had been shown and experienced. However, this time, looking into it, I saw myself as I had dressed in the morning and my breathing quieted. I stared into it for quite some time, but nothing happened. Then, by happenstance, I turned away to see where the animals were (right beside me) and then turned back to see Eben standing there dressed in mid-eighteenth century finery smiling back at me as though he and I were the best of friends. Before I could even think any further, he stepped out of the mirror and into the room. I looked down at myself quickly and saw I was still in my modern pants, shirt, and jacket.

"Well, my lovely, here we are again, just as we were the first time. It was so kind of you to invite me to visit, even though your husband and I have not spoken in years. And it is a very good thing he's away, isn't it! We now have time for us, you magnificent creature!" He took a giant step towards me and then went through me! I turned to follow him and saw a beautiful young woman

149

standing by the threshold of the room with a gracious smile on her face. Her skin was as clear as a bell and her beautiful auburn hair was coiffed in an upward sweep. Her dress was a pale blue silk with dark blue laces at the cuffs. The neckline was squared off with a v-shaped lace insert over the light blue silk going from her neckline to her waist in the same dark blue lace.

"So we should not be seen here together, Eben, I gave the servants the rest of the day to themselves. Please, dearest, take my hand before I faint at seeing you actually here!"

I watched in complete awe as he did so and together they headed for the staircase, where they stopped, kissed, and then ascended from my view. Without waiting a split second longer, I went to the sofa and sat down unable to control my breathing which was now coming in long gasps. Feeling lightheaded, I put my head between my knees, gathered my total self together, sat back, looked for the cats, who had not moved one iota, turned towards the mirror which had moved itself upwards again over the mantle, closed my eyes and fell immediately into the strangest sense of knowing I had ever experienced in my entire life. I've no idea how long I sat there or even how long the scene that had unfolded before me had lasted, but somehow I didn't care. This was proving to be the weirdest place I'd ever encountered in my life and now it was beginning to gnaw at me.

Without waiting another moment, I ran upstairs and pulled my drawing pad from underneath my mattress, sat on the edge of the bed and sketched Eben in both his guises and the woman as well. Then I drew his entrance from the lowered mirror. There had to have been a door there at one time and yes, that was an outside wall, but I thought the fireplace was as old as the room itself. Was there a different house on this property at one time? There had to be a way of finding out without asking Maude or George. I didn't want them to know what I'd been into, either up here or in my earlier life. And somehow I knew that Harry knew all about it, but either wanted me to make the discovery on my own or not to know at all. After replacing my art work, I went into the library and searched the shelves for a telephone directory. Nothing was there. However I was not going to be daunted so I returned to the small table where a telephone sat around the curvature of the banister. There it was. It was so thin it was hidden in the drawer of the telephone table. Grabbing it quickly, I finally went into the kitchen for a cup of coffee without caring if it was hot, cold, fresh, or stale, and sat at the table with the directory. I was looking for someplace that would house old plans and designs as well as property delineations; the library was the first place I found. Oh, there was a newspaper office but I was not certain it was there in the early 1800s or even kept records on microfilm and I was in no mood to go through tons of back issues should they have even kept them, so the library it was. Unfortunately, there was no land office as such, but maybe a City Hall. No, only a Town Hall, but I decided to investigate that too. Before figuring out which place to hit first, my mind settled down, and logic prevailed. I picked up the phone and began dialing. Just as I was about to enter the last two numbers of the library, there was a horrifying yowl from the living room. I dropped everything and ran like wildfire into the living room.

The felines were sitting in their very same positions and the mirror had once again dropped to my eye level below the ledge of the mantelpiece. The cats were like statues, ears straining to pick up the merest sounds. Just as I got there, the woman and Eben came down the staircase, kissed again and, holding hands, walked toward the mirror, where he kissed her again, bowed low, and exited as he had entered—through the mirror. As soon as this scenario was complete, both animals stood up and gave the longest series of feline stretches I'd ever seen. Then without another word marched towards the kitchen and out through their special door without even glancing at me.

I took that to mean I could continue with what I had been doing and called the library. A lovely woman, who identified herself as Sarah, answered and after I explained what I was looking for, told me that yes, the library had been the repository for all of the information ever culled about the town and all the surrounding lands, estates, or farms since the area was first settled in the late 1600s, and she also told me they had been very busy with the aid of the school children in scanning as much as they could into their computer system. I was suddenly the happiest person in the world! Most of what I wanted may just be at my finger tips! However, Sarah explained I could not gain access from the "outside" without first coming in and joining the library, which I told her I was more than happy to do and would be there as soon as possible. Oh, Joyous Day!

I ran upstairs, got my ID together, the car keys, and even remembered to change into my driving shoes and put on a clean blouse, not just a tee shirt, and headed for the car. There, already sitting inside were Nappy and Peaches. I couldn't even question how they had gotten in as the windows were closed even though the doors were not locked. Somehow that too would eventually be answered, I hoped.

The drive into town was uneventful in all respects. The land on either side of the road was level farming area with trees planted sporadically along the shoulders of the road to maintain the land, the road, and the atmosphere of this part of Maine. As I'd never been there before, I took my time just riding slowly around familiarizing myself with the layout. It was a lovely town with beautifully tree lined streets, plenty of areas for flowers, dainty and typically New England-type stores, some attached to others, some separate. It looked as though the town had gone up in stages, which I was pretty certain would prove to be the case. However, one thing was definitely clear. The largest store was located just as one was about to enter the town itself, so as to make it easier for those who wanted only one stop shopping. It was new and bright and even looked as though it contained everything one would need including food, clothing, and any kind of farming equipment and supplies required by the inhabitants of this area. However, for some reason, I knew there also had to be a specialty shop somewhere in the town itself because George had brought me some highly specialized items on his shopping trips—things that even in a medium-sized city were not found in the local supermarkets, so I went in search of that first.

It was tucked away on what I thought of as a side street and not near any of the parking areas. But there, inside this little store, painted a soft yellow and white outside shutters, I saw Harry. Luckily, he seemed very busy and did not look up, so I skedaddled out of there to find the library.

The Library has to be called such with a capital "L." It was massive and exquisite with six Doric columns holding up a massive marble roof along which were carvings I could not really see while driving. It was five stories tall and I was certain it had a marble-lined basement as well; loads of storage room for everything even in this old community. It looked to take up about two and a half city blocks!

As the layout of this town was so beautifully done, there was a parking area just across from the Library. I pulled in, parked the car, and opened just my door. I intended to leave Nappy and Peaches inside, but no such luck. As soon as I leaned over to get my purse, they flew out of the car and ran up the seven steps to the Library door, sat down, and waited for me to join them. Luckily, no other cars were coming down the street at that time, so I took off after them and gave them a good scolding before opening the door to enter this magnificent building. I didn't even remember to look up to see the carvings as I had planned to do!

We no sooner entered when one of the librarians came at a trot exclaiming, "Oh, you two beautiful cats! Where have you been hiding? We've all been missing you, and if you go downstairs, Ah am sure you'll find much to keep you busy!" She turned to me and added, "Tis the season when the mice want t' find a warm place to nest for the winter and these two have always come to lend a paw at getting rid of them," she giggled at her own choice of words. Without waiting for any further directions, Nappy and Peaches ran toward the back of the main floor and headed for the work set out for them to do. "Ah am Sarah and you must be the famous Dr. Emma Epstein! Ah have read almost everything you've eveh written and am absolutely pleased as punch to meet you," she said taking my hand and almost shaking my arm out of its socket. Her accent was most definitely not "Down East." It was from the Deep South! Sensing my incredulity, she continued at the usual fast Southern pace. "Ah migrated up heah with the man I met and then married who came to visit in Charleston. It was such a lovely weddin' and mah whole family could be there, and then we moved heah and ah settled in with no trouble what-so-ever. But you're not heah to heah about me, Dr. Epstein, are ya. So tell me how I can help."

While Sarah was chatting away, it dawned on me I had not told her my name when I called, but this being a small community, I gathered everyone was well aware I was staying at the Spruce's house and that of course it had probably sparked their curiosity. What interested me more was that Nappy and Peaches were well known in this building, and very possibly all around town, so I asked her first about this. She told me that they had been arriving yearly at this time to help maintain the collection in the basement and keep everything free from the field mice that somehow managed to get in—and that even though the entire building had been searched quite thoroughly over the years, no one could find the mouse holes. In fact, she had begun to worry about them since it was rumored that two cats had been doing this since the building was erected. "The same two cats?" I asked.

"Yes, Dr. Epstein! We've even photos of them goin' back to the old sepia rotogravures! Of course, ah personally have found it quite amazin' but left it at that 'cause this area has so many strange and wonderful things goin' on in it all over the place," she whispered quietly in my ear.

"Well, then Sarah, I guess I've not only come to the right place, but found the right person to speak with. But first do you have files or articles going back to when the Spruce family arrived and even before? The place has been growing on me and my curiosity has finally gotten the best of me, so time for some research," I said with what I hoped was laughter in my voice. I didn't want to divulge any of the strange goings on that I'd experienced. I just wanted solid information.

"Why, a' course, we do! In the basement. Why don't ah just show you the way!" she said leading me toward the back of the building the way the cats had gone. She led me to the back and I walked down the marble stairs to the stacks. Everything was so very orderly, I couldn't believe it. There were signs pointing to every area imaginable and I headed for the earliest section only to find my two feline friends sitting and waiting for me at the beginning of that aisle. The looks I received from them were hilarious! It was a mixture of "What took you so long" and "We're ready, are you?"

With tails held high, they led me down the aisle to the furthest section which was full of boxes. Inwardly I groaned. I always hated having to go through boxes of old clippings and information, but at the end of that aisle was a desk, chair and praise be, a computer. I immediately sat down and Peaches jumped in my lap just as I turned the computer on. This was a new computer that took only seconds to activate. Instinctively I hit the "enter" tab and the Table of Contents appeared along with space to enter what I was looking for, so I typed in "Spruce House and Family." What came up blew me away! The gist of it was that the family moved into the area in the early 1700s and the dynasty was begun by Harris Jonathan Spruce and his wife whose name was not to be found anywhere in these archives. It did make mention of a fishing fleet begun by this Mr. Spruce, and the opening of a fishing station where people could come and buy the catches, but that was all.

There were several houses upon the same huge expanse of land the current house inhabited. In each of these houses, the family had encountered sometimes terrible and sometimes mystical occurrences as though the land itself was cursed from some other time or other place. The people themselves were well regarded in the community and it was not until the Salem Witch Trials that rumors about them began to circulate in the neighboring areas. Of course, it was the women in the family who were immediately blamed as were the women in Salem, but that proved not to really be the case, since most of them died early in their lives from a wide variety of problems including childbirth and diseases not understood back then. This led me to assume that Mrs. Harris died early as well, but there were two children. Again, no names were given so I couldn't begin to draw a family tree.

In order for the Spruces to live harmoniously with their neighbors, they began giving much of their land away to those in need. I gathered this was in a way compensation for their work and any ills that had occurred. The result was that homesteads were built and farming was done with much of the produce not only taken into the small townships to be sold, but also brought to the Spruces as payment for their generosity. The result was that things quieted down until the mid to late 1800s when one Eunice Spears, age 17 was married to Harry Jonathan Spruce, son of Harris Jonathan Spruce VI, and Martha (surname not entered).

Harry, like his father and many of his ancestors had taken to the sea and left his new wife to her own devices. The image of Eben came immediately to mind and the scene that had last unfolded before my eyes. As this realization hit, Peaches began to knead on my lap and Nappy began running around in what seemed like celebratory circles to my mind. Then before I realized what was happening, both cats stopped, sniffed the air, and ran off to do their duty. I next heard a yowl and then frantic scampering as their quarry either escaped or eluded them completely. Peaches, unfazed returned to my lap just a few minutes later and fell into a happy catnap. But I still heard Nappy's claws clicking away on the marble floor.

I read further on to find that the manor house, as it was being called then, had undergone some structural changes as deemed proper by the family. The original front door was where the fireplace was now situated with the brick outer wall. But that was back in the mid 1800s. However, as the terrain on that side of the house was not level due to the rockiness of the land on that side, that wall was totally bricked up and the front door was placed where it is today. That meant that a circular driveway could be added without too much disturbance to the land surrounding the house and the gardens. One article also stated firmly that the Spruce Family was the first one in the area to own a roadster! However, I found no other mention of the family from the 1800s.

This set me thinking and I went to the obituaries for that time period. Sure enough, in 1863 one Spruce member died. The headline read, "Mrs. Eunice Spruce, nee, Spears, age 22, passed quietly in her sleep on October 26, 1863. The Spruce family is in deep mourning. After a suitable period of time, it is hoped that Captain Harry Jonathan Spruce will be returning to sea." Nothing else was said, but there was an etching and sure enough, Eunice Spears Spruce looked exactly like the woman on the Widow's Walk, There was a second obituary stating that Mr. H.J. Spruce VI also died. No mention was given as to why or how.

I gently woke Peaches, put her on the floor, stood up, and began to walk around through the rest of the aisle. Actually, I wasn't looking for anything; I just needed to walk off the angst that had suddenly been building inside me. I knew what had happened. I knew how they both died and why. And what was more, I knew who did it. She was murdered by her father-in-law and the son murdered him. That was all there was to it.

She had lived there for five years with her husband often gone and no progeny ever mentioned. Not the sort of wife this family wanted. As there were no other children besides Harry, an heir must be produced. I was also certain that her illicit affair with Eben had become known. In small communities there are very few ways of hiding things no matter how secluded an area was.

Someone always knew what was going on. That was an actual fact of rural life. One would always be seen at strange times that did not coincide with the usual schedules. And in retrospect, since the Spruce family gave much of its surrounding land to homesteaders, I was sure someone was always out and about.

I stood there just staring off into space while all this information traveled through my mind when Nappy brought me back to reality by yowling at my feet. He then stood up, balancing on the shelves and started pawing at an unmarked box. "All right, boy!" I said. "Thank you. I guess you are showing me the next step in the puzzle, and I'm wondering does it include anything about you two." I asked, petting his neck. A very succinct and loud, "Yowl!!!!" was his reply. So without any further stalling on my part, I picked up the box and took it to the desk.

This box was different from all of the others in that section. It was sealed. Without even thinking about going upstairs to ask Sarah about it, I took my keychain out of my pocket, opened the tiny pen knife attached to it and slit the tape. After all, from what I had gathered over the years, sealed boxes were found in evidence lock ups, and this was a library, so I felt no guilt about it whatsoever. I gently put the top on the floor. The box was full of files all in order by year going back to the late 1790s. I took a deep breath and pulling my pad and pen towards me, sat down. As I was doing this, my peripheral vision saw Nappy and Peaches both sitting like statues of Bast in the box top.

I began at the beginning. The handwriting was old and the paper, brown. I took the first file out gingerly and laid it open. I then very gently began reading and turning these old pages slowly all the while trying to decipher them. I was seeing the history of the Spruce family from their crossing the Atlantic from England and Scotland. The first Mrs. Spruce was of Scottish descent and was pregnant, but did not tell her husband before boarding. It was a terrible trip for her, but she did not die in childbirth. She did, however, remain very weak for many months afterwards. What was fascinating to me was that these people were not poor and had a cabin! And they also had two cats! The descriptions of these felines were carefully noted by a feminine hand and it was exactly like my two companions. When I came to read that section, two loud purrs erupted at my feet.

"Yoo-hoo, Dr. Epstein, the library will be closing soon!" I heard Sarah calling down the staircase. "Yah can come back at any time yah know. Ah know there's a lot of stuff down there to interest yah, so feel free! And there's no appointment needed," she added with a delightful laugh.

I put everything back in the box and pressed the tape hard to make it look as though it was never touched; although I had no idea why I did this. I then gathered my things and went back upstairs thanking Sarah as I left the building. As soon as I got to my car, I looked inside and there were my feline companions curled comfortably in the back seat as though they had never left. All I could think of while driving back to the house was, "Stranger and stranger. Things are becoming stranger and stranger!" And yet, somewhere in my mind things were beginning to make sense! Strange sense, but sense nevertheless.

In retrospect, as I neared the house, it was the felines that interested me most of all, but all of that evaporated for the time being, because there was HJS's car and I knew I had to keep my mouth shut and stay calm tonight at all costs. Don't know why I felt this as being imperative, but I did. As I pulled into my parking space, I said to the cats, "Not a word of this to anyone is that clear? We just went for a drive to see the countryside." The response was a double yowl!

When I entered the house, the most delicious aromas emanated from the kitchen. "May I enter?" I asked, "Or is your meal to be kept secret?"

"You may come in for your coffee," he answered with a deep-throated laugh. "I just made a fresh pot, knowing you!" He turned with the biggest grin on his face and poured me a cup. "Have a seat and tell me all about it!"

"About what?"

"Where did you guys go today? Maude said you left hours ago!"

"Oh, I just drove around to see the countryside and then stopped and sat under a lovely pine tree in a small forest." I knew I had to say something like that, because I felt he would check the odometer and see that I'd not really gone that far. "In fact, it was so lovely and the sun was still bright, I must have dozed for a while, because before I knew it, I was getting a slight chill and the cats were curled up beside me," I lied. But looking at him, I knew he bought it.

"Just like you dear Emma. Just like you! Well, dinner will be ready in about an hour and a half, so if you want to bathe, change, et cetera, now is your time to do it. Oh, and hors' d'oeuvres will be served in the music room first!" I must have looked astonished because he continued after looking at me, "I thought we'd do this up brown as they say!"

"Fantastic! I'm off to get ready," I said taking my mug with me and heading towards the staircase. But before I reached the first step, two growling yowls reached my ears. "Sorry guys, you must be famished," I said turning back into the kitchen. ""Harry, just hand me their bowls and I'll take care of this." He did so, shrugging his shoulders. I poured out their food, left them to it, and headed upstairs calling over my shoulder to the cats, "And I promise no matter how good Harry's cooking is, I won't forget dinner for you two! And maybe you will even have a taste!"

"Over my dead body," I heard him say as I continued upstairs.

✍

Dinner was a huge success as was the "cocktail hour" that preceded it. I felt so relaxed I even offered to do the dishes but was disallowed. "After all, dear Emma, when you do the cooking, then you clean up and when I do the cooking, I clean up. That's fair and just," he said with laughter I his voice. Our conversation during the evening had been just wonderful. We seemed to renew our old selves in one another just by our proximity and sharing the food, liquor, and the demeanor caused by the entire evening. Not a word was said about the mirror or anything else, and yes, the felines did get to sample his cooking from both our plates, and they loved it! How easy it is to spoil pets, whether they are really ours or not; and believe me when I tell you neither of them begged.

163

Not really. They just curled up by our chairs and waited us out.

"You know, Emma, I think it's a good idea if we both retired early. Tomorrow is supposed to be another magnificent day and maybe we can go around together."

"That sounds fine to me, Harry," I replied, all thoughts of going back to the library vanishing from my mind.

"Well then," he continued rinsing the dishes off and stacking the dishwasher, "Why don't you go on up. You do look a little tired even though you napped in the pine forest and after all, it is your vacation." I took the hint, went over and kissed his cheek and headed upstairs. Then the realization hit me hard. We had gone into every room but the living room. Both of us had stayed far away from temptation!

As I entered my room with the felines at my heels, I felt a cool breeze. I knew I had closed the windows, but something else was blowing. We three gingerly stepped inside. Nappy growled deep in his throat and Peaches skirted behind me.

I turned on the light and there was Eben seated on the bed as though he was waiting for me. But as I continued to enter, he made no move. It was as though I was not there. It was as though I was not the one he was waiting for. Now is the time, I thought to myself and sat down on the opposite corner of the bed so that I could face him. He had both feet planted firmly on the floor and I sat with my left leg curled on the bed and my right foot planted firmly on the floor.

I looked him squarely in the face. "I can see you, Eden, just as I saw you at the shack, which means to me that you can see me." I spoke gently but authoritatively and kept my voice soft.

"You are not her," he responded with despondency.

"No, I am not Eunice. She was of a different time, over one hundred years ago. I am Emma."

"I AM Eben!"

"I know you are Eben," I said.

"No! You do not understand! I AM Eben!" I knew he was not getting angry. His voice was quiet and full of love and I thought he was just asserting himself. "You do not understand, Miss Emma, excuse me Dr. Emma—I AM Eben. I know who I AM and that is how I can come and go and know the time or era, as you would say that I am in." I just stared at him. "What I am trying to tell you is that all one really has to do is to know who they are and claim it. I AM THAT I AM and so it was written long ago. Ah . . . I see you are still staring at me in disbelief, so I will continue."

"Wait a moment, I AM Eben. Before you say anything else, if you are trying to tell me you are so holy or sainted or whatever, why do the felines react negatively to you? What did you do to them? From what I've been able to find out thus far, they too, are ancient and not only in their lineage, but in carrying all their past knowledge with them as you seem to be capable of doing. They also seem to have the ability to come and go without any problems of getting to where they are supposed to be."

Before I could go on with the beginnings of my diatribe he put up his hand to stop me. "We three have known each other over these centuries as well and I admit, I often teased them mercilessly and this has become a game between us. Look at them now." I did so. They were curled up sleeping peacefully between our feet with their tails happily slapping every once in a while. "And don't let them fool you. They know everything that is going on here," he continued softly, "And do not be fooled by your dear friend, Harry Jonathan Spruce. He directed you here to rest and recuperate while your sabbatical is active, because he requires your help but cannot say why. It is just something within him which he senses."

Eben stopped and just looked at me. The two of us sat there without moving. The entire house was silent. I didn't even hear if JHS had come upstairs. It was as though I was in a vacuum. Suddenly my mind became filled with everything I'd experienced from the moment I'd left the city. Only this time it did not come in waves, but in a logical order, and I heard and saw in my mind's eye, every incident that had transpired since I reached Maine including all of my "trips" through that dreaded mirror. When I became cognizant again I was comfortably situated in bed with the coverlet keeping me company. No one else was in the room, not even the cats.

I awoke happy as could be. The house was still silent and my watch said it was only 6:30 AM. How wonderful, I thought and reached down to pet the felines. They stirred and stretched and jumped off the bed as I joined them, ready for my morning exercises. After I'd put myself together for the day I was going to spend with Harry, I dashed downstairs and got breakfast for the three of us. I kept it simple. I didn't want the odor of frying bacon to awaken him. I wanted the peace and quiet. And I wanted a view – a view of the glorious sun gently awakening the rest of the manor house, so I took my mug into the music room and stretched out on the chaise longue there, sipping and watching the sun's rays shining on the tops of the trees.

⁂

"Harry, where has everything gone?" I asked in complete amazement.

"I don't know what you mean, Emma. When I stopped using this place, I guess the family cleared it out."

"Look, Harry, before you arrived, I found this place with the help of the felines, and it was filled with books, toys, and even an old rocking horse. And you even brought me here and you yelled at me because I touched one of your precious books!"

"I did?"

"Yes, you did. Don't you remember? It was only a few days ago." I looked him squarely in the eyes. Was he playing with me? What was going on here? Was I really still sleeping? Is that why I saw I AM Eben? Then before I could gather myself up, he grabbed me and pushed me to the floor. He began pawing me while saying, "Emma, don't you realize It's you I adore? The others were your friends and I came along because you were there. Didn't you notice all the attention I paid was really to you? Why do you think I gave you this place? It was so we could be alone!" He proceeded to attempt to rip my sweater off and my pants and tried pulling my shirt up over my head, but that was not to be. I was not going to be raped by him or by anyone. Not now, not ever!

Before I realized it, I'd kneed him in the groin and he toppled off of me screaming in pain. I don't know where I got the strength from, but I then socked him in his jaw, slapped his face good and hard, got up, straightened myself out, stormed out of the barren playhouse and ran for my life back to the house. Having to pass the library windows, I glanced in and saw myself still asleep on the chaise longue!

A dream! It was all a dream! And it really wasn't me he had attacked, it must have been Terry. Or at least that's what my sensible mind told me. But I also heard in my left ear a voice that said, "You are now able to slip between the realities as well. This is why you were brought here. This is why you came. It is all up to you now to undo all that has been done and put to rest those . . . " The voice faded away as I saw Harry standing over me gently shaking my arm and calling my name.

Like a bat out of hell I flew back into my body, yawned. I wasn't in the music room at all, but in my bed! How wonderful!!!

. . . Or Child

The day broke with silvery cool sunlight pouring in through my windows. I tossed the coverlet off of me, arose, and went to look outside. It was a typical autumn day, ever so slightly overcast, but with streaks of this silvery light shining through the thin clouds. I just stood there rethinking everything that had gone through my mind the night before with I AM Eben sitting on one corner of my bed and the felines curled up between our feet. One thought kept playing over and over in my brain: Harry's little play house and the young Terry who often played with him.

As I was doing my morning stretches and other routines I knew what the day would bring and where I had to go. Since Harry usually slept late, I knew I had the house basically to myself and quietly went down to make coffee and have some cereal. Even though the thought of bacon and eggs made me salivate, I knew better. Harry would awaken and I knew instinctively I needed at least two to three hours without him, and this time, in my real reality, the clock said it was 5:30 AM. Time was on my side. Of course I took my coffee mug with me and went directly into the long avoided living room; curled up on the settee facing the fireplace with my feline companions. As I entered, neither of them moved—not a tail nor a whisker. It was not until I placed my cup on the nearest table that they even stirred. I quickly returned to the kitchen, put out their breakfast, grabbed the small ladder, and returned. Their eyes were open, their beautiful heads were up, but they made no move towards their breakfasts. They knew what I was going to do.

I placed the ladder securely under the mantle piece and climbed up. My companions just jumped up and sat there looking from me to the mirror and back again. "I want to see Harry's play house from the beginning of its usage through to the end, when he no longer went there." As I said this, with my heart beating very quickly, I felt a presence in back of me and I knew it was I AM Eben, there to help guide me.

The mirror clouded over for a moment. When it cleared, there was the play house I all its original glory. I did not go into the mirror, but silently willed it to take me inside. There was young Harry this time about eleven or possibly twelve years old sitting at his small table which was filled with books, not toys! His attention was so deep in what he was reading he did not hear the door open. "Harry! I've so much to tell you I'm coming in whether you like it or not," the young Terry said, flinging the door wide open with a bang and running over to him. "Put that book down and listen to me! Mama and Papa—yours and mine, are planning things, and I don't like it one bit!" Terry was about ten or eleven with long blondish-brown hair that fell in long ringlets down her shoulders and back. She wore a head band, and her dress had a small buttons on the collar and cuffs, while he was dressed in pants, a blue shirt, and a sailor's tie under the collar that had been folded into a sailors knot just below where the shirt collar, which was open at the neck, met. Without any further ado, she burst into tears!

"They are taking me away, Harry! Very far away! And I don't want to go and no one will listen to me and I will never, ever see you again!!!!!!! Oh, Harry what are we to do?"

The scene faded, or I should say the film stopped. All that was needed was a "The End" sign on the mirror, but I suddenly understood it all. Maybe it was I AM Eben's influence or just the plaintiveness of Terry's cries, but I knew. Something terrible had happened to squelch the land deal for the Inn as originally proposed to her parents by Mr. Spruce. Or was it just that? No, I knew it wasn't. I then saw Harry running up to the house but Terry was still in the play house when the door flew open again and another person entered. Without warning another video began playing out in my mind's eye. I saw Terry's parents out for an evening stroll and looking up in horror at the Widow's Walk. They saw Eunice and the beating, and were scared out of their minds. Right! What next? I thought to myself as I grabbed my coffee mug and took a good long gulp. What I had been seeing was relatively recent history. I had no idea if they knew their daughter had been raped but guessed they did and this was just the icing on the cake as far as they were concerned. I wanted more. Back to the library or not—I knew it was basically my decision, but somehow the impetus wasn't there. Maybe tomorrow, but not right now.

Before I could turn my attention to any noise from upstairs, I felt myself being urged to climb the ladder again. The felines were still sitting on the mantle piece so I followed this inclination. What transpired when I looked in the mirror was astonishing: We, the cats and I, were on a large vessel in the middle of the ocean in what then passed for a stateroom. Looking outside the porthole were many families, all bundled up from the cold and ocean spray. The cats were busy prowling around the small cabin while Mr. and Mrs. Harris Jonathan Spruce were curled up on the one mattress sound asleep. Within a matter of minutes the scene changed from day to night with a storm raging outside and people clamoring to be let in to the lower decks of the ship. The thunder, lightning and horrible cries from the people raged through the night as the captain and crew did their best to keep the ship steady and their passengers as safe as possible. Tumultuous rain beat against the small porthole causing it to make hearing almost unbearable until the woman, Mrs. Spruce, began to scream in agony. Her labor was beginning. Mr. Spruce ran to the door and yanked it open and yelled as loudly as he could to cut through the voices of the frightened people who had taken shelter in the passageway that it was time and the midwives were needed. I saw him turn back to look at his wife as he said, "Steady there Maryanne. You must be brave. They are coming!" As he said this three women pushed their way into the small cabin and tossed him out into the passageway with the others.

Night turned into day and then into afternoon. The sun was shining; the passage way was clear except for Mr. Spruce and groans and crying were still coming from the cabin. He had sunk to the floor holding his head in his hands and cringing with each of her moans. By late afternoon there was suddenly dead silence and then the wail of an infant. He pulled himself up just as the door opened and the three exhausted midwives left the cabin. "It is messy in there Sir, but we will be back shortly. You can go in and see your son," one of them said as she exited.

"Is my wife...." He almost couldn't finish the sentence.

"She is weak but alive," the last woman said as she went down the passageway. "Don't forget now, we shall be back in just a short time with sustenance for the both of you." This woman turned towards him and placed her hand on his arm, smiling at him all the while.

"Thank you, Miss Eunice. Thank you," he responded to her touch with a small smile of his own and the hurried into the cabin to see his exhausted wife holding their son to her breast while trying to keep herself alert and awake. But that did not happen. Maryanne took one look at her husband, smiled wanly and fell into sleep with the child in her arms falling into sleep as well.

In the next sequence The Spruce family was settled in a small stone house. A fire was burning in the large fireplace in the kitchen area and a woman was turning a large spit on which was the hind limb of what looked to be a deer. A kettle was situated on a small stone hearth which had been built on the inside corner of this fireplace and the water was just about to boil. "Eunice, I need my tea, and Harris needs to be fed!" a weak voice called from another room in this dwelling.

"Coming, Mrs. Spruce in just a few minutes," Eunice answered. This had to be the same Eunice from the ship, and when I looked closely at her, I could see a similar resemblance to the Eunice who walked the Widow's Walk. Just then, I heard the sounds of water running upstairs, so I scrambled down the ladder, grabbed it and my mug, and headed back into the kitchen to await Harry's arrival so pleased that the library came to me!

જ

"And what time did you get up, Emma! Your face is shining and you look as though you ran five miles in three minutes!" Harry said as he bounded into the kitchen and headed immediately for the coffee.

"Oh, not too terribly long ago, Harry. And you look like you slept very well and I'm glad. You needed it. Now, what would you like for breakfast?" I said, pulling myself completely back together after a quick glance at him, as I reached into the refrigerator for the butter. "Want some toast? I could use some as well and if you want eggs, how do you want them?"

"Are you a short order cook, now my dear?"

"Well, why not! I'm suddenly hungry as well but I only want some toast, a slice, or two of cheese and some tomatoes on it."

"Ah, so you've been up for ages and have been waiting for me for breakfast. Emma, you really are a dear woman!" He sat himself down and contemplated for a moment. "I'll have what you're having. And then we can continue with our day as I've been planning it out!"

I took out the Swiss cheese and a tomato, put the bread in the toaster but did not turn back to him as I said, "I know we talked about seeing more of the area today, JHS, and I know you are leaving at the end of the week, or at least that's what I think I remember your telling me, but I'd rather not go driving through the countryside today if you don't mind too terribly. I just want to hang out for a while. Besides, the weather doesn't look that great

174

out and the thermometer is reading temps in the forties! A little chilly for sightseeing and not much sun either. Do you mind terribly?" I said turning to face him.

His eyes were glaring pure anger but his voice, always under control intimated it was fine with him. But I knew differently. I knew that if I went anywhere he would be sure to follow, so I thanked him and poured myself more coffee. We ate in silence and after I did the dishes and put things back in place, I walked towards the back to the music room, where I parked myself. Yes, my feline companions came with me and curled up beside me on the roomy chaise. I had to think. Was this one of those "closed" communities like so many of the hill communities in the South? Was intermarriage and intermingling a part of their co-existence here? Were the names just passed down from one family line to the next to keep the caste order? Was the Eunice of the Widow's Walk an offspring of the midwife and then servant Eunice? Was Papa Harris, as my mind called him, having an affair with midwife Eunice? Did he have any offspring from her as well as his son by Maryanne? Was this all just coincidence or were these individuals, like I AM Eben, able to cross time lines and eras. And most important, if the latter was so, was there cognitive awareness in these people of past relationships and experiences? After all, Eunice was beaten by her father-in-law! Was there cognitive sense memory there? Is that why he exploded when he learned of the affair with Eben, or was it just a paternal protection for his son? And what was even more critical to me was that all of these people I had met, with the exception of Sarah, who was not born here, related? And if so, was it Papa Harris who began this dynasty—Puritanical religious beliefs notwithstanding? After all, we've all known for many years that each and every religion, no matter how strict, has never ever been followed to the letter as long as love and hormones were involved. Someone always gave in or was pushed into doing so. This seemed to be the law of the land in our so-called modern world and the roots of this had to come from quite a ways back. Look at how many books and plays were written about this "forbidden" love. Of course, all these questions brought my own marriage and divorce back full force and once again, I realized that the vast majority of us were not really meant to spend a lifetime together, although in some species it seemed to be the natural way of existence except when one lifetime partner died, then the next in line (the next strongest) moved up the ladder to take the place of the lost mate. Ah, life! We've allowed religion, through misinterpretation, to make it so very complicated and to rule us.

As all of this was floating around in my mind, I quickly deposited each piece of information in its own compartment—the file cabinet in my mind—yawned widely as my companions followed suit, and fell promptly into a deep sleep. Once again I saw myself floating free of my body and looked back to make sure that the all-important silver cord was still attached to it. I was taken back to my first encounter with the mirror at The Hounds Tooth Inn. I saw myself in that riding habit, heard a young JHS call to me in that Irish accent; then I saw myself in that beautiful dress with Marie fixing my hair. Next I heard her say, Mlle. Eunice, not Emma, as I had thought JHS had called me . . . and that was Eunice's face before me, not my own.

Being in an altered state has its advantages. My mind recorded these encounters, but my sleep was so deep, I did not worry about them nor was I awakened. Instead my own mind worked with the speed of lightning bringing to bear the Time-Space Continuum where everything can happen at the same time; where one can go in and out of realities because everything does occur simultaneously, creating a myriad of probable realities all of which have their own life and activity. I knew I was deep into this phenomenon, and just continued to float in it while my human brain continued placing the information I was receiving in the proper files in my mind.

The next sequence took me back to the town library and the files downstairs where I saw Nappy and Peaches sitting by the box with the tape. Suddenly, like magic, the box top was on the floor by the desk with the cats sitting in it and I was rifling through all it. I had remembered where I stopped before Sarah called downstairs about closing time and I immediately went on rummaging. But for some reason, even though I flipped through pages and pages of very old paper and various other things, no writing appeared.

Just as I was about to mentally go back through that box; I flew back into my body with a bang and was sitting on the one of the sofas! "Emma, what's wrong with you! You're sleeping the day away! EMMA! EMMA! WAKE UP!" Harry was shaking me so roughly I sat up suddenly afraid and immediately had to put my head between my legs to let the dizziness and nausea subside.

"Oh, my God! I'm so sorry," he said as he gently rubbed my back. "I thought something was wrong with you. I've been trying to wake you for over five minutes!" He was very apologetic. I nodded my understanding. So that's why I saw nothing on those pages, I thought to myself, still in the bent over position. He must have been shaking me which not only brought me back so quickly, but disrupted what I was seeing. I took a few deep breaths, sat up, patted his hand, and looked around. The cats were nowhere to be seen.

"Its okay, Harry," I managed to say as I attempted to stand up, teetered, and sat right back down. "I must have been in a very deep sleep not to have heard you."

"Didn't you sleep well last night, Em?" He was once again rubbing my neck and back very gently.

"I guess I didn't sleep as well as I thought," I responded with a small smile. I do remember tossing quite a bit and I even had to pick the covers off the floor when I awoke. Sorry I frightened you, but I'm okay now, and I know you really want to go for a walk, so just give me a few minutes and I'll be ready to join you," I said finally standing firmly on my own two feet and pushing my energies back down into Terra Firma.

I went upstairs, threw cold water on my face, ran the comb through my hair, grabbed a sweater, and met him in the vestibule. As I reached the bottom stop I heard myself say. "All that matters is that we get some air, Harry." That stopped me cold for a moment. I was frozen in time. I hadn't verbalized that phrase in years and years! Was I, the Emma I knew to be in this current reality, going backwards in time too?

"You are so right, dear lady," he responded as he helped me into my heavy sweater, opened the door and took my hand. The air had that wonderful crispness that portends the coming of winter and just breathing

178

it in made me feel together and alive. I was ready for anything! But nothing untoward happened. We just walked briskly through the gardens, went towards the back of the house and the woods, but did not enter. As Harry turned, I said, "Couldn't we go to the playhouse just one more time, Harry? I loved it so, and seeing you as you are now and imagining you as a youngster is delightful!" He looked at me with his head cocked to one side and grinned. I was instigating a repeat of what I had just experienced! How weird! Even the verbiage was the same.

"Okay, if that's what you really want to do, Emma, let's go!" He turned left and headed down the old trail towards the playhouse. Being the gentleman he was, he held the branches aside that could have gotten in my way, and by doing so this time I saw I AM Eben standing in the middle of the path. Ah, there was a reason to repeat this one, I guessed, but Harry took no notice. If he also saw I AM Eben, he made no mention of it and walked right through him. I gave a slight nod, which Harry thought was my way of thanking him for holding the branches until we reached the uncovered trail which led directly to the playhouse.

"Every time I come here, Emma, I find it absolutely wonderful. Thank you for suggesting it. It brings back such memories! Some good, some bad, but that's all a part of growing up. Did you know I had a friend who often came here too?"

"No, I didn't know that," I said. We were standing at the closed door.

"Well, I did. It was Terry, now the owner of The Hounds Tooth Inn when she was a girl." I just looked at him to continue. We had talked about this yesterday—that I did remember. "Her parents were friends of my parents, but after about a year or two they moved away, why I don't know. However, after she married and her husband died, she moved back here."

"Of course, I met her, Harry. I stayed there over night, or was it for two nights, as I mentioned a day or so ago. I can't quite remember. I only remember being very tired after driving all the way up here. She and her son, Jess, were very helpful. And of course, that's where I met the cats! Didn't I tell you they were there with Terry and Jess to begin with, and then came here with me? They just jumped right in the car and would not move. We all thought it was a riot, but neither of them was upset about it!" I rambled on without filling in any of the other details that were filed away in my brain. Something deep in my heart told me to just continue as I was doing and not to add anything else; not even the supposed car trouble I had upon trying to leave.

"These cats seem to roam around with whomever they choose, even though their parentage is with my family. I remember my parents telling me that once when I was looking for them and couldn't find them. Of course, they returned a few days later, but no one knew where they'd been or what they'd done. Very interesting animals, wouldn't you say?" he asked as he finally opened the door and ushered me into his once private territory with a great sweeping gesture of his right arm. I half expected to see the cats sitting inside, but the playhouse was devoid of felines. In fact, it was devoid of everything. Had someone come down here and cleaned out all the toys, books and other paraphernalia? If so, who was it? George?

Harry? And why had I AM Eben, my Watcher, I had begun calling him in my mind, been standing on the path? What was he trying to tell me? The "rape" sequence with Harry began again, and I did as I previously did and then ran back to the house. That's when I heard, "So now you too can switch between realities and . . ."

⚘

"Emma, are you not well? You look so strange!"

"No, I'm fine. Harry I've a question for you." He turned and came back towards me. "I think I was day-dreaming, well sort of," I began slowly. "You and I went for a walk and we ended up at the playhouse, but when we went in, it was completely empty! Can you imagine that?"

"Empty? Never! I left instructions it was to be maintained just as I'd left it when they sent me away to boarding school! How strange," he almost whispered. What else did you see? Do you remember?"

Ah, how sweet of him to give me an out! "I remember standing there for quite some time looking at the empty space, and then leaving and waking up here." I looked at him to see if he bought what I was saying and then asked if he still wanted to go for a walk.

"I'll go alone, Emma. You stay here and rest. I'm just going to the playhouse to see if it's still intact. Do you mind?"

"Not at all, Harry. Not at all. I think I'll just go upstairs for a while." I responded, arose, and with my feline friends, did just that. Once I heard the downstairs door close I pulled the chair to the window, sat down and looked out into space. I waited until I was cool, calm, and collected and then called on I AM Eben to come and visit. For quite some time nothing happened and I was getting bored waiting. Just as I was about to get up and go back to the mirror, he appeared, sitting on my bed, resting against the pillows with his legs crossed at the ankles and as comfortable as could be.

"To answer your unasked question, Doctor, you have been doing a great deal of time traveling in a wide variety of ways. I believe that if you think about it, you've always had this ability and have used it in your work to great advantage quite often, and without even giving it another thought. It was something you were born with. It was given to you as a gift from God before your actual birth on this planet at this time. And even though you've used it before, it was not in the same way or with the acumen that you have now. Does that help you?"

"Yes, it does, somewhat," I said standing up and beginning to pace because my energy level was suddenly excessive.

"Ah, you are feeling the full effects of it, I see. When energy flows consciously into you, this is what happens to you. You want to expel it, so pacing or running is what you want to do next. I think what you should consider are two things: What you or any part of this planet—or any planet for that matter—desires is the energy you call God. And this energy wants to experience everything through you, as well as through each and every part that lives in physical form. You are experiencing the push to continue because the time is ripe. You have yet to finish your conversation with Maude and she is alone now since George went into town, so get going. And yes, I will always appear as needed. And again yes, you are correct, but I will let Maude fill you in." Once again, he vanished before I could even blink!

Within a matter of moments, I picked up the telephone and called Maude inviting her over for tea, coffee, or whatever else she wanted. I told her I knew she needed a break from canning and she accepted with joy, telling me she had just finished her last batch of tomatoes, jarred them, and washed everything. Inside of ten minutes, she was there and we two were sitting at the kitchen table like old coffee buddies, except we weren't drinking coffee. Each of us held a stiff glass of scotch and soda. And we were filling each other in on what we'd been doing. When I told Maude I'd gone to the gorgeous library in town, I thought she'd drop her teeth. And I also told her the cats were with me and worked relatively hard at ridding the basement of vermin. I didn't tell her about the sealed box, just about going through the stacks downstairs to find out some more of the history of the manor house, and she was agog at what I told her I'd found.

"Ya mean our house used to be the original? Oh, my goodness! No wonder it's so solid. Ya know it's withstood really terrible storms and winds without even a window casing cracking, although in one storm we did lose a window!! Oh, my Gawd!" She took a big gulp. "I ken just see them all livin' there together until the big house was built! Were there any other kids then?"

"I'm not sure I remember seeing any names other than Mr. and Mrs. H.J. Spruce and the baby boy, but I do intend to find out." I only assumed that when the manor house was being built, the young Harris was old enough to be working somewhere or at sea or even married! After all, people did marry very young in those long ago days. 'You are right, he was at sea being trained,' I heard inside my head. 'He was twelve years old then and was what we now call a steward.'

"Ya know I always thought it strange the big house was set way back from ours, and I do know the shape of the land must a changed from time to time 'cause of the storms. It all sorta makes sense now! Thank ya, Emma. You is a real friend acause these questions have been goin' through my mind for years and years!" Maude reached across the table and patted my hand affectionately and then reached for the bottles I had there. She poured us both another hefty drink.

"So tell me, Maude, what do you know about our current friend, Harry?" I asked very shyly after she had taken another swig at her glass.

"Oh, him! He used to be a holy terror when he was young when his folks wasn't around, but then he found a friend—the lady who now owns The Hounds Tooth Inn, and he quieted down considerable! Oh, yeah, there was a time when things didn't go so smooth with all of them, her parents and his, and by that time, he was old enough to go to boarding school, so that's where he went, and the other family moved fer across the country as I told yer t'other day until I guess Missus Terry got it in her head she really liked being here instead. Thar was also somethin' happened in the playhouse, but it was never proved it was his fault!

"I know she were married out west, but don't know wha' happened to him. Rumor had it he died early and she came back with that lovely child, Jess. And I'm told by those who've gone there to visit, my George bein' one to do so, he looks more like his pa than like his ma and handsome he is. Just don't know why he hasn't found a girl of his own." She sat quietly for a time and then said, "Maybe 'cause that Inn takes a whole lotta work and no girl wants to work that hard today! I know you stayed there before you came up here acause it was a long drive and sure mighty tiring, and if you dawdled on the way up, you would a arrived there about dinner time. No sense in driving elsewhere, 'specially if you'd not been here afore!" As she spoke her accent got thicker and thicker, and I knew it was time to get some sobriety into both of us, as the men would be arriving, so . . . time for really strong coffee and some rolls. I quickly put the bottles away, washed and even dried the glasses, started the coffee, and took four rolls out of the freezer popping them in the microwave. All the while Maude kept on speaking of young Harry and comparing him with Harry today. It was quite amazing the change in the individual. What a different person he had become. As a spoiled, lonely child he was really a brat, but now that he'd gone through boarding school and subsequently university, and had been living in the city, he'd changed completely into a caring man.

"Do ya know if he ever married?" she suddenly asked me.

"He did, but he's never really spoken about it, Maude. I don't think it went well."

"Well, he should a married his own kind like Missus Terry!" she retorted hotly as though she was his parent and I guess watching him grow up as she did, which made her older than I was even though neither of us looked our ages, she did feel a parental responsibility forwards him. I know she worked in the manor house when his parents were alive, and still kept the place up even though I'd not bumped into her cleaning while I was there. At least not yet. "Ya know, we folks here do better with our own kind," she continued. "After all, look a George and me! We been together for over thirty years now and we're still going strong!" Once that was said, she looked directly at me and began to giggle like a young girl! That started us both off giggling like school girls, and almost choking on our now buttered rolls.

We were just in time. We heard the truck coming up the driveway and Harry calling out to George to come into the house and join him for a drink. Within a matter of moments they entered and we laughed even harder as they came directly into the kitchen and saw us with the coffee and rolls.

"Ah-ha, I see you've beaten us to the punch, you lovely ladies, you!" Harry said as he headed for two more glasses and the liquor. I guess we all need this today for one reason or another," he said as George entered, went over to his wife, and gave her a loud kiss right on the top of her head. This made us only laugh harder. They, of course, drank the Scotch neat and after downing two glasses each, they too were relatively smashed.

"Now how do you know we'd been drinking, Harry. After all," I said in our defense, we were just gabbing and laughing at life itself. How dare you accuse us of tippling?"

"That's right!" Maude chimed in. "Aren't we allowed to gab with one another? And besides, don't even ask what we were laughing about," she said placing a great stress on the "T" of "don't."

"Hey, now girls, let's keep things calm. We meant no harm, and of course the two of youse can do whatever you wish on your own time. Let's all be nice to each other. I do not want to sleep on the sofa t'night! Ya know my legs don't fit on it a right, Maudie, so just . . . "

"Okay, okay. We were just teasing you," I put in before the male ego tempers began to fly. Harry, would you reach for two more glasses and we'll join you. People should most definitely not drink alone. Oh, and I think I'd like mine with soda, of you don't mind." Maude nodded in agreement and before I knew what was happening the four of us were having a grand time. Harry even brought out a variety of cheeses and crackers and the nibbling led us all to thoughts of dinner. George looked at Maude and together they arose.

"You two set the table and we'll be back in a Down East second. Maudie was cooking up a storm with a beef stew this mornin' and I bet tis well ready to feast on. We'll go get it and let it heat up here unless you two want to come to our place. Either is fine by us."

I let Harry take the lead here. After all, this was his house. "We'll come to your house, George, and bring the spirits of all kinds, and we've a beautiful cheese cake for dessert, that is, unless you'd another thought," he said looking at me.

"The only thought I just had was to make a huge salad and bring it with us. Will a half hour give everyone enough time?"

"YOWL!" was the response we all heard as both cats jumped on the table. "Well, it seems we are all in agreement," Harry's laughter boomed around us all, "But I do think 45 minutes would be better for us all, don't you

George? After all, we men want to be clean and neat for you ladies, and I know Emma takes her time with salads!"

"Let's make it an hour then," George added as we were all still laughing. I'm in charge of something, I know—whatever it is Maudie tells me to do, and I've a lot to unload from the truck." As we all agreed on the time, the Everett's got up, I grabbed their glasses before they both headed to the sink to wash them out, while Harry bounded upstairs leaving me to finish the clean up and start the salad.

"Would you two kindly get off the table and get yourselves ready too?" I asked my feline companions, but neither of them moved. I stood still and listened closely, but nothing was coming into my head or my ears. I looked at them, and they were looking first at me and then they swiveled their heads looking at either side of me. I didn't move. I sensed something was about to happen, but I did glance at the kitchen clock. It said 5:05 PM. When I looked again, it said 5:45 PM and Harry was standing in the doorway.

"What a beautiful salad, Emma! And you did it so quickly!" He came over to the large salad bowl that was on the sideboard and took a leaf of spinach. "That dressing is remarkable! What's in it?"

"Oh, this and that, and whatever I could find, but let me run upstairs and freshen up, and while I'm doing that, why don't you get the wine and whatever else you would like? There's a large canvas carry bag in the inner door of the broom closet." I said nothing else and ran upstairs as though I was on fire.

Once in the sanctity of my room, I still did not feel safe, so into the bathroom I went and locked the door. Where had that time gone? Who made the salad? Where were the tops of the radishes and the cores of the red and yellow peppers? And what was more, I had no memory of going into the cellar to retrieve any sort of mushrooms whatsoever, so how did they get into the mixture? Bean sprouts? That was another mystery.

I washed my face, combed and brushed my hair, added some lipstick and rouge because I felt absolutely pale, and used the facilities. When I went to wash my hands, I looked in the mirror again. There, in back of me was I AM Eben!

"Hope you all like the salad. It was fun 'cooking' again and don't worry; I didn't use your energy. I've my own when I want to use it! Aren't time warps fun?"

"HOW DARE YOU!" I hissed. "Just what gives you the right . . ."

"Hush now, Doctor. All will become clear before Harry leaves, which he will do as I said before. But don't worry. You will be understanding more and more of it beginning tonight. Just remember we are all little children at heart no matter how old or how young we may seem to be." Again he vanished as I heard Harry calling me.

Dinner was a howling success all the way around, but the most interesting part, as we were all slightly tipsy again from the wonderful Cabernet (three bottles gone) with dinner, was going into the Everett's living room for coffee and the cheesecake made by yours truly, I think, because once again, I had no memory of making it, but it sure was my recipe even down to the hand rolled graham cracker crust and Harry swore he didn't buy it at any time and George said the same thing, yet it was there in the refrigerator and I knew it. I had even said we would have cheesecake for dessert when the whole idea occurred! Oh, well—just another conundrum.

We were sipping our coffee and having our dessert when I decided to take a close look on their mantle at the framed photos. Maude came and stood beside me pointing out their relatives. It was then that I noticed a few of the frames seemed to hold more than one picture and I mentioned it to her. She picked up the one I pointed to, opened the back, and pulled out the three pictures stuffed there, whispering in my ear, "He's not one of our favorites right now, so I moved it in back." It was the picture of the leader of the group of people from The Hounds Tooth Inn!

"I know you mentioned him," I whispered back—the men were talking sports so they weren't paying any attention to us. "And that you usually see him once to twice a year, but you never told me his name."

"Gideon, the dreaded," she whispered back, and then hid the photos again while I broke out in laughter at her tone and facial expression.

"Hey, what are yer doing over there, girls? Laughing at the clan, are ya?" George chimed in. "Well, many o' them there should be laughed at, ninnies that they are, especially that old goat, Gideon. Did ya show her his snapshot?" He came over to us just slightly unsteady on his feet, found the correct frame in a nanosecond, opened it, and said, "I bet ya dollars to doughnuts ya saw him when youse was at the Inn, right, Miss Emma?" He shoulda been there with his passengers going to Boston, they was, for their yearly." He pulled the picture out, took it over to Harry, and continued speaking. "Ya remember him, don't ya, Harry? He's the one who introduced you to that little miss, who is now the big Missus Terry! He's the one who introduced your parents to hers and then started the whole ruckus that got you sent to that nincompoop boardin' school! And remember, he lived only about three more miles down the road between your house and hers!"

"Ya, and I call him Gideon, the dreaded," Maude chimed in, "'Cause he loves nothin' more than to mix things up fer people and there he is, your cousin, George, the son of your favorite uncle, also named Gideon, but who was good and kind. Pity God took him so early on in his life, but the sea claims its own. And it's no wonder the son is as he is with the mother he had, always bringin' bad people into their house!"

"Now don' ya start, Maudie! Leave him in peace!" George said testily and before anyone could erupt further, something made me say, "It is what it is, and people are what they are no matter what the influences in their early lives. We all come in with things to do and we all seem to choose the right families, because they, the parents, have things to learn from us as well, and sometimes they do learn and other times they just go on the way they were programmed to do. Remember the old song, 'That's Life?' I believe there is so much more meaning in that title than anyone has given it credit for— and in the lyrics too!"

To say that put a stop to the conversation is not enough! George suddenly began singing, 'That's Life', grabbed

191

Maude gently, and started dancing! Harry jumped up, almost forgetting he had his coffee cup in his hand, quickly put it down, and gently grabbed me around the waist so that we could join in the dance as well. We twirled and twirled, two couples harmoniously singing that old wonderful song. The next thing I remembered was waking up on my bed, still dressed, but without my shoes. I looked at my watch and it said 2:00 AM. There was not a sound in the entire house. Not even the cats were with me, which was very strange. They had come over for dinner but departed after they had their fill. Where were they now?

I sat up and looked around me. Everything was still the same and I thanked God for that. I propped the pillows in back of me for support and took a few deep breaths, long and slow. I did not close my eyes nor did I intend to fly out of my body and go tripping again. Instead, there seemed to be other plans for me. The room suddenly filled with the brightest light I had ever seen. I even had to shade my eyes from its intensity and as soon as I did that, the light pulled back and became a stage with characters walking back and forth. At first they were blurry as they seemed to be traveling with the speed of the light. Then little by little, they slowed down and I could make them out. There we two couples were dancing and singing and twirling, twirling, twirling until we were replaced by another two couples, dressed in clothing from the 1920s: these were Mr. and Mrs. Spruce and Terry's parents who were then replaced by still other couples, this time many of them, dancing the waltz in long gowns and the men in the formal wear of many different centuries.

More and more people joined in the waltz which slowly became frenetic. It went on and on becoming more and more frenzied, until the couples began to fall all over themselves. I was witnessing a kind of Danse Macabre, encompassing every one involved in the life cycles of these people. Suddenly the scene changed and I was watching them being born, growing up, interacting, dying, and being born again and again and again. It was as though these people did not stray from their own circle, yet intermarriage occurred only with those most distant. It was rare that a new face was introduced into this family circle, but when it was, it seemed as though they were incorporated genetically and became as the others. What kind of power did these individuals contain? What was it that allowed them to be able to do this? I wasn't afraid, but my body began to shake. Yet fear was the furthest thing from my mind. I knew I was safe even without the felines by my side.

The franticness of this sequence began long ago— long before the Spruces boarded the ship that brought them to America. I did not recognize the area I was seeing where the first members of this group lived. No language was being heard and the landscape was completely unfamiliar to me. As I said before, I had done extensive traveling throughout our planet, but this was like nothing I'd ever seen. Even the sky was a different color, red with greenish hues, and clouds that were silver. The landscape had many pointed and jagged obelisks surrounding these people and their home. Yet the home was so much like the Everett's I was taken aback. And this home kept changing as though with the times, having additions added on, walls taken down, and rooms made larger and/or subdivided. My first thought was that this was another planet somewhere and these people came here en masse, as did quite a few of our first cultures after Earth cooled down and became habitable. But those groups came with a different kind of knowledge, knowledge that would enhance the progression of Earth for the most part.

I yawned and stretched my arms out wide. When I put them down by my side, they landed upon two cats who twitched considerably at being touched in their sleep! Now when did they come in? I had no idea and my mind began to wander back to the sequence I had witnessed, some of which was still going on. And then it dawned on me! I remember seeing such a place myself in my own dreams and again in my deep meditations. This was no planet. This was what has often been called the Oversoul, or the Soul Body. So the Spruce family and "friends" came together as one and planned to stay as one! How absolutely unique!

I know well we meet people from our pasts, from this past and other past lives, and so often we just pass as ships in the night, usually because we've worked out everything we needed to work out with them before, and sometimes, they do become great friends. But this group possessed a power beyond my comprehension. They remained a unit, probably having lived as such for much of their existence here and wherever else or rather, whenever else they came together on this or any other planet.

The light changed again. This time it was softer in its yellow hue and then suddenly became speckled with red. The stage in front of me showed the playhouse and two youngsters, a girl and a boy putting together a puzzle. Suddenly they raised their heads as though being called. The boy quickly put on his jacket and ran outside. I knew what I was going to witness before it happened but that was fine. I needed to see it because it needed to be dealt with; since Harry and I were dear friends, not passing as "ships in the night" this lifetime, but as friends, it was my duty to help him out now. He had already helped me greatly in this lifetime—now it was my turn to set things right. That's what all this was about. I was now certain, and the sudden rumbling purrs I heard seemed to agree.

The playhouse was again in front of my eyes and the young Terry was staring at Gideon who had entered a few moments after the young Harry left. Without any waiting, he sat in the small chair and began to help her with a puzzle that was on the other side of the table away from Harry's book. Then as he handed her a piece to put in place, he grabbed her by her wrist, pulled her out of her chair, and threw her on the floor. He raped her just as I had been 'raped' in my semi-dream state, but she had no recourse. He tore off her clothes, raped her repeatedly using every orifice, and as soon as he was finished with her, he laughed hideously, pulled up his pants, and strode out. Before that scene ended, Harry reappeared but this time with his father, who, seeing Terry, began to beat his son about his ears, head, and buttocks so violently, I thought Harry was a goner. All the time, Harry was screaming, "I didn't do this. I love Terry." That was the only time I heard anything. Everything else was visual.

The very next sequence was back at The Hounds Tooth Inn with a bus load of people walking to the back of the in to the housing there. Gideon was leading them and Terry was standing there waiting for him. She did not smile; she just took the papers he handed her and turned to face the back of the Inn where Jess was standing waiting for her and left.

જ

To this day, I have no idea how long this went on. I know that when the sunlight shown through my window I didn't feel tired at all. In fact, just the opposite! I awoke with energy. In fact such a great amount of energy I was bathed, dressed and out of the house within twenty minutes with my car keys in my hand. I hadn't even stopped for coffee or to feed the cats, but psychic animals as cats are, they were standing by my car ready to jump in because they knew exactly where I was going. Library, here I come! But first, I did stop to fill up my body tank with fuel as well as the car's tank and something for my companions who graciously accepted their late breakfast and were fastidious about eating in the car.

The Library was open and the felines headed immediately downstairs to do their assigned tasks. Sarah greeted me with open arms and shooed me downstairs as well. I no sooner got myself situated when my cell phone rang. I had automatically placed it in my bag before I left just in case. Amazingly, this was the first time I carried it with me. "Hello," I said as quietly as possible. "Emma, this is Harry," as if I didn't know his voice, "I just wanted you to know Sam's coming by this evening for drinks and then we're going out to dine. Do you care to join us? It is a business dinner though."

"Don't you guys just want to be alone and have an all male re-bonding evening?"

"Well.....I guess we do, but I thought I should ask you just in case."

"Not to worry, Harry, I'll be home in time for cocktails so I can get a hug from him too. I promise!" and I disconnected before he could ask me where I was, what I was doing and his usual caring questions.

Without any hesitation I went to the 'sealed' box and opened it, again putting the cover on the floor beside my chair. I slowly went through the entire box and found the original deed for the land, the first cabin, and the wish from Mr. H. J. Spruce that as soon as possible, a large house be built approximately one and one half acres from the present site to prevent any possible water damage from the sea or the weather. I also found the original articles of ownership to a shipyard being built five miles north of their present location that then had approximately three seaworthy ships. Along with this were advertisements for a crew. So Papa Spruce was on his way to creating a shipping business for the area in which they had settled, which I gathered must have been settled by farmers first who had also built a small town area incorporating the needs of the inhabitants. I was also pretty sure that there were those who did have small fishing vessels, but nothing the size and scope Papa Spruce was building. After a few pages of invoices, there was an article about the success of the first voyage of the 'Maryanne' and her success not only as a large, seagoing vessel, but returning with quite a catch on board. She had been fitted with many nets and brought back fish and lobsters pleasing the community so greatly that a store was quickly built near the docks so that people could purchase the catches from this ship and all the smaller fishing boats as well.

Then I came upon the Maryanne's log. Papa Spruce had noted he named his first ship after his ailing wife in hopes it would please her enough to recover and gather her strength from the birth of their second child, a girl named Meta. He had set sail soon after her birth leaving his trustworthy cousin, Gideon, in charge. He continued that he prayed every night not only for their safe return but for the health of his wife and new child. He did mention he couldn't wait for his son to attain the proper age for a sea voyage, thus setting the pattern for his family's riches. The rest of the log spoke of the training and quick comprehension of his crew and of their fishing abilities. The dates illustrated they were gone for only 3 weeks.

The next item was the death certificate for his wife, Maryanne, who died a week and a half after he left. No mention was made of his daughter, Meta, who must have survived. Then there was something I just knew I had to read carefully: a report from Gideon. I must have let out a gasp because my feline friends came running, their eyes shining, and smacking their lips —they must have had lunch! They cleaned their faces and whiskers while sitting in the box top while I read on. All had gone fine except that Mrs. Spruce was not recovering from the birth as expected. Nothing Maude or Eunice did seemed to help her and she succumbed in her sleep. Meta was wet nursed by Maude who had an eight month old of her own, Other than that the little homestead was fine.

Oh, I was so very disappointed. I was certain Gideon had a hand in something nefarious! But then again who knew for certain. Did he give Maryanne something to drink when the other women were busy elsewhere? I was certain from the excursion I'd had during the night that these people didn't change much from what I'd seen and that was their main problem! I also felt very strongly about the transference of personality traits and had always done so since I witnessed it over and over again within a myriad of cultures. Of course, this might have been slightly different unless this Gideon had named his male offspring Gideon and then the youngster, being influenced by his father, continued the pattern of unabashed cruelty. All of this was really quite possible from what I had witnessed and discovered thus far. My conclusion: The children did inherit the sins of the parents for the most part within this clannish society—unless they did get the chance to go elsewhere—until our entire society progressed and grew into what we are today.

I finished going through that box, found nothing more of interest, removed the cats from the top, and put everything back together, gathered my things after completing my notes, and went upstairs. Stopping by Sarah's desk, I thanked her again and left.

The Not By Chance Occurrence

I, or I should say we, arrived home with plenty of time for me to collect myself, take some cocktail franks from the freezer, and set the cheeses out to become room temperature. Of course, I also put out crackers and arranged the cheese boards. I knew better than to do anything about the cocktails themselves. Harry would handle that. Then taking a stiff drink for myself upstairs, I changed into something more appropriate for a cocktail hour. And of course, I made certain the felines had food in their bowls as well.

I decided that this evening would be a grand affair and as such, I even put on my full make-up. Something I had not done since I arrived. This allowed me time not only to take stock of everything that had happened so far, but to primp while I was doing it. What a pleasure! I felt no pull from the mirror or anything else. I didn't even hear any wee, small voice in my head or ears. I just felt calm. In fact, I felt calmer than I had in the few weeks I'd been there. Nothing was pushing at me.

Just as I was about to take a deep breath, I heard a scratching at my door. I went to open it and the two cats, also calm and content entered. I looked at them and thanked them for asking to come in since it was their habit just to appear when they wanted to, a feat I no longer questioned.

My first inclination was to sit in the chair by the window, but instead I sat on the edge of the bed. The cats came to sit by my side and we enjoyed a great love-fest. They purred and cavorted and gave me such gentle love bites I almost cried with joy. Then knowing the time of arrival from the guys was fast approaching, I took my glass downstairs, grabbed my jacket, and decided a quick stroll around the house was best for me to do in order to get in some much needed exercise. I was pleased I had decided to wear my best black slacks and a ruffled white silk shirt as well as sturdy flats. Heels are never a good idea in the country, so they stayed in my luggage, but the flats, being patent leather were fully acceptable. I took my time looking at the beautiful architecture of the manor house and, when I got back to the front, I peered up at the Widow's Walk. All was quiet there too. Very interesting, I thought to myself since the sun was setting. But before I had time to ruminate, I heard two cars coming up the long driveway. And before I realized what was happening, Sam had jumped out of his car and swept me up into his arms, which, as I may have stated before, was no easy feat!

"God, have I missed you, you magnificent woman! And here Harry is having you all to himself! How dare he!"

"Oh, Sam, now really, you are just too much!" I gave him a big wet kiss on his forehead as he put me back on the ground. "You know, you never joined us when Harry decided to join us girls—oh, just that once, which I guess was enough for you, as Lynn had had a very bad week, and you and I only met a few times for dinner, and always with Harry, so what's this about?" I said taking his hand and leading him into the house.

"I just missed talking to you on the phone, Emma, or have you forgotten our weekly calls?"

I squeezed his hand as I led him into the living room saying, "We never talked about anything serious, just our work, and Harry's work, so what is this about? Don't tell me you've fallen in love with me, and me only gone for three weeks!" I really wanted to laugh, but knowing the male ego as I do, I stifled it as Harry entered with Sam's luggage. "Ooh, are you staying here too?"

"Until Sunday, then we'll both leave you in peace and quiet as we are going to do tonight because I've a business dinner and Harry, as a semi-investor in his own work has been invited too. You know how difficult publishing can be! This may even be another writer I can gather up for my stable," he smiled as he said that even though he had tried to get my books, but academia had other ideas for me. "And don't wait up for us either. We just may be terribly late," he said mockingly. "After all, you gals certainly tripped the light fantastic quite often, and now it's our turn!"

"Ok, you two," Harry said as he came downstairs after putting Sam's luggage in the bedroom far down the hall from my room, "Let's take everything into the music room. It's always so much nicer to have drinks in there watching the day slip gently away." Then he turned towards the kitchen. "Emma, how can I ever thank you! All of this looks wonderful. Why don't you two grab the cheeses," he said handing us the platters, "And I'll zap the franks and don't worry. Sam has been here before so he knows the layout. Oh and there are cocktail napkins in the little drawer of the small round table, and you will also find coasters there, too. See Sam, I told you she was really a gem of a person!" he called after us with a lovely relaxed laugh in his voice.

As Sam and I entered the music room, we were greeted by the felines with loud purrs. "I'm not sure whether it's you they're happy to see or the cheese," I said, putting the tray I'd been given on one of the tables, "So I guess we'd better watch them carefully," I said half jokingly as Sam placed his tray next to mine. I then got out the napkins and coasters and the two of us moved our chairs closer to the table.

"I was here a long time ago and I really don't think they would remember me unless they are part elephants,"

"Sam, what you should know about felines and probably all other animal species, is that they do have memories and if they are very bright, they have fantastic memories of people they like, and that often includes wild animals as well! As a matter of fact, the three of us just had a big old love-fest upstairs for the very first time even though they've been with me every day and have followed me around as though they were dogs. It was just a delicious time, and it is very special to be approved by felines and thought, by them, to be a member of their family."

"Really?"

"Yes, really! And even the wild animals, if they get to know your scent and that you mean them no harm, will allow you to stick around. Haven't you read anything about Jane Goodall? Or anything about elephants no matter whether they are in the wild or are those who have been retired from circuses? National Geographic and The Animal Planet always have stories about the intelligence and memories of animals. And I thought you were an animal person, Sam!"

"Only teasing you, Emma. That's all. Only teasing you," he said coming over to me and giving my hand a squeeze.

Just as he did this, Harry called, "Pigs-In-Blankets coming in. Come and get 'em while they're hot!" He placed them right on the same table and then took our drink orders. The sunset was magnificent and the conversation was light and airy and full of fun. Even the cats seemed to enjoy it, their tails twitching in delight, and their tummies fully of snippets of cheese and franks.

Three drinks later, and with the platters almost empty, the men said they had to leave and helped to gather everything and take it into the kitchen. I shooed them out so they wouldn't be more than a little fashionably late, wrapped what needed to be wrapped, cleaned up, wiped off the wooden cheese boards with a damp cloth, and stacked the dishwasher. I knew I had enough to eat but decided to make a sandwich anyway, took it and a large glass of water, and went back into the music room where my feline friends were waiting for me.

I hadn't noticed that the chairs and table had been put back in their original places by the guys, but guessed the manor house itself did it. I was well aware that the three of us left this room at the same time and unless the men snuck back and rearranged it, which I somehow doubted because I heard one of the cars start up almost immediately, I felt it was not my place to question anything right now. It was time just to be and accept. The beautifully carved and comfortably designed chaise longue, covered in a serene golden Damask material, was placed so that one could easily see outside. On the side of the chaise was a small but sturdy table, so I retrieved my sandwich and glass of water and placed them on it. Then I settled myself on it and looked around the room dreamily. My two companions had ensconced themselves on the big chair, and were happily wrapped in each others paws, sound asleep.

I gazed out at the glorious night sky and for the first time since I arrived, marveled at its magnificence without being bombarded with street lights. My immediate thoughts were how absolutely vast the universe is and how lucky I am to be a part of it. I knew I was here for a reason and that I was specifically in this room for a reason, but I didn't give a damn as to what that reason was or why. It was just as it was meant to be and that was all there was to it.

I waited patiently for something to happen. Nothing did. I looked at the cats, because animals sense things far more easily then humans, but they were still wrapped around each other in deep sleep. I reached for the glass of water and was about to take a sip when I felt I had better put it down. I did so immediately. This one small action awakened the felines who then came dashing over to me and jumped on the chaise and sat by my feet. Each of them placed a paw on my legs as though holding me down when a torrential gust of wind blew through the room. I knew the windows were closed so this did not come from outside. Therefore, something was about to happen again. I took a few deep breaths to ready myself for whatever was going to occur and cleared my mind. Nothing happened. All became quiet for what seemed like hours, but in looking at my watch, it was only a matter of a minute or two.

Then the gust came again with even more force. I looked around the room, but nothing was moving, only the wind. I immediately thought of Amelia from "Othello," saying, "Tis' only the wind," when answering a distraught Desdemona, and began giggling. It must have been my giggling that caused everything to come to a head. I was no longer in that room. I was in a small house similar to the Everett's home but without the modern conveniences. It was very warm and I began sweating profusely. Eunice entered with a pan of water and a cloth and wiped my forehead and arms and chest, fix my pillows, kissed me on the forehead and left. I had become Maryanne!

I slept fitfully and when I awoke, Eunice was there with a bowl of soup which she gently tried feeding to me. I took a few sips and began coughing so hard, I know I coughed up blood. I saw it spew out of my mouth and all over the cloth spread over my chest and under my chin. She removed the cloth, put the bowl of soup down and began cleaning me up as best she could. Then, after trying to make me comfortable, she too, left the room. Pneumonia? Is that what she died from?

Again I slept, but was awakened by Eunice and a strange man whose skin was not as white as mine. He looked ancient, had long hair streaked with silver, and wore a jacket which exposed his bare chest. The jacket looked vaguely familiar and I stared at it until my mind clicked. It was one of my husband's jackets. He was also wearing my husband's pants! Oh, I thought to myself, he must be one of the natives, and as though he was reading my mind, he smiled at me and took my hand in his. He nodded to Eunice who went out of the room for a moment and brought back a large bowl and a small cup. The cup had a steaming brew in it while the bowl contained leaves and other things that had been heated, but were now cooled. He placed his hands in the large vessel and extracted a variety of leaves and placed them upon my chest. Immediately I felt better, and even stronger. I even, with his assistance, sat up higher than I had been, and saw my son, Harris Jonathan Jr., my four year old, standing at the door.

"Oh, Mama, You look so much better! I knew he could help you!" he said, as the old medicine man beckoned him into the room. He then gently lifted my son up so that he could kiss my cheek and I could stroke his face. Then he turned and beckoned Maude, who was holding my infant daughter, Meta, to enter. She did as he instructed, and I placed my hand on my daughter's head and face, caressing her gently. The old man then pointed to the door and the children were removed.

He sat down beside me, changed the poultice, and also held the cup for me to sip from. It tasted strange and acrid, but I knew it would help so sip it I did. He stayed with me for what seemed to be hours, changing the leaves and feeding me his brew. When he finally left, the moon was high overhead. When he had come, the sun was just reaching its zenith. So this wonderful soul had spent almost 12 hours helping me to heal. What a blessing. He came back for the next two days and each time I was able to spend more and more time with my children. Of course I did not feed Meta. I knew I still had the infection in me, but I was stronger each day. So much so, I was overjoyed when I could finally move out of the bed and stand up— holding on to the post, as well as having help from all concerned. I knew Jonathan (I had always preferred calling him by his middle name) was at sea, but had to ask how long he had been gone. Eunice told me it was almost a week. And with that, his son, Harris Jonathan, Jr. said he missed his father terribly, but now he had me! I was overjoyed and filled with love and thanked all concerned. I know I told them so before fatigue overcame me again and they helped me to get back into bed.

The next three days were wonderful. I even was able to walk slowly and asked to be allowed to go outside to breathe the fresh air. My son was on one side of me and Eunice on the other. I was even allowed to sit on the bench by our doorway and let the sunshine wash over my embattled body. The old man came back twice more to check on my progress and even left his brew to be given to me as often as I wanted something to drink, which proved to be quite frequently all of a sudden as my hunger and thirst returned. Eunice only allowed me to eat and drink a little at a time, because, she told me, my stomach had not had anything substantial in it for many weeks now and too much at once was no good for it or for me. I knew she was right because I remember my own dearly beloved mother telling us that when we were little and someone got sick. It was just really common sense, but when one is recuperating one does not think sensibly!

I sat in the sun until it warmed my entire body. I felt so much stronger I stood by myself and with Eunice beside me walked with more ease back into the house. Harris James Jr. had gone to play quite some time ago. One cannot fault a four-year-old for needing to release the energies within him.

That evening, I sat in the main room for supper with my little family surrounding me and I felt grand. I even asked for a second cup of the special brew the old man had brought me, but Eunice said I had had enough for now and could have it before I went to sleep. I complied with her judgment and asked then to be allowed to sit in the comfortable chair and read for a while to my son. Everyone applauded and of course I was granted my wish. I read two stories to him and he fell asleep in my arms. Eunice picked him up and carried him to his bed and then returned to help me to mine.

I fell instantly asleep too, dreaming of my beloved aboard his new vessel, when I was awakened by a slight noise at my doorway. There stood Jonathan's brother, Gideon, who had arrived on a later ship from England, as he had remained there to be with their parents until their parents aged as they were then, had passed. I turned and beckoned him into the room. He asked me how I was feeling and suddenly needing to talk, told him about my lovely day sitting outside, having supper with the family, reading to my son, and even that I was just on board the Maryanne with Jonathan in my dreams. He smiled warmly at me and kissed my forehead and then asked if I wanted anything. I said I was thirsty and never did drink the second cup of the herbal tea I had been given. He smiled and said he would bring it to me. Within a few minutes he was back holding the cup Eunice had left on the table for me to drink later. He said I should sip it slowly and I did. It tasted different, more acrid, but I thought that was due to its being so much cooler than what I was used to imbibing. We chatted for a while as I finished it all, as he insisted, and then he wished me a further good night's sleep and said he would come by tomorrow to see how much stronger I was then! I beamed at him, thanked him, and, sitting up, gave him a kiss on his cheek. He helped me back down, fluffing my pillow, and departed.

The next thing I knew I was floating high above the bed. I turned and saw myself lying there peacefully. I stayed where I was for quite some time waiting to see my body turn on its side, but nothing happened. Then panic took over. Was I dead? Why didn't any part of me move? I floated out of the room and saw Eunice sitting at the table with Gideon, speaking softly to him, and holding his hand. Ah, I thought, she has finally found someone. Then I floated to where the children were sleeping. I smiled at them both and bent down to kiss them. Junior suddenly awoke screaming, causing Eunice to run in to see what was wrong. I heard him telling her I just kissed his forehead and she, fearing he had contracted my illness, touched his brow to find it damp only where my lips had touched him; my daughter being an infant used to noise within our little household, slept on. She had always been a good sleeper since her birth, just the opposite of her brother.

I watched as Eunice comforted him and put him back to sleep. Then I felt myself drifting further and further out of our home to find the vessel named after me. I saw the seas were rough and I saw my beloved husband, Jonathan, at the wheel and heard him say the age old phrase, "Steady as she goes," to the crew and to the wind. I smiled at him and wanted so to get close, but could not.

I do not know how long I floated in the air but I did sense and see the sun beginning to rise. That's when I heard the scream. I flew back to our house and tried to enter my bed and the body there. I could not. Eunice was standing there screaming and screaming. Maude came running in as did my son. Meta was left in her crib. Then Eunice ran out of the house, still screaming and crying, and I knew. I was no longer to be there. I also knew it was Gideon who had done this to me. I also knew his name most certainly did not mean One of God. This Gideon was the hewer of life. He had taken mine, and I knew why. He and he alone wanted to own everything he could. I also knew I had to keep a strong watch on my son. Gideon wanted to get to him too, but not yet. It was too soon and my husband would have suspected his brother. They had always had sibling rivalry between them as Gideon was, in his own way, very selfish; staying with their parents was a ploy. He knew his brother would do well. After all, my darling was the first born, and Gideon knew he would receive nothing from his parents except their love and thanks. However, when he arrived here in the new country, he did have money of his own which he said their parents gave him to start again here in the new country. My darling never questioned that. Gideon's need to own and control everything told me I had to protect my son at all costs. He took my life because I was a threat to him, since everything would come to me in case of Jonathan's demise. Thus he threatened my entire family, especially, my son. I vowed to follow him until the end of the sands of time.

I was still floating but the landscape had changed. I was seeing the building of the manor house and the building up of the town, including the wonderful library. I saw my children growing up beautifully and kept a severe eye on Harris Junior. Every time Gideon got close to him, I made certain he was not alone. Maude's husband, a man named Ethan George Everett, was always close by. My darling daughter, who began to look very much as I had looked as a child, stayed close to Eunice, who I gathered had become their surrogate mother. She never had any children of her own. She had remained unmarried, and she cared for Meta as I would have done. She also did very well with my son who, when he was almost thirteen years of age, accompanied his father on his first sea voyage. His life took on a different meaning for him there and then. A seaman he had become, and a seaman he would stay. I thanked God for that in no uncertain terms, as I knew he was now safe and protected—even when he was on land. Gideon hated the water and would not go near it, and he also feared those who did. He thought them God-like and would not even deal with them. This was my first blessing.

My second blessing occurred when I witnessed the marriage of my daughter. Meta met Cyrus, who was helping to complete the library in the town. I again thanked God he was not from this area. I knew she would be well, and I also knew that when his work was over, he would be taking her far away which, for her, was safe and good. However, there was still this in-between time that was worrisome. I stayed with her as much as possible, and kept whispering in her ear to stay far away from

Gideon. I was also able to instill my fears of Gideon being near Meta, to Cyrus, making me feel doubly blessed.

I watched my daughter's wedding with glee and saw the lovely small house Cyrus had constructed in town for them and was pleased. However, before the wedding, there was one occurrence that did frighten me terribly. I saw Gideon sneaking up in back of my newly wedded Meta, who was watching the waves roll in. I knew what he had in mind, and put my thoughts into Eunice's head that Meta was in trouble. Suddenly I heard Eunice call her name and turning as she did, she saw him, nodded, and ran off to safety.

Then, as fate would have it, I saw my son's wedding as he too, had met a lovely young woman who understood all about the sea. Her name was Mary and soon they had a child, a daughter, whom they named Maryanne after me. I was elated. Even my then hard-to-please beloved was happy. Both of his children had settled down well, and his mind was at peace. I thought he too, knew or sensed everything evil about his brother. I guess he had always felt that way, but never expressed it openly to me during our years together, and knowing that he knew, caused me to move on. But before I completely did that, I saw the manor house finished and decorated just as I would have liked it to be, saw my beloved walking through the rooms when he was not at sea, and watched him relax and play with his granddaughter. I did not follow Meta and Cyrus, who then moved away to be with Cyrus' family, but I knew they wrote frequently, and both my darling Jonathan and Eunice were overjoyed. Meta and Cyrus had twin boys and all were doing well, happy and healthy.

It was time for me to go. My watching was over. Or so I thought. I knew suddenly that I was really Emma, who had become Maryanne. But, try as I did to return to my own body, I could not. I was caught in this web of the Spruce family. I looked longingly at the manor house and peered into the music room windows where I saw myself unmoving, just as I had seen Maryanne on her deathbed. There was something different here, though. Nappy and Peaches were beside me still, as though they were guarding me. And even though I know their family lineage traced back to the crossing with the Spruces, I had not seen them since.

I turned away from what I was about to consider a sorry sight because I did not want to die; at least not yet. There were too many things I still wanted to do. Suddenly I AM Eben was beside me. Again, I thanked God, but this time very verbally! "No, you have not passed over as yet. And the time that has passed since the men left for their business dinner has only been fifteen of your minutes. Follow me. I will guide you," he said taking my spiritual hand and pulling me along after him.

This was like seeing a kaleidoscope but not with patterns. I saw decades pass beneath me and members of that family born, grow, work, partner, and die. During this occurrence, I even saw the felines coming and going. Time had no meaning here. I AM Eben was right. I just let him pull me along for what seemed ages and ages. When we finally stopped I saw Harry and Sam, but they were old men fending for themselves in the manor house which was simply a mess. No one had been in to assist them and looking over, I saw that the Everett's home was boarded up, causing me to think both of those wonderful people had passed. I AM Eden said nothing. He just stood beside me and let me watch.

I could see them talking, but I could not hear them. Then the two old men got up and each using a cane slowly climbed the stairs and entered what had been my room. There, they had laid out all of my drawings and notes. Again, I thought I must have died too, but I AM Eben touched me and I saw him shaking his head. Ah, I thought, I had left this hidden under my mattress and someone must have found it after I left. Suddenly they both looked up towards the ceiling in alarm. The doorway to the Widow's Walk was right overhead and it must have thrown open and slammed against the turret wall. The two old men hugged each other in great fear and as quickly as they could, headed downstairs and out the front door. One went north, the other south, so that each could have a singular view of the Widow's Walk while we stayed in the middle. Again a kaleidoscope of events presented themselves to me. I even thought I saw George and Maude Everett on the Widow's Walk and hoped my mind was playing tricks on me. I could not imagine those two fighting up there—him killing her and tossing her over or bringing her downstairs to die. My own thoughts were stopped and I looked at the men. I felt as though I were watching a tennis match, my head swiveled so much. Both looked horrified and then, when the picture show ended, both men hobbled back inside, their heads bent low.

The scene changed again and I was back to the one I had first seen. The woman called Eunice being beaten by Harry's great-grandfather. I also split at this point—I was watching this not only while in the ethers, but in the living

215

room looking through the mirror. The cats were beside me on the floor while I floated up to the mirror to watch. This time there was a clarity I had not had before, as my etheric body-mind was experiencing this sequence from both vantage points. I was also given a prequel with this sequence while looking in the mirror. It was very fast, but I caught it. Eunice had been walking in the farthest part of the garden when Eben came upon her and pulled her into a bushy area. What neither of them realized was that Mr. Spruce, the father, saw this as he was coming up from the area in which the playhouse had been built. He stopped and watched, then went back the way he came as this Eunice and this Eben departed and she went into the house and up the stairs to the Widow's Walk to watch for her husband.

She walked back and forth looking out towards the sea which could be seen as the sun was dipping low in the West causing a magnificent glow on the manor house and the grounds surrounding it. It was then that Mr. Spruce, the father, returned and surreptitiously came in through the side door where the fireplace is now. She neither saw nor heard him. She was gently singing to herself while looking and pacing back and forth and this time, there was no storm.

As the sun set, the door to the Widow 's Walk slammed open, and the beating began, accompanied by the father's yelling and screaming at her. He hurled her to the floor, stomped on her, and kept on yelling so loudly, I thought any neighbor would come running. But the only one who seemed to hear was her husband who was walking up from the docks. He had reached the property and hearing this, looked up to see his father and his wife. He began running as though he were on fire. He flung open the door, and ran up to the Widow's Walk, where he took his father, knocked him down, picked up his bloody and beaten wife, and carried her hurriedly downstairs, and laid her gently on the sofa. He did all he could for her, bringing in a basin and cloths to try to ease the bloody mess she had become, but nothing worked. Her internal injuries were so severe she bled to death internally in less than an hour.

His father hobbled into the living room just as she expired and began screaming at his son, calling Eunice a whore and a slut and the one person who was demeaning their good family name. He even rushed at her dead body and began hitting her again. His son then grabbed his father with all of his strength and almost beat him to death as well.

The young Harris ran upstairs to their bedroom, took the comforter from the bed, ran back down, and wrapped it around his wife. He then ran to the smaller house, banged on the door wildly until it was opened. A man, who looked very much like George, probably his father or grandfather, I could no longer discern the time sequence within this complicated community structure, opened the door, listened and then ran to get his horse, and rode off bareback, probably to get medical and police assistance.

With this, I felt myself come back together as I was no longer needed on the Widow's Walk. I was like the proverbial fly on the wall, seeing all the action that ensued: the doctor came, pronounced Eunice dead, and tended to the father's wounds as best he could, as he too, had sustained some internal injuries. The constable also arrived, took copious notes from both father and son, and was about to cart the father off to jail when the doctor said he could not be moved and instead, asked the constable and George's relative to help get him to his bed, where the doctor did his best to medicate the older man and give him pain medicine. Upon leaving, the constable said he would return in two days' time to arrest the father for murder.

The next day dawned gray and overcast, but that did not deter the son from burying his wife. He then took his own horse and rode to the church where he told the preacher all that had transpired and begged for forgiveness for beating his father so drastically. This was granted him by the reverend, and notations were made in the community book as to Eunice's passing. He then rode through heavy rain to Eben's home, banged on the door. There as no response. He tried the door handle and found it open and entered the dwelling. There, in the middle of the foyer was Eben. He had fallen in the fetal position after taking his own life plunging a knife into his belly. The young Harris quietly backed out of the doorway. Soaking wet, he mounted his horse and returned to his house, where he, after tending to the animal, went to his rooms and gathered all he thought he would need, and readied himself to leave forever. He did not stop into his father's room, nor did he pay any attention to the moans he heard coming from there.

He went downstairs and prepared himself something to eat, but could not get the food down his gullet. Instead, the tears poured forth as copiously as the rain that was still falling outside. Four hours later, he tiredly climbed the stairs with a bowl of soup, opened the door to his father's room, placed the bowl gently on the nightstand, and then fell on his knees besides his father's bed. I heard tears and the slurping of soup. Then I saw the felines and the scene went dark.

Once again I heard I AM Eben's voice in my ears but did not see him. "Do not despair, Dr. Epstein, you will go home again." I had no idea what that meant, and then I heard loud purring right beside me. I looked down and there they were, floating with me, my two faithful companions, and all fear left me. It was then I realized there was nothing to fear at all anyway. There never had been. All of this was natural and one did not have to be born psychic to experience in this way. It was just another part of living. All things live all the time, no matter what dimension they are in.

Therefore, according to the syllogism I was beginning to form, there is no such thing as death. Death was not an absence of life; it was just a change of life. "Like menopause," I said aloud, and then I began to roar with laughter! I laughed so hard I found myself doubled over and holding my sides even though I really had no actual body to hold on to, yet my mind said I did have a body, otherwise I would not have been able to hold it! How strange everything was beginning to seem to me.

Suddenly I was being pushed and I looked to see who was doing this to me. It was the felines! They were pushing me first upwards, then sideways, and then downwards. "What is going on with you two?" I heard myself say. Two very loud "Yowls" answered me. "But I've no idea what that means!" I said. "Look into their minds and you will understand," a very different voice than I AM Eben's responded. I stopped and squatted down, bending my knees. How easy that was to do while in this bodily form, and what a pleasure to be able to do it so lithely! I looked each animal in his and then her eyes and new images came flooding into my consciousness. I saw the entire scope of the history of the Spruce family and knew they represented the vast majority of people in this world, no matter what skin color or creed. It was not a question of intermarriage and repetition; it was a question of morality. It was a question of seeing the wheat through the chaff or seeing the reality of the situations, all of them in one humongous bubble and that this bubble had to be burst, but not like a messy cyst or abscess. It had to be cleansed first, so that when the bubble burst, it would be clean and wholesome. I also saw that the past would not be obliterated, but it too would be cleansed, and what haunted the manor house and the surrounding property—all the Spruce's had owned or had a hand in building or dealing with—would be released.

But how could I do this? I still could not get back into my physical earthly body. I was still stuck in this reality and even though it was a real place, it was not where I wanted to be until the end of creation, whenever that was. I again saw my body in the library, safe and secure, and I noticed also that the moon had not risen as yet. The cats were still beside my physical form, so I was safe. Then, in the wink of an eye I felt myself being whisked away. Whisked! Now, what I wanted more than anything else was a glass of whiskey. Funny how one thought leads to another! I pictured myself sitting in our local bar in the city with the girls, and I saw myself holding a glass with ice and that beautiful amber brown liquid! But that lasted only one moment! I had to move on to solve this problem.

The next thing I was aware of was sitting in a classroom with a desk and three chairs. I was the only student. I looked around me and the room was filled with golden-white light, laced with a soft pink and a sprinkling of purple. It was gorgeous, and I thought that if every classroom in the world had light like this, the students would excel in everything! I waited patiently for the teacher, but instead two souls entered. They both greeted me at the same time and finished their greeting with "Yowls!" and pulled each of the other two chairs close to me. Oh, my God! They were Nappy and Peaches! I almost fell out of my seat!

They both came over to me in their humanoid forms and stood on each side of me. I don't remember what was said, but I do remember their eyes were glued to mine and whatever I was to learn I learned through their mental communication. When they finished, they both stood back and nodded to me. I stood too. They instantly became feline again and guided me back to the music room in the manor house. There I was, still lying on the chaise and I saw my body shift ever so slightly and my hands clasped themselves over my heart. So I was not dead, just dead asleep. What a joy and a relief, but I still could not re-enter my body.

"Ok, what's next," I said aloud and my companions answered not in meows or yowls, but in English! "Use your mind, Emma. It's all there. The men will be back in half an hour and when you awaken, which will be quite shortly, you will know what to do and what to say to Harry. Oh, and don't be afraid to lay it on! Sam knows what's been going on. He knows as much as Harry because Harry has told him over all these years of friendship why he cannot stand this place unless someone else is here with him. Not even George and Maude are enough to counteract everything Harry has seen and knows. It's all part of the family history, and they too, are a part of the 'family.' Why do you think you placed your hands over your heart just now? That's your starting point." With that said, Peaches gently pushed me from one side and Nappy from the other until I was fully back in my body. I felt my breathing in my physical body becoming normal again, after it had been laboring to oxygenate my out-of-body form.

Just as in a normal awakening process, I stretched, pulled myself together, and suddenly felt the need to run to the bathroom, so up the stairs I ran and made it just in time. After freshening up, I hurried back downstairs, made certain everything in the kitchen had been cleared away, and went back to the music room. The chaise had been moved back to its original position and my whisky tumbler was on a table next to a great reading chair. A reading light was pulled in back of it, and a good mystery book was open on the table. I settled myself, picked up the book and began reading. I finished the chapter just as the guys pulled up and came into the house.

"Wow! What an evening it has been," Harry said coming over and kissing the top of my head. "And I see you've kept yourself busy too. I see you've almost finished the book as well. Were we gone that long?"

I looked at my watch. Only about four hours had passed. "Not that long, HJS. I started it earlier before you arrived, and put it back on the shelf by mistake," I responded. "And from the looks of both of you, everything went very well, and your deal has been concluded, and a new business partnership is about to be blessed. How wonderful for you both. Can't have the two of you idling your lives away, you know. It's not good for either of you!" I really knew very little about whatever they were becoming involved in but as long as they were happy, that's all that counted in my book. They had each done very well before in a myriad of businesses and amassed more than enough money to live on. Men should never be idle. It's not good for their male egos and come to think of it, it's not good for anyone to be idle. That only causes illness and dis-ease.

"We have everything signed, sealed, and almost delivered, Emma," Sam said, "So don't worry about us. As you know we're fine financially and this is just another investment that will pan out and pay off handsomely—a fifth publishing outlet. And the guy we're involved with and his family are lovely folks and trustworthy. I checked them out thoroughly before I came up here—ran a D&B on them and contacted all the States Attorney Generals involved."

"You aren't only quite an editor, but quite the entrepreneur as well, Sam. You do all the leg work and Harry seals the deal, I bet!"

"Right you are!" both responded together. "And besides reading and having a drink yourself," Sam said pointing to my almost empty tumbler, "What else have you been doing this evening?"

"Let me put it this way, guys, it's been a long day and I think we should each have one more drink to celebrate and then bedtime! I can fill you in tomorrow or, if you really are not tired, let's celebrate and then I'll tell you!"

"That's a great idea. A celebratory drink is in order and then we'll see how we feel," Sam got to his feet and went to the kitchen. We heard some clinking and clanking around for a few minutes and then he returned with the ice bucket, a few bottles—Scotch and wine, and the leftover cheeses and crackers.

With glasses filled and raised, we toasted each other and then settled down to nibble. And as my sandwich was still there, I used a cheese knife to cut it up so we could finish it off too. After all, I had wrapped it in foil so the bread had not dried out.

As our conversation began to dwindle, in walked the cats. They greeted both men and then came to sit by me Nappy on my left and Peaches on my right, each pressing close to me. It was time.

The Secrets Begin To Unravel

"Hey, what's going on with you and the cats, Emma? They come in, say 'Hello' to us and then go right to you! Harry was asking me about that when we left to go to our dinner meeting. He was stymied by their reaction to you and he told me they came with you from Terry's place. Can you fill us in, do you think?"

"Sure, Sam, but I suggest both of you get ready for the ride of your life!" And I began: "During my time here thus far, I've experienced everything you have Harry, and you too Sam, and even more. I became so curious about the graveyard, especially the one for the felines, and the playhouse and things that I saw that transpired there, I finally spoke with Maude a few times to get filled in, well, sort of. But that was not enough and a search through the photo albums here and our experiences with the mirror—you do remember those, right, Harry?" he nodded. "Well, I had other experiences with the mirror even before I arrived here. I'm sure Terry and Jess would be delighted to fill you in with those, especially Terry, because I told her all about them before I went into a state of collapse. Oh, and there was Jess and the car, when I wanted to leave and the cats were already in the car even though I had locked it. The car kept stalling because someone had unseated the spark plugs, well, sort of, but that's the least of what I found out.

"In looking carefully at George, I realized he reminded me of the leader of the group of people at The Hounds Tooth Inn that night. Terry told me they were only staying overnight and would leave early the next morning for Boston, but she did not seem happy about having him at the Inn at all. So, being curious, as you know I am, and having gone up to the Widow's Walk my first evening here and actually seeing the lady walking back and forth before George came to rescue me, and then the arrival the next morning of the mirror itself . . . well, you can easily guess what state I was in.

"It took me a while to calm down, especially when I awoke that first morning here and experienced changes in Time. However, the cats were my constant companions and seemed to be guiding me everywhere. Thus the peace and quiet I was to find here did not exist for me. And no, I wasn't miffed or upset. I was excited. I knew there had to be answers to the myriad of questions floating around in my mind. I also knew I'd gone about as far as I could go in speaking with Maude, and by the way, we became very good friends, and none of our conversation involved 'girl talk'. You know she adores you, Harry, and is still very worried because of all you've experienced here, especially at the playhouse with Terry when you were both young, and the wrath that followed. But dearest friend, that was not your fault; I know you didn't rape Terry, but I now know who did. No, say nothing! I'm on a roll so let me get on with it." Sam got up and refilled their glasses. I declined liquor, so he sat down again absolutely transfixed as I continued.

"To see if there were any papers dealing with the history of your family since its inception here, I went into town, and I saw you in that terrific little shop as I was exploring the town and finding my way. I guess you were buying whatever you needed for the delicious meal you cooked for me that evening. Oh. My God, that seems like ages ago, but it was only a few days ago!"

I stopped and tried to stand to stretch, but the cats pressed against me signifying to me I had to continue. But I asked Sam if he would get me a large glass of cold water, and not one in a highball glass! He did so without batting an eye, and even ran to the kitchen to fetch a pitcher of water and three large drinking glasses in case anyone wanted some. Once I had taken a good long drink, I continued.

"I was greeted by Sarah and her delightful Southern accent and she chided the cats for not coming earlier to do their work in the basement readying it for winter. Amazed as I was at that, I didn't even question it. And after asking her as to where all the deeds and other papers could be found, she took me to the basement as well, and showed me what had been collected there since the beginning of the town and the arrival of your family. Did you know there is one long corridor of stuff belonging to the Spruce family in the basement?"

"No," Harry said in a very small voice.

"Well, there is and one day you really should take a look at it and what is more, there was also one box Nappy pointed out to me, but it was sealed with tape and hidden back on the shelf to begin with." Both of them opened their mouths but before they could even pick up their teeth and speak, I continued, "By that I mean, I guess I overlooked it as I was seeking land deeds and such, so I went to the early binders first. The information in that box was and is priceless. Your first American ancestor came over with his wife, Maryanne. She was pregnant and it was not an easy crossing. By the way, he also made a notation about two felines describing the forerunners of these two. Anyway the child was born and a woman named Eunice was the chief midwife with a woman named Maude also assisting. The child, a boy, was named after his father, Harris Jonathan Spruce, Junior, and yes, before you say anything, Junior was notated instead of Harris Jonathan Spruce II. They settled closer to the water and built what is now the Everett's home, but it was really one very large room to begin with and probably the partitions were first separated with curtains before walls went up. Eunice stayed with the family as Maryanne was still very weak from a difficult birth. Your ancestor decided not only to enlarge the house and to secure it from storms by using stones instead of wood, but he also was an entrepreneur. He decided to start a ship building business. Many of the others who had come earlier farmed, and some of them did fish and sell their catches, so the site was there and the scene became easy to set. And while this was happening, his brother, Gideon, who had stayed behind to care for their aged parents joined the group after their parents had passed, about a year and a half later, but did not live with them."

I stopped cold. "Do either of you need a break? The expressions on your faces are astonishing and you look like you're about to fall out of your comfortable chairs," I said with a giggle. Neither of them said anything. So I stood up. I was finally allowed to, as the cats stopped pressing against me. I told them I would be back as quickly as possible. I needed to be more comfortable, and not only with my clothing. I also needed a break. My mind was being flooded with what I should tell them in images as well as words, causing me to relive everything myself. When I returned about ten minutes later, having changed into my comfortable zip-up robe, they were still sitting there with their mouths open.

"So, I surmise you are beginning to see the patterns here! Good! Because this community seems to have been built by your family, Harry Jonathan Spruce, and the people first written about in the journal seem to have stayed and kept their first names so as to remain a part of the tribe, so to speak. To try to keep the people and the time line straight for you, it took about four years for Maryanne to become pregnant and give birth again which coincided with the first ship in your ancestor's fleet to be completed and manned. The child, a girl, was named Meta and the ship was named 'Maryanne' after Papa Spruce's wife. The ship sailed approximately three weeks after Meta was born because Mrs. Spruce, Maryanne, had had another difficult labor and Papa Spruce, as I had begun to call him, was worried about his wife. Of course, many more had arrived from England and settled the area by then, so the town grew as well, more farmland was being cultivated, and the fisheries were going well, too.

However, since Mrs. Spruce was too ill to nurse Meta, Maude became the wet nurse having had her own child just a few months before. Oh, she married a relative of the person who was also called George Everett. Papa Spruce left with great trepidation and his log is in the box as well.

While he was away, Eunice and Harris Jonathan Jr., had an idea and went to the local Shaman who brought herbs already prepared for Maryanne. He visited every day for a while and directed that she be given the brew he had concocted twice a day, and she grew stronger, enjoyed the company of Junior, and Meta, and she had the strength to finally sit outside in the sunlight. But that night, after Eunice had gone for a while, Gideon came to visit and gave her the cup of brew she was to drink before sleep. She said it tasted more bitter than usual and passed in her sleep."

"Oh my God, Emma! How do you know all this! Was it written down? Did everyone know Gideon killed her? What are you into? You've done some very strange things in your life. After all, your books seem to tell us this. Now what? You put yourself back there and heard and saw all of this happening?" Harry had gotten up and started pacing back and forth, his face filled with rage as he spoke. "What the fuck are you talking about? How the hell do you know this? Maybe it's time . . . " Sam got up quickly and came over to me as though he were afraid for my life. Just as he reached my side, Harry came close to me with his hand made into a fist to hit me, but then forced it down, and stormed out into the night. He slammed the front door with such force, the whole house shook. He could be heard storming around the house cursing, while Sam just looked at me as though Harry and I were totally insane. Almost twenty minutes later, we heard the front door open and close. Harry walked slowly back into the music room, sat down, and began to cry holding his head in his hands. I got up, walked over to him, and squeezed myself next to him, pulling his head onto my lap. I stroked his head and back until he calmed down somewhat. Then I kissed him on his head saying, "I think we're all very tired; too much to eat and drink, and too much excitement for one evening. It's late, so let's all retire for the night. What do you say, Harry? He only nodded his head in agreement and the cats added their consent by two good yowls making us all giggle just a little, breaking some of the tension. Sam came over and helped him upstairs while I piled everything on the tray and did my usual kitchen duty. I turned out all the lights as I left the music room, finished cleaning up, locked the front door, and also went upstairs.

The next day, which was the day before Harry and Sam were scheduled to leave, broke misty and quite cool, even for mid October. I was sure I would see frost on the pumpkins somewhere if I got in the car now and drove around. But it was really too early for that. My watch said it was just 5:30 and the rest of the house was deadly silent. My two sleeping companions were the only other ones awake, and even they looked at me through sleepy eyes which were really slits. Their facial expressions told me I had no right to be up just then, and they were not in the mood to move. I smiled to myself, arose, did my exercises, leisurely bathed and dressed, and then as my stomach started to growl, felt the need for my favorite brew and something to go with it. So, leaving my companions still curled up together, I went downstairs, made coffee and an English muffin with peanut butter and jelly to satisfy my hunger, or at least try to. I sensed today was one of those days when I would be perpetually hungry, gave out a great sigh, because those days had always portended too many upsets and a great deal of work, and I hated them. But as I'd been this way since I was about three years old, it was a part of me and I of it, and there was little I could do about it except go with it.

I boldly took my coffee cup into living room along with the ladder. I knew I had to use the mirror at least one more time, and by myself in peace and quiet. I set everything up, looked for the cats, who did not join me, and even though I felt strange about that, I climbed the ladder after placing my coffee mug on the mantelpiece. As I began to peer into the mirror I heard the galumphing of paws on the staircase and within a matter of moments, both had joined me. I smiled at them and thanked them for joining me. Telling them made me feel safer. I could swear they both smiled back at me.

Looking in the mirror I mentally called on I AM Eben telling him I felt it was safer for him to appear to me via this route then in person just in case someone woke up and came down to hear me talking aloud to him. Without a moment's hesitation he appeared and nodded in agreement, so there I was standing on the ladder with the cats beside me, appearing to be looking into the mirror, all the while communicating mentally.

He began: "You did very well last night. Harry will come around. He had a tough and restless night with many strange dreams, but his super-consciousness or as some call it his Higher Self is helping to put everything together for him."

"Thank you. I really was worried because I know the two of them must understand what's been going on here and how it can all be taken care of!"

"Let us say it must be taken care of for the sanity and sanctity of all concerned. It is imperative that you continue right after breakfast and as you see . . . "

"The weather is on our side. Yes, I do see, I AM Eben, and thank you." I was so in tune with I AM Eben I was beginning to finish his sentences for him.

"It is we who thank you, Dr. Emma Epstein, for undertaking this daunting task!" With that said, he disappeared, the cats lithely jumped down and headed into the kitchen ready for breakfast. But I called him back. "I AM Eben, did you really take your own life over Eunice's death?"

He came back into the mirror, looked at me, smiled, and said, you will see soon enough. Please remember probable realities and how they work within the Time-Space Continuum. Now, go and feed yourselves," he concluded using his hand to shoo me away.

The Revelations Begin

Everything began just as I AM Eben said it would. Sam was fine and said he slept well, but Harry was really beyond belief. Tired and grouchy are the nicest words I could think of. Yes, I understood fully, but his attitude towards me and me alone was one of pure detestation. He even spat out his breakfast order using a few choice words to go along with it. I tried to pay no attention to it, but in truth it was getting to me and when he called me "The biggest bitch on wheels" using the 'C' word as well in the very same sentence. I turned away and was on the verge of tears. Then directly in my ears I heard, "Pay him no attention and do not react to him at all. He will ask your forgiveness quite soon. Tell him to put another teaspoon of sugar in his coffee. His blood sugar is very low and all this verbiage is a result of his physiological lack." I swallowed my pride and the oncoming tears and did as was suggested, even putting the sugar into his coffee for him, and throwing Sam a look that told him to keep quiet.

We could see the sugar was working as well as the food. His color began to return and Sam gave me a hidden 'thumbs up' sign, but there was no apology or other response from Harry. I knew then it was all up to me, so without waiting any further, I began: "Last night you found out stuff that really knocked you for a loop, didn't you, Harry, and that wasn't the worst of it by any means. I'm now going to bring you up to date on the one called Gideon as you knew him when you were a child. And please forgive me if I said it last night, but I don't think so. It's just that I saw it all as it really happened and you, poor dear, were the one who was blamed. It was Gideon who raped Terry. Not you. You were long gone and couldn't even hear her sobs and protestations. When you were a kid and decided to run, you did so with the wind at your back. Your mistake here was that you didn't go immediately to your parents. You snuck upstairs to your room for comfort. And what was even worse, to your way of thinking, was that Terry didn't even stand up for you. She couldn't, Harry. She was too traumatized and in truth, blanked it all from her mind for years. However, when her family went out west and she married, there were problems, and she knew she had to deal with them, so she sought help from a very good and wise therapist, and the truth was brought out. But by then it was too late to help you. So you were sent away. Punished for something you didn't do. And please remember, your parents were really old school, and never really gave you all the love and attention you craved and deserved. They most certainly did not follow in the paths of your forbears in that matter. They were both too involved with themselves and their social standing, and left you in Maude's care much of the time, didn't they? No, don't respond. That's just a rhetorical question that I figured out for myself, because Maude thinks of you as her own, as does George, but in his own way. He too, did everything he could think of to keep you happy. It was he who built the playhouse, and without permission. He just did it, and when your parents saw it, they thought it was a wonderful place to put all your things and get them out of their way and out of the house! I know kids don't often realize until they are forced to review things in their adult lives, but I feel this is true for you." He nodded with his head hung low.

"Now don't say anything. Just continue to listen for a few more minutes, please. I have to go back in time to the one who walks the Widow's Walk. Her name was Eunice and she was married to your grandfather. It was his father, your great-grandfather, who killed her because she had had a long and torrid affair with a man known as Eben. And none of it was her fault really. She was young. Her husband, your grandfather, was a young seaman, and she knew all this before she married him and yes, she did love him, but she also needed love, and only received hostility from your great-grandfather. Because of her beauty and youth, he really wanted her for himself. I wouldn't be surprised if he tried, but I know he was not successful, and that's why, when he found out about the affair, he followed her up the stairs to the Widow's Walk. She was waiting for your grandfather as his ship was scheduled to arrive that day, and she kept watch for it with great excitement. But she never got to see him actually walking up the path to the house, because her father-in-law went after her and beat her to a pulp. Your grandfather heard her screams and, like you with the wind at your back, seemed to fly to the circular staircase and began to beat his father until he was down. Then he picked Eunice up, brought her downstairs, and tried to tend to her wounds. But her internal injuries were too great, and she passed away in his arms.

"By the time your great-grandfather managed to descend from the Widow's Walk she was dead, and your grandfather took the rest out on his father, and after a short time your great-grandfather also died from the wounds inflicted by his son, your grandfather. Here it gets a little confusing. Give me a moment because the realities seem to have clashed in my mind and I want to get everything straight." I took a very deep breath, relaxed, breathed deeply again, and then saw what I needed to see.

Your grandfather then rode bareback to the church to confess his sin and the sin of his father. The minister rightfully, forgave him, but told him to notify the constable of this terrible tragedy. He did so, and brought the doctor to the house to verify everything. The minister accompanied them as well. Last rites and a hasty burial were performed for both Eunice and eventually your great-grandfather.

"Knowing the constable would have to report all this to higher authorities, your grandfather then rode out again, bareback in the rainstorm that had begun, and went to Eben's home to notify him and confront him as well. Eden was shocked beyond belief and told your grandfather, who had been named Harry James Spruce, instead of Harris Jonathan Spruce, to gather up his belongings and flee before he was arrested, tried, and charged with patricide. The first time I saw this, Eben had killed himself, but I think it was his remorse and loss I was seeing, not his actual suicide.

"Your grandfather agreed and even forgave Eben in a rather strange way by thanking him and then barring him and any of his family from the manor house property forever. This has still been true to this day, by the way. But I'm getting away from what occurred, and unless anyone needs a break I'll continue because I'm on a roll again!" I was rather proud of myself until the cats got up and headed out for their morning business and perimeter search.

"He did as Eben suggested, went home, cared for his horse, dried himself off, and then, since the rain had let up, notified George's father on the QT that he would be away and also told him what had happened and swore him to secrecy. He hurriedly packed what he thought he would need, but this time he saddled his now dried-out steed, put food in the saddlebags just in case, and headed south to Boston. He stayed away, hidden in the midst of the crowded city for over six months.

"Meanwhile, back at the manor house, everything was maintained by George's father and his family. No move was made by anyone to go after the young Harry, although the crime had been reported to the traveling judge, who, upon hearing all the evidence from the constable, the doctor and the minister, with the exception of course, of Harris—deemed the crime to be justified in that the perpetrator was trying to save a life. It was thought by the good minister that the time away would do Harry good, because he would see how others managed with the harshness of life, so no move was made to locate him."

"If all was forgiven, I don't understand why he was left to suffer so," Sam said beginning to gain a faint idea into some of the reasons for the current occurrences.

"I think you are right, Sam. This was trauma heaped upon trauma and all of this trauma is not only negative energy, but tends to repeat itself strongly. That's why we've so many therapists and counselors assisting our young people when they return from the war zones. At least we've finally learned one important thing. We know now that most of these do not fully recover from their experiences without ongoing treatment."

"Okay, so get on with it," Harry grunted. "This is beginning to sound like a very good TV series and nothing more. Hope you've written it down. Maybe you could sell it and make a fortune."

"Now Harry, stop it!" Sam said reaching for his friend's arm and applying gentle pressure. "After all, you did confess to me that you asked her here just for this purpose and even though she didn't involve you in her escapades, there's no reason for you to be so hostile. Remember, she's always basically worked best alone." Harry sat up straight and finally looked at me. Then he got up, grabbed the coffee pot and refilled all our cups and since the pot was now empty, took the time to wash it out and set up another to brew. Sam and I just watched him in amazement.

"I'm so sorry, Em. I had no right to treat you the way I did. I know in your heart you forgive me, but . . . "

"You needn't say anything else, HJS," I responded, taking a sip. "But since you're up, could I have a large glass of cold water? All of this talking and remembering makes me very thirsty." And as soon as I said that, the felines re-entered, went to their water bowls, and lapped up huge amounts of water. That made us smile and even laugh a little, helping to break the tension even further. As Harry placed the water by me, the cats came over to me as well, placing themselves one on each side of my legs.

"Ready now guys? I'm getting more: I then continued with what I was being given as they settled back in their seats: "Your grandfather, Harry, was finding out how the other half of the world lived in a bigger town, found work to support himself doing all sorts of menial work, and while he was at it, he also met a woman. She was rooming next door to him and they became fast friends. Her name was Maryanne, just like the first Mrs. Spruce. And yes, he married her. She convinced him that he should return to his family home, claim whatever was his to claim, and serve whatever term he had been sentenced to. And he, being totally besotted with her, readily agreed. So back they both went, into the open arms of the Everett family, who quickly filled them in on the legal decision made in his absence.

"Both he and Maryanne felt blessed beyond belief, visited the minister and the constable, left a letter of thanks for the traveling judge, and began a life of helping others. It was this Harris, your grandfather, who was responsible for the town library. He used the family money that had amassed after his departure. But he did not do this alone. Soon others within this growing community added their moral and financial support, and with their various connections, brought in the marble that was used. One entire area of the library basement was dedicated to everything his family had ever collected. Neither he nor his wife really cared about the papers. They just bundled them up and readied them for transport to the library whenever it was finished. And no, he never went to sea again. He only ran the now large company of sailing vessels and the fishery, which was also becoming a cannery, as this process was then being developed.

"In time a son was born and they named him Harris Jonathan Spruce. Maryanne also had two other children, but they died young; one from accidental drowning while swimming in the ocean and being caught in a rip current, and the other from cholera. It seemed to your grandfather that only one child was fine and Maryanne agreed.

"As the town and the surrounding areas grew, your grandfather and grandmother decided to give parcels of land with actual deeds, not just word of mouth, to the descendents of those who had worked the land since their arrival on these shores, neither asking for nor taking anything in return. They were the philanthropists of their day. I know you want me to get on with it, but you needed to know this about your grandparents first, because they tried to impart their beliefs and work ethic to your father.

"However, Harry, we each are born with a specific set of ethics, which are not always what our parents want from us. And as to your parents, nothing your grandparents did or said changed your father's mind. And yes, they did spoil him, but he was always self-centered and married a similar kind of woman, your mother." I took a deep breath and said I thought we should stop now, take a long break and if possible, a walk, weather depending. It seemed the men felt the same way. We all arose from the table at the same time and headed to our separate rooms without a word being said.

I returned downstairs first to find Maude cleaning up the breakfast dishes. "Well, I see it's beginnin' to come out now thanks to you, Emma. George and I have been all on pins and needles since last night. Even the animals is wary of what's to come." Since this was the first time I'd actually seen her in the house cleaning up—she also had the duster out and the vacuum cleaner—I was surprised and couldn't answer her for a moment or two. "The cats even came by this mornin', somethin' they rarely do, so we figured the time was ripe and somethin' big was up," she continued. "Maybe I should come back later to do these other things. What do yer think, Emma? Although it is time to change the linens," she added.

"I think I'll head out for a long walk, so when the men come down, would you please tell them? And yes, you're right. Everything is coming together now, but don't be afraid. As a matter of fact," I said as an afterthought, "maybe you and George would like to join us in about two hours, that is, if you can and he's not busy. I think there are things you need to know as well," I said surprised at myself for saying so and then realizing the invitation had been put into my head. She nodded vigorously in response, saying, "The linens can wait another day, but I'll dust quickly and phone George if I may."

"Of course you can use the phone at any time," I said, walking into the hallway to grab my jacket and an umbrella just in case it was needed. This time I headed for the old ramshackle hut where I first met I AM Eben. I had no idea why my feet hurried in that direction, but they did. Upon reaching it, there was nothing there. Not a trace of the hut. Not even a piece of wood! I had turned around and was about to leave when I heard a whooshing sound. Turning back quickly, there was the hut and there was I AM Eben in all of his sloppy glory standing there with a big grin on his face. "Well, Dr. Emma, I bet you had no idea where this was going to take you. Are you enjoying it? We all rather hope you are, because in truth, it's fun to watch the others as the words come pouring out of your mouth! Sometimes we're laughing so hard, we have to play catch-up with things we may have missed!"

"Oh, you mean to tell me you guys have a re-set button or automatic replay available?"

"Where do you think the original idea came from, dear lady? But enough of being silly. You are doing splendidly and we are all very proud of you!"

I walked right up to him and asked who he meant by *all*. "Oh, every one who has ever been involved in and with this clan, but don't worry. We're all behind you one million percent because, my dear lady, as you clean up something as messy as this, you are also clearing up a myriad of other similar situations.

"Now, I suggest you get in your car and go to that lovely gourmet shop in town. I took the liberty of sending them an order from Sam for platters of food and sodas— no liquor today, please—and yes, it's been paid for by Harry, of course. Now, don't ask how. Just do it." And with that everything vanished again and I was standing by my car with the keys in my hand. Just then I decided to give up and give in. No more questioning about the how's and why's, just go ahead and go with the flow.

The entire trip only took forty-five minutes and I didn't even need help carrying everything into the kitchen. It had all been packed so that a simple method of stacking was easily accomplished. I put the sodas in the refrigerator and since it had an automatic ice maker built in, there was no need to do anything else except shove the platters in as well.

That done, I called upstairs to see if anyone was there. "I'll be down in a moment," Maude replied, and she was as good as her word coming with the duster and carpet sweeper. She quickly stowed them away and told me the men had gone out for a walk and should be returning momentarily. I told her what was available as far as food was concerned and she ran to the telephone to call George. I heard her asking him to bring the heavy duty paper plates and cups so that we'd have less of a clean-up. Then she began gathering utensils and napkins and put them on the living room table. I took out the ice bucket and had it at the ready on the kitchen table and made another pot of coffee and set the water to boil in case anyone wanted tea instead. Now why had I put everything in the refrig? Silly, I thought as I opened the door and took out the boxes, opened them up and handed them to whoever was standing around, gesturing that they should be taken into the living room.

Within twenty minutes we had all gathered in that room. The men had first stopped in the kitchen to get coffee and George took tea instead. We women also took what we wanted. I took a large glass and filled it with water and ice. As we got comfortable and chatted just for a very short while, George turned towards the mirror and blithely said, "Mirror, Mirror on the wall, who's the fairest of them all?" We all laughed heartily and then Harry added, "I think that should be changed to "Mirror, Mirror on the wall, what have you got to show us today?" As soon as he said that, the mirror, having our complete attention on it, moved and began to shake. We all shut up and just watched it. The shaking went on for about a minute, but it did not break.

"I think it's done showing us anything else," I said as the cats came bounding into the living room as though the house were on fire. They both leaped onto the fireplace and peered into the mirror and then turned to look at us. It seemed all they saw were their own reflections. What a blessed relief. Out of the corner of my eye I saw I AM Eben standing by the entry into the living room, nodding his head in complete agreement.

"What the hell was that all about?" Harry asked.

"You know very well, Harry. It follows the dream you just told me about," Sam responded. "Why don't you tell them now?" Harry shook his head, so Sam took over. "HJS dreamed the mirror broke. It didn't shatter into a million pieces, it just fell apart, crumbling like sand, and that woke him up in a cold sweat. He told me he was so shaken up, he couldn't even scream, but something got him up and he went into his bathroom, saw the mirror there was fine, took a glass of water, instantly returned to bed, and fell into a deep, peaceful slumber. And I've a feeling that's what's just happened, but without the mirror turning into sand. What do you guys think?"

We all just looked at him and nodded at the possibility, but I got up and went to get the ladder. "Ok, Harry," I said placing the ladder by the mantelpiece. "Go on and see if there's anything there but you!" Harry stood up with great reluctance and went over to the ladder.

"Could you come with me, Emma?" I nodded and climbed it while Harry brought over the strong chair and stood on that. Both of us saw only our own reflections. But I asked mentally if the mirror was "dead" as far as giving us pictures or allowing us to enter. There was no direct response. Not from I AM Eben or the cats or the even the mirror itself.

"I can't say for certain if this mirror has had its final say, but for right now, it is not pulling me towards it. However, before we begin where we three left off last, George, Maude, do you have any questions about this stuff at all?" We three looked at them and waited patiently for their reply, while George looked at Maude and Maude looked at George. Very slowly they turned to look at each of us.

"We do know what's been happenin', Emma," George began and then they alternated first George and then Maude. "We also know what's in the library cause we been downstairs ourselves and saw it for ourselves."

"We also know the history here having lived here all of our lives and my Pa told me all about Harry's grandfather and father and their wives and what went on."

"And I been friends also with Missus Terry since she was a youngster acause we also played together, but not with young Harry here. My folks would often drop me off by Terry's house when they had to go somewhere and Terry and I whispered about the strange things here at the Big House, as we called it."

"So you know the history pretty well," I interjected. "But did you know the names you have now have been passed down through each generation and that your namesake, Maude, was the wet nurse for the baby Harris Jonathan Spruce, Junior, born on board the ship during their crossing to reach here and again for his sister, Meta?" Her mouth fell open, so I quickly filled them in.

I suddenly felt as though I was back in the classroom, but not a lecture hall, and surprised myself by asking if anyone needed to use the facilities as we were about ready to begin. No one spoke, so I said, "Back in a few minutes, folks, and while I'm gone, I place George in charge of the class and seats are to be maintained and no noise!" I dashed out and up the stairs laughing with everyone else who was still seated and giggling too. Ah, what a wonderful tension breaker and healer is laughter!

When I returned a short time later, I felt as though we were going to one big party, made myself a half of a sandwich, took a few bites, and then sat back down in the comfortable chair I had chosen to begin with. Suddenly there was a knock at the door. Sam got up to open it and Terry entered. "Thanks for calling me Emma. I know I need to be here too," she said as she sat on the sofa beside Harry.

I was beyond stunned. I had not called her, but I took a big gulp of water and knew who did. Was I AM Eden in charge, and was I only the conduit? "Welcome, I said. So glad you could make it Terry, and help yourself to anything you want, because we really should get started. Oh, George and Maude know what's been going on as they visited the library and read through stuff. How about you?"

"I've been through much of that stuff too, and Maude called me earlier as well, and filled me in. I hope you don't mind."

"Not at all," we seemed to chorus together, and waited just a few moments for her to settle herself.

"Okay, then. Here goes! I think I have to tell you what happened to me the other night when you two men went to your dinner meeting so that you will all understand where this is coming from." I related my journey including the inability to return to my body for what seemed like days but was only a few hours. I even included the meeting in the 'school room' with the felines becoming people. As I spoke I kept looking from one to the other and found not a shred of disbelief as amazing as that was. They all even turned to look at the cats who were still sitting on the mantelpiece. "This is how I found out the rest of your family history, Harry, including the stuff about your grandparents and parents, because Maude did not say a word against them and neither did George, and as a matter of fact, neither have you in all the years we've known each other.

"Now I've come to some conclusions as a result of all of this. And it's really simple! No one in your family—and that includes everyone in this room—ever thought about forgiving any of your ancestors, many of whom brought with them the traits that still needed to be cleaned up. This has often been called Karma, and it's really not difficult to take care of especially in such an insular group as this. In fact, in this year of 2012, it's very simple!"

"Impossible!" said you know who, falling into his pouting mood again, and standing with his hands on his hips. Terry reached up for his arm and gently pulled him back down beside her.

"Thanks, Terry. you've come to my rescue once again," I said and then continued. "All that came before on this planet really ended with December 31, 2011." I stopped cold for a moment. "I don't know where I got this from," I said shifting my gaze to the mantelpiece, "But I've a rough idea. I think these felines have stayed around in one way or another since this family began and they know stuff we humans had never even thought of. I think most animals are like that, but I don't want to get into an argument about animal intelligence versus human intelligence. However, if you've ever had a pet, or as they should be called, 'animal companions,' you'll know how sensitive they are to your needs as well as to their own, and how wise they can be when they wish to be. And those two," I said pointing to them, "are really beyond belief in their sensitivity and their knowledge. I fully believe it has been passed down to them through their generations, and given to them by their parents when they were kittens.

"But since I was told to tell you when all the old stuff ended, I guess all that's new and exciting began as of January 1, 2012, and here it is Friday, October 19, 2012, and yes, I am fully aware that according to the Mayan Calendar, the world is supposed to end, etc. All that stuff has been all over the Internet, the news and other media, but with the new Mayan tablets found last May, it looks like the world will not end after all and if you've noticed, the weather has evened out. Hopefully, all the hot spots on this planet will calm down as well. Now the question is—by fixing the problems within this insular community, can we help these changes to continue? I think we can if you are all willing to do so, to stop harboring your dislikes and, in some cases your real fears and hatreds, of some of your clan and of those who were the initial perpetrators. Are you willing to really do this?" I stopped speaking, wiggled around in the chair into a more comfortable position, stretched out my legs and just looked at them all, one at a time. I made their eyes meet mine and held them there.

It was then they decided to take a break and dove into the food. I even joined them again, and gentle conversation accompanied our break. Then I heard Terry mention Gilgamesh while talking to Sam. I did a double-take because the same thought had also come into my consciousness.

"Hey guys," I said, "Terry just mentioned Gilgamesh. Do you remember that ancient legend?" They all nodded, so being the professor again, I told them that the legend of Gilgamesh was written at a specific time and for a specific purpose. In the latter part of the legend, this King seeks eternal life and is told: "The life that you are seeking you will never find. When the gods created man, they allotted to him death, but life they retained in their own keeping." I said that was used to keep Gilgamesh and all who came after him in line.

"It was the same kind of ploy used by the ancients, who created idols to whom the populace brought food and gifts so that the leaders could be fed and cared for without having to work for it. This was just another method of preventing the people from finding out who was really running things, and to keep them in line and from thinking too deeply. This is still going on today. So many try to keep religion and spirituality apart because, should it be found out that the spirit really does live on forever, then there is no death, just a different way of being.

This of course, started a long discussion and I let them go at it until George said that the minister and the Bible all speak of life after death. I agreed wholeheartedly, but pointed out that since there is life after death, this is something we can easily reach into and find out for ourselves, because all energy is fluid and available to us.

This has always been true for those who really searched and worked at it, but now it's a cinch for anyone who really wants to do it! They all looked at me as though I was totally insane, but suddenly my stalwart friend, Maude stepped up to the plate: "You mean to tell us that this is the reason we can all see what's-her-name walking these days? I've even seen her during the mornin'! And George has seen her too, although he's not one to talk about it easily. I've to pull it out of 'im and I can tell, acause he comes in a little shaky and grumpy, and it's not the grumpy of a hungry man!"

"That's right and thank you, my friend."

"And Jess saw it too while he was driving by, and he also saw something else he said was strange, but I paid no mind to him. After all, you know how young people are these days," Terry chimed in.

"But Terry," I began, "The morning I left your Inn, Jess seemed to have the psychic strength to stop my car from going. You were inside, if I remember correctly, and we sort of had a psychic tussle. Of course, I didn't realize why it was happening. It is true that it could have been the power from the mirror reaching out to both of us. I don't really know. But what is so important is that it happened. Can you call him and ask him what else he saw? I'm just curious."

Without any hesitation, she whipped out her cell phone and called her son, asked him about the incident and listened with her jaw dropping open. When she disconnected, she just looked at all of us and stared. Finally she said, "He saw Mr. and Mrs. Spruce, your parents Harry, walking along the road. He thought he'd gone into a time warp, because he never even met them.

He only knew it was them through the photos I have in my bedroom, just like the ones you have here," she said pointing to a group of framed photographs on the sideboard against the wall by the entryway. Then as he went farther up the road toward the north, he saw a man dressed as though he was from another century, and this guy waved at him and smiled." I smiled too, knowing full well it was I AM Eben pulling one of his tricks, but I said nothing. Neither did anyone else for quite some time.

"Okay. I'm sold, so what do we do?" Sam asked. "I don't think Harry can handle much more of this and in truth, neither can I." Everyone began to speak at once and the general consensus, including my own, was that we had all had it. But once again, everyone sat quietly. Then all hell broke loose!

Synergy Begun

Noises drowned out our thinking, and the manor house itself began vibrating; chandeliers shook, doors opened and banged shut, windows seemed to fly open bringing in gusts of wind and cold air. Then within a few moments, they began shutting again. Everything was rattling and rocking and rolling, making all of us duck for cover and shield our heads, but nothing was breaking. The door to the Widow's Walk kept on banging open and shut, and all the lights kept turning on and off. "I AM Eben," I said mentally, holding my hands firmly over my head while kneeling behind the chair, "Stop that!"

"I'm not doing anything!" I heard loudly and clearly deep in my consciousness. "They are afraid—all of them!"

'Then what the hell is going on?" my mental voice asked.

"I am asking around," I AM Eben responded, "But I personally think all of your research and all of Harry's and Maude's and George's knowledge, as well as what Terry knows now and remembers from her childhood and from overhearing her parents, has called forth everyone and everything that has ever existed on this land from its beginning to the present! All that ever happened here has come to the surface! I am with you now. In fact, if you do not mind, I think it more propitious for me and everyone here if I entered your body and directed things from here on. Is that fine with you? We have to ask, you know, before we do such things." I said nothing because I suddenly was frightened myself, for myself, so he continued. "I will not harm your body. I will just be acting as your guide, close up and personal, as you say in your day and age. Some psychics do participate in this form of channeling, you know. Ah, I sense your next question. Yes, your voice will be your own unless it is necessary for me to burst forth!" I think I nodded at that point, but I'm not certain whether it was mentally or physically because all of a sudden, I heard in my ears a 'swishing sound' and that was all.

Everything was still shaking like mad, but I managed to get to my feet and went around helping everyone else to their feet and then back into their seats. Even though things were still going on, when they saw they weren't being hurt, they held on to each other and to me, steadied themselves, and sat down. When we all realized the food platters were still in place, something began to dawn on them. It was Harry who opened up first.

"What have we gotten ourselves into? I mean, we've all had experiences over the years and it seems quite a few of you have delved into the entire family history! What did we do, wake the dead?"

"In a manner of speaking," came from my mouth without any thought. "As was said before all of this racket began, there really is no such thing as death, and oftentimes, although not always, those who have passed over can come back just to let you know they are still around, and I don't mean 'ghosts'. Those are usually souls who have not crossed over completely for one reason or another, like Eunice on the Widow's Walk. Her sudden death prevented her from realizing she was no longer among the living in your reality, so she's stayed in hers. Terrifying events can cause this to happen."

"Yeah, and look at all the stories around here, especially in the New England area, and in many of the old mansions and homes in Great Britain," Sam added. And remember all the 'ghost stories' we would be told around campfires when we were young? Anything spoken of so often must have a reality somewhere. I mean, after all, this has been going on for years and years and years! And remember how we all loved them when we were kids. We couldn't wait to be scared!"

"Right you are," Terry added, taking a deep breath and resettling herself more comfortably on the sofa next to Harry. "And out West, we used to use those times as special treats for the kids, and then toast marshmallows and Smores over the campfires—especially on fishing and hiking expeditions, and what was more, everyone went to sleep without any nightmares. And look at us now! We're sitting here amid such cacophony and strange stuff going on, and we're really all fine—and what's more, nothing in our time has been destroyed!"

"I'm certainly glad you two feel that way, but what about you two? Well, Maude and George?"

"We've been so used to all of this, and what with the repetition, as you call it, Emma, of our kinfolk and the names attached here . . . we've just taken it for granted, haven't we, George? I mean, we've talked about it many times and never reached any conclusion." George, being the strong silent type, nodded in agreement.

I smiled at my newest girl friend. She was really "with it", as the younger kids say, and she just confirmed everything that had been going on in my mind. "Yep! You are right on, Maude and I thank you. The crux of the situation is right here!" I no sooner said that then the house began to shake violently again. "Ok, manor house, or I think I should call you The French Blue House with the White Trim, because I've a sneaking suspicion these colors have always been used here. I need to tell you, for all of us, we mean you no harm. We also mean no harm to anyone who ever lived here or in this area! And dearly beloved Spruce House, we all do love you and your history. You are a great part of the history not only of this country, but of all humankind." With that said, I took a very deep breath, and the others, including the felines, all of whom were watching me like hawks, did the same. Everything shook some more and then was silent. "Thank you, Spruce House." I said and the others added all of their voices in chorus to this—even the cats with copious yowls and then loud purrs!

It was then that the house began to speak: "Help me! Help us!" was the plaintive cry coming in on a gentle breeze. We all heard it, and I think we all paled. I know I did. I even felt dizzy and nauseous. I was so dizzy; the room began to spin around me. Then I felt I AM Eben close by my side. He felt so close, I wasn't sure whether he had materialized and the others could see him, but he steadied me so I could look at my companions. Yes, they too, saw him. Their eyes were wide in amazement. I cannot say 'awe' because he was not fearsome, nor was he glowing with a bright pure white light around him. He was just there.

"I AM Eben, ladies and gentlemen. I knew Eunice, the one who walks. In fact, I humbly accept that our relationship is why she was so brutally murdered. It is the usual story. She was young when she married, her husband was a seaman, her father-in-law wanted her, but she would have none of it. I was a lonely bachelor and a friend of the family. We fell in love after she came to me for help and advice. You know the rest."

"No, they don't, I AM Eben," I said. "We've not gotten that far."

Synergy Completed

"Well then, I will sum it up for everyone, if I may." All heads nodded in agreement and the cats' tails twitched up and down. "To continue: Eunice was waiting for her Harry to come home and was watching for his ship. She did see it in the distance, but we had been seen together in a compromising way earlier in the day by her father-in-law, and when he returned home, he flew up to the walk, and began beating her just as Harry was walking up the road. He saw this and ran like the wind. The Everetts were not home, so only he heard her screams. By the time he arrived, she had suffered serious injuries. He attacked his father and he went down. Harry brought his wife downstairs, tried to help her, could not, and she expired. His father struggled downstairs, and young Harry just kept pummeling him until he too, after having been attended to by the local physician and consigned to bed rest, died two days later, also from severe internal injuries. Then as a storm was coming on fast, he came to me, furious of course, and almost began hitting me. I told him to see the minister, who in turn brought the constable who had to report this to his superiors. The doctor was also called in to pronounce Eunice's death and that of your great-grandfather.

"I saw to it that both were buried in the family plot and told Harry to disappear into the city, which he did. After six months, Harry returned with a new bride, Maryanne, and by that time, all legal problems had been solved and Harry was absolved completely. Does that about cover it, Emma?"

"Yes, it does, I AM Eben, and thank you. So you see what your grandfather did and what your great-grandfather did. You are a result of the union of your grandfather, Harry, and his second wife, Maryanne as you know. And I think subconsciously, you've been carrying that guilt with you because I am sure your parents, knowing the story, did speak of it, and children, even newborns pick up everything and store it away in their brains."

"Is this what is causing all this disruption?"

"Yes, and everything that came before which you have experienced, even when you, Harry, were accused of raping Terry by a distant relative who had the same name as the one who killed the first Mr. Spruce's wife, Maryanne. And that one, Gideon, is still around. One day Terry will tell you all about her problems with him, but that's for a later time when you two can figure out what to do about it. I know there is no statute on murder but I don't know about rape. However, I feel in my bones something can still be done about that one named after God!" I said hotly. "All that matters is the truth, the whole truth of the one body of consciousness for each of us, including him, and I think it is up to each of us to find this one body of consciousness for ourselves."

"Now how in hell are we supposed to understand what you just said no less do it?" George finally chimed in.

"I'm not certain, George, but you all just saw I AM Eben, right?" he nodded. "Maybe we need to ask him to guide us in this."

259

"Listen, Dr. Emma, you can ask anyone you wish but Gideon is my relative and all this talk . . . "

"The talk is true, George. And I am so sorry you had to find out this way," Terry said calmly getting up and going over to him. She knelt down beside him touching his arm as she did so. "We were both young then, but you well know he was always a hot-head. His parents always said he drove them crazy, if you remember, and that was way before troubled kids were recognized in school and stood the chance of receiving help. And before you say anything else, George, you are not to blame, he is. He knew exactly what he was doing and he didn't hate you, he hated Harry and still does. I know he is jealous of the friendship I have with Harry and with you, even though I rarely get to see you unless you are driving by and stop in for a cup of coffee. You know how word travels around here. You cannot even sneeze without someone calling to find out how your cold is! This is one of the most fantastic grapevines in the country!"

"Maybe it's because you are all so insular," I added seeing the confusion on George's face, smiling as I spoke.

"Maybe so," he responded a little less sullenly. "Even when I go into the big market the chattering that goes on in the aisles is beyond my ken! And then they all seem to go for tea or just sit outside on the benches and continue to talk, talk, talk, and if they see me, they try to stop me to find out what's new around here, but I keep me to me! And what's more it's not only the gals, it's the men too!"

"So what are . . . " Harry stood and as he did so, the front door flung open with a bang and Gideon stormed directly into the living room as though he owned it. Once again, the house began to shake violently. "So you are the root cause of all of this," Harry screamed and lunged for Gideon with his fists raised. He had been on the boxing team in college and his movements were still quick and his body, still relatively agile. But he only landed one punch to Gideon's midsection before George and Sam pulled him off, while we women flew out of our seats to do whatever we could. The punch was so strong, Gideon doubled over trying to catch his breath.

We gals grabbed Gideon, even Terry, and led him to the sofa. He was a big man, taller than George and weighing about 215 lbs. so it did take the three of us to sit him down. I first made him sit up straight and then, as the breath came more easily from him, pushed his head between his legs. While I was doing this I saw from the corner of my mind's eye, these two growing up together and the constant fighting in school, in yards, on the roads— everywhere. All they had to do was to be in close proximity and the fighting began. They automatically threw themselves at each other. No apparent provocation seemed to be required. So, they were both at fault here along with everything else, I said to myself. Then something made me look at the mantle piece. Both felines were curled up, paws folded under the chests, grinning at me.

While I pondered this, he regained his composure and said, "I am Gideon just in case you didn't know." The house shook again even more violently this time with doors banging, windows opening and slamming shut again. It felt as though we were on the epicenter of an earthquake! And this time, knick knacks did begin to fall off the book shelves and we even heard things falling upstairs.

"And I am Emma," I said by way of reintroduction. He opened his mouth about to speak, but could not. "And I AM Eben," Eben's voice said penetrating through the din. "And now that we are all together it is Time. Sit everyone, listen, and see for yourselves.

❧

The living room became a huge turbine with a screen attached, turning and turning so that everyone could see what was on the screen. It revolved slowly at first and then sped up and then slowed again. It showed everyone the beginnings of this family, not only what I discovered, but even centuries before. Then it jumped from the scenic pictures of Earth to another planet, where everything was in hues of browns and yellows and then to another place where the basic colors were blues of all hues including the French Blue color of the manor house today. Once again, as everyone was able to see these changes and the interactions of the Beings and/or people involved, the repetitive pattern was there. Since the very beginning of Time this group of individuals had been together torturing each other in various ways so much so that it became a part of their genetic pattern and was passed down from generation to generation, no matter where they were or whether they were corporeal or not.

I have no idea what length of time elapsed. I only knew I was awed beyond belief. So many things were now fitting together in my own mind from not only my life's work and research, but from my own personal past. Upon this realization was when I felt two furry bodies on each side of me purring gently with their paws on my thighs. The pictures kept coming but it seemed that each individual in the room was beginning to see his or her own beginnings separately from the others. Individuality was the key here.

Then suddenly the entire room went dark and the screen was no longer visible. I was seated where I could see the outside and that too was dark. Darker than the darkest night. When I tried to see the others I could not. I heard nothing. Not even a cough, sneeze, or a breath. It was as if each person was contained in his or her own bubble. I seemed not to be contained in anything. It felt to me as if (I know, double syllogism) the cats and I were the only ones in this vast darkness. I could still feel their warmth and the pressure they applied on me. This was like nothing I'd ever experienced before. Darkness has its own quality, but this had no quality what-so-ever. It was so dark I almost could not feel myself but I had no fear even though this darkness felt beyond what death could feel like to those individuals who did not believe in going through the Tunnel of Light after they had left their physical forms. I sat quietly and waited for something to happen. My hands drifted to my sides to pet my friends and as I touched them, they were gone and my space suddenly filled with light.

This light was unlike anything I had ever seen before. It was not the light of Earth and the sun, it was not like a klieg stage light, it was not like the light I'd often seen in my meditations or when I'd been allowed to travel astrally. It was cool, yet warm and pervaded every cell in my body. Yet it did not hurt in any way. In fact, it felt as though my physical form was being bathed in it. Actually, cleansed would be more like it. And while this was going on, my life to date passed through my mind and this light, cleansed all the negative things I had done and experienced, including my temper tantrums as a child straight through to my divorce and any untoward arguments I'd ever had that had hurt anyone at any time. I even felt as though this light, no that is not right; this LIGHT would automatically be with me from this time forward and forevermore. I suddenly knew I would still be responsible for my own actions and reactions, but this LIGHT would help to keep me on the path I was still to take and yet, allow me to be my human self as well.

I then heard a tinkling laugh within the LIGHT and knew it was True and Truth all at the same time. "Are you the ONE LIGHT we've all been striving for?" I asked aloud. The laughter was warm and welcoming and its response was a magnificent glow akin to the most beautiful sunrise or sunset ever depicted anywhere.

We were all together again, seated as we had been. Even Gideon was still sitting on the sofa still sitting in a slightly bent over position. The screen and turbine were gone. The cats were back on the mantelpiece and all seemed quiet and well with the world. However, no one moved or spoke. I looked at their faces but could discern nothing. In trying to see their eyes, they all seemed to be deep within themselves, thinking. As they came back to their current reality one by one, the light in the room also changed. This light was soft and warm and loving. It was rejuvenating. It was healing. I looked up and outside. It was snowing. They too, all turned and looked outside and as though we were of one mind, we all got up and went out the front door to stand in the first light snow of the impending winter season. The flakes were soft and we just stood there, not getting wet, but allowing the cleansing process to continue. Then like children, we all began laughing and running around and finally reentered the house and resumed our seats.

"Aaah! I see the class has come back from recess," I AM Eben's voice rang out. "We do hope you all had a good time and are now ready to get back to the work at hand." His voice was soft, and yet commanding; we all sat there as though we were back in elementary school. I personally felt as though I had a name tag pinned to my shirt and a handkerchief in my pocket. All I was missing was the Hall Pass.

"You have each seen your beginnings, your foibles, your many attachments to this life from the beginning of this family, and you now know who and what has been 'running' your lives. What you are each surmising is true. None of you have been running your lives. You have been caught in the same pattern of repetition that the majority of inhabitants on your planet are caught in. And each time you came back to this planet and to the other places involved, you did so with the very same problems to be worked out, but you've not been successful in doing that . . . UNTIL TODAY!

"As far as I am concerned, this peregrination was well worth it, because what you learned and what you are going to do about it shortly will have a great effect upon everyone else in the world—or I should say in any and all worlds in which you have ever been involved. I believe Dr. Epstein has something to say, don't you Emma." He stopped speaking and another warm glow over took me. I felt wonderful as the realization of what was and what will be came flooding back into my entire being.

"We've never really spoken about this, dearest Harry and Sam, but the girls and I have, many times. We are all at the beginning of a new cycle on this planet. That's why there is so much upheaval. Look outside. The snow has stopped and the sun is brilliant. Open the window wide and you will see the temperature has risen again. It had to be below forty degrees for the snow to have fallen before, but now it is back into the fifties! Amazing weather patterns, some with awesome consequences have happened that really began last year in 2011. But now we are nearing the end of 2012 and I know you have all heard rumors and prognostications even on the very serious news programs as to what is coming. It is you who are coming. It is you who are here to create these changes. And yes, it is an awesome task, but you are all up to it." Gideon turned sharply to look at me. "Yes, even you, Gideon. Your past is your past and it is over and done with. I think even Terry understands that now and to hold on to the past is only going to undo you."

"But..." both Gideon and Terry said at the same time.

"There are no more 'buts' of any kind." I AM Eben countered.

"He's right!" Harry said. "We were forgiven by that Light! Everything is okay now."

George rose to his feet and started pacing. He did this for quite some time and we all watched him, especially Maude, but no one said anything. We just watched him as he was trying to put it all together for himself.

266

"This is the stupidest thing I've ever heard! I think we were all put under some sort of spell. Probably something in the food, eh, Gideon? What d'ya think? After all, we're kinfolk. Oh, you didn't eat. I forgot that, but you are you and I AM me and we was brought up in the church and that's all there is to it. We follow what we were taught even if we don't go regular."

"But that's just it!" I said before he could continue. "You already said it, George. You said, 'I AM Me' for yourself even if you didn't use those exact words, the meaning was clear, and that Gideon is 'I AM Gideon', even though you used the plural!" It is the 'I AM Presence' that's so important because it tells everyone who you are and what you are a part of. You've even heard it in church, but it was said differently. We are all part of God or whatever you wish to call that energy, and it is a part of us. Therefore, I AM is the closure of the syllogism of the how, who, what, where, and anything else. We are all One. And the Light we saw . . . you did see it, didn't you, George?" He nodded looking at me strangely. "That is the Light of Oneness." After saying that the entire room began to change and even though we were all seated in the seats we chose, the furniture we sat on, the walls, the rugs, the bric-a-brac changed through the preceding centuries.

The house itself also changed. It began with only the first floor and started being built upwards. The fireplace was no longer, and everyone saw there had been a door there. More rooms were added as the years swiftly passed until we were once again in our current time. What had fallen on the floor and rugs was also put back in its proper place, unbroken. So, I thought, the manor house wanted to be included in this also. That was fine!

Then the living room was peopled with those who came before. They strode in and out on their daily work and missions. We saw children being born, people passing over, others growing and leaving—the entire history of the property wanted in. So be it! Everything on this land was entitled. It too had suffered.

If we humans think that inanimate objects don't feel and react, it is we who are crazy. Scientifically, everything is made up of molecules and each molecule is a living, breathing organism in its own right, and this includes all new things created from plastic and other man-made products. They may not vibrate at the same speed as our molecular structure does, but they too react to the circumstances surrounding them. Therefore, everything that lives, breathes, and vibrates has life and in this instance, especially, everything must be included in this brand new Light of Oneness.

"Oh, God!" George moaned. I don't understand this, but I see it and I know I am the same man who entered this room about two hours ago. It was about two hours ago, wasn't it, someone?" Tears began to roll down his cheeks.

"Come here beloved man and sit down beside me again," Maude said patting the cushion next to her, since she was seated on the smaller of the two sofas in the room. Dutifully, he did so as she continued, "I love you more than life itself, George. I always have and I always will. But according to my watch, it has only been about one hour we've been here. Do you all agree?" Everyone looked at their time pieces and their mouths dropped open again. It was only about an hour with the exception of Gideon who had entered only during the last fifteen minutes.

"Ya mean we ate all that food only a hour ago and the snow and the screen and the sun and the temperature rising and the house an everythin' in it changing? Oh, God, I am going crazy and so are all of you!" George wailed again and tried to pull away from Maude, but she held him firm in her embrace.

I got up and went over to them. "No, George, I don't think you're going crazy at all. No more than the rest of us. I do think what we've just experienced was the expansiveness of time and that all things happen at the same time but our own physical forms in our own times keep them apart."

"Huh?"

"Now look at your watches everyone," something made me say, and I looked at mine as well. "You see, George was right. A little over two and a half hours has really passed. You are most definitely sane. As a matter of fact, I think you are the sanest one of us here!"

"Wha do ya mean by that, Emma?" he said, sniffling and pulling out his big handkerchief to wipe his forehead and his nose.

"Well, you refuse to be fooled by anything besides your own reality whereas the rest of us instantly believe what we see as truth. But the truth lies within us all and we can now go on and clean up this mess once and for all as we were asked to do, don't you agree, dear George?" He took a deep breath, sighed, and then nodded.

Without a moments hesitation we were all walking in a magnificent garden full of blooming roses, azaleas, morning glories with their trumpets wide open, acacia bushes, lilac bushes, forsythia, gardenia plants, cherry blossom trees in full bloom, hillocks of heather, every kind of garden and wildflowers one could imagine and tall, stately elm trees with aspens encircling the entire garden wafting gently with the breeze.

We were gathered towards one side of this beautiful and fragrant spectacle and before we knew it we were all holding hands. Slowly, we began to form a circle and Maude, in seventh heaven as she loved gardens, began to dance. We all followed her lead because it seemed the thing to do.

I was wondering whether this would lead to some sort of Bacchanal but no, the dance was slow and graceful and soon ended. We dropped our hands and just stood there becoming encased in the Light we had all witnessed before and in the middle of our circle appeared each and every individual who had been a part of this family. Slowly they came one by one being led by Nappy and Peaches, and stood before us.

It seemed as though the main job here became Harry's, George's, Maude's Gideon's and Terry's. Sam and I were just there to lend our support. We were peripheral to begin with.

No one spoke at all. The 'ghosts' from the past stopped before each one of them. I had no idea what was going on, what their faces were exhibiting or if any one said anything to anybody. All I saw was a constant stream of entities, mostly human in form but some not. These entities were all those they had each experienced in his or her own way.

When the long, long line of these souls stopped coming, Nappy and Peaches circled Sam and me. These souls then came and stood before us en masse I believe to this day both of us spoke our own minds silently to these individuals, doubly forgave them and thanked them as well, because they became the wayshowers for all of life, everywhere. At least I know that's what I said. Sam and I never discussed it. Not then and not now.

I only know we were all back in the living room looking and feeling rejuvenated; so much so Harry, George and Sam hied themselves to the kitchen where we women heard a lot of clinking and opening and closing of cabinets. They soon returned with trays laden with sodas, cheeses, crackers, glasses, and of course liquor. With that, we women gathered up the platters and things from our earlier repast took them to the kitchen, made short shrift of them, and hurried back into the living room.

We drank and gobbled up what the men brought and then I remembered the freezer which was full of a wide variety of frozen foods. "Come on, girls," I said, "It's time to feed these men and quickly too. You know how unruly men get when really hungry." That was the tension breaker that was sorely needed. We all began to laugh and chatter and we ladies, with the help of the defrost button on the microwave stirred up a hearty casserole, in a very short time full of veggies, steak, and the mushrooms I went down into the cellar to retrieve. We worked on automatic pilot each of us immediately taking over a task. It was Terry who browned the meat and the mushrooms while Maude and I did the vegetables and made an excellent cream sauce to be poured over everything.

After dinner was served and eaten, the evening went the way any party usually does. Terry had called the Inn and everything there was fine. Gideon finally sat next to her with his coffee and the two of them whispered on and off for quite some time, while the rest of us just relaxed and chatted about nothing of any great importance.

By nine o'clock everything was cleaned up, put in the dishwasher, the cats were fed and the company left. Harry, Sam, and I just looked at each other. Being of one mind, we took our jackets and climbed the stairs to the Widow's Walk. All was quiet. It even smelled fresh and newly cleaned. There were no leaves there. There was no tug or pull up there at all. We looked at each other smiled, returned downstairs, hugged, and bid each other a peaceful night's sleep.

Once in my room, I plumped up the pillows, tossed off my shoes, ran to the bathroom, washed up, did my teeth carefully, and changed into my nightgown and robe. When I came out, there were the felines ensconced on the bed waiting for me with the biggest grins on their faces. I sat on the bed but did not throw back the covers. Instead, I followed their gazes as their heads turned to my chair by the window.

"You well know I AM Eben, Dr. Emma, and that I too have been blessed by all you did."

"So you are on your way now?" I responded to his comment without hesitation. I think I had been expecting this somewhere in the back of my mind.

"Soon, Doctor Emma Epstein, soon, but not quite yet."

"I have one question, I AM Eben and that is, will we all remember what happened today?"

"To your dying days you and the others will remember and now, because their hearts are open—wide open, they can allow the Divine Joy of being to shine forth. And what is more, it will touch everyone they meet and enhance them whether those people realize it or not. That is how strong this Light is.

"But to answer your question properly, I will be here as long as you are here. You do have a few more weeks before the snow begins and you decide to head back to your home and life there."

I sighed gloriously. I liked this soul. I wanted his company, but when I wanted it, not when he thought it was appropriate and just popped in. I still had not had a real vacation—one where I could do what I wanted to do when I wanted to do it.

"I know your thoughts and I will not bother you. We will make time when the time is ready, Doctor. And yes, you will have your peace and quiet. You most certainly deserve that. Oh, and one more thing, if you wish the felines to accompany you, they will. They have told me so."

I smiled and reached to pet each one of them. "That is really going to be up to them. It is their decision, not mine. This is their home but maybe I will be lucky enough to find two like them in the city! Oh, no!" I said suddenly sitting straight up, "Don't tell me Peaches is pregnant! That only means it is their time to pass on according to the history here and I don't want to be responsible for that!"

"Yowl!!!!!!" was the first response.

"No, they are young yet and have many healthy years ahead of them so do not worry."

"But what about the library and all they have to do there as well as here and Maude and George adore them too!" I countered.

"We will let them choose. Two more will take over the duties at the library and at the Inn and . . . "

"No, I AM Eben. I adore them and it seems to be mutual. But I insist they remain where they are useful. City and apartment life is not for you two," I said showing them mental pictures of my place and life style.

"Chirrup, burp" was their response together. They understood.

"I just stopped in to tell you to sleep well. You did a yeoman's job and tomorrow will be a day of parting and the peace and quiet you crave will be yours." With that said, he disappeared in a flash of subdued light.

All That Matters

I awoke without any alarm at all. It was eight o'clock and everything was quiet. I tiptoed to my door, opened it a crack, but didn't even smell coffee. So . . . I was the first one up—again! Even the felines were still asleep on the bed, curled up together at the foot. Oh well, a woman's job is never done! By the time I'd readied myself and done some of my exercises, but not all, the felines were sitting by the door ready for breakfast. We went out into the hall and downstairs. As soon as I put the coffee up and fed the cats, I grabbed the ladder and went into the living room, placed it by the mantelpiece, and started to climb it. I stood there, I admit with great trepidation, but belief is 100% of the battle and according to everything that occurred yesterday, the mirror should just be a mirror. "YIPPEE!" I screamed at the top of my lungs. All I saw was me—the very same me I'd seen in the bathroom mirror. No untoward lines, at least nothing that had not been there upstairs, nothing in the background; it remained stable.

"What's wrong!" was the shout from upstairs. "Emma, are you alright?" Harry came bounding down the stairs two at a time.

"Nothing's wrong and that's what's so exciting dearest Harry. Come on up and see for yourself. I'll be right here beside you and tell me what you see!" He did as instructed (what a good guy)!

"I . . . I . . . I see me and just me! Oh God, how wonderful! Must call George and Maude and see how they are and then Terry and Gideon, too!" His excitement was so great he missed the last two steps of the ladder bumping his ankle bone, smiled and ran to the phone while I, knowing what was coming next went to prepare a good old fashioned country breakfast, including pancakes, eggs, bacon, ham and yes, even sausages.

I heard Harry on the phone, but I paid no attention to what he said. I was too involved preparing everything. When he came into the kitchen, he filled me in saying all was well with everyone.

"That's all that matters," I said as I handed him a cup of coffee and after a big gulp, he began setting the table and even put out all the necessary condiments.

As soon as the bacon began sizzling, Sam came downstairs smiling broadly. "Good morning, you dear people! Where are those wonderful animals—ah, here they are," he said as they came bounding in from their outside trip. "Oh, you gorgeous creatures, do you know I dreamt about you two? And what a time we had!"

"What did you three do?" I asked just a little jealous.

"We went everywhere on the property together. I saw the playhouse all pristine and neat, and your books and games and that old rocking horse just as you left them. Next we were standing by an old dilapidated shack that stank from fish and there was that I AM Eben person looking all grubby and then that changed and became spanking new and I AM Eben had vanished. And then we went to the graveyard, to the tree in the back, Harry where you and I used to hide behind, and suddenly, all the gravestones looked shiny and were erect! Amazing!" He said this all in just about one breath, and he was talking so fast the giggles hit me right in my solar plexus. "What's with you two?" he asked as Harry also began laughing. We both filled him in—I while flipping pancakes and putting the food on platters and having a high old time. "I guess everything is now cleared up," he continued. "And it looks like you do have a family home after all, Harry. Amazing! That's the word for today. Simply amazing! And we all did our part to clean up this eons old mess!"

Both Harry and I agreed it was amazing and so did the felines by thumping their tails in a delightful circular motion. However, in looking at Harry I knew one thing was not good. But first things first. A hearty breakfast, more coffee, and then we would talk. We all ate as though we were possessed. I even outdid my usual self and made a third batch of pancakes which we three devoured and as a special treat, I also made two more strips of bacon and gave them to the cats who, by now having been completely spoiled and liking people food, inhaled them. The only thought that crossed my mind was, all that matters is that we are satisfied now.

After breakfast, Sam said they should go upstairs and pack, but I suggested we go into the music room for a short while with our coffee. "Not the living room, Em?" Sam asked.

"No, I think we had enough of the living room yesterday and I think a different view is called for, don't you?"

"When you're right, you are right, Em!" he responded graciously and led the way. The morning was one of those wonderful autumnal sparkling ones with crystal clear air—so clear everything outside seemed to join in the crispness, whether it still had leaves or not. We gazed out happy and satisfied until I said, "Ok, Harry, I've known you long enough to know something is not quite right in the 'State of Denmark' so out with it.

"Ok, but don't badger me, either of you. It's Gideon. Terry and I both feel that what went on here yesterday really didn't affect him at all. She did feel some relief when they went their respective ways, but upon reflection, she said he wasn't hostile but overly solicitous which frightened her even more and took her back to the rape. But I did tell her not to worry. He wouldn't be around for another few months and I would ask George to keep an eye on her and on Jess. Somehow she was more worried about Jess then herself."

"Maybe that's because Jess has been acting as her protector every time he's been around, and the time is fast approaching when he will be making a life of his own," Sam said.

"Sounds logical to me," I said, "And there is one more thing to consider even though it wasn't really discussed yesterday, but it was illustrated. We can really only be responsible to ourselves and for ourselves. Yes, we can look after and help others when they ask us to do so, but what we are is what we are and sometimes no matter what's coming down the road in our lives, we don't get it and therefore don't make any changes. All that matters is that we are there for each other when needed.

"I think it's just like raising children or pets. Each individual has his or her own personality quirks and flaws and if they cannot get over what's eating at them, or what they think was given to them when they were born, there's very little we can do except to try to set a good example. I know that seems over simplified, but that's really all that matters—we are here as the wayshowers as was said yesterday, but we are also human." With that, the felines banged their tails harshly showing their disapproval of my summation.

"I think, Emma, that there are those people who are born without consciousnesses and really don't give a hoot for anything else but their own selves. Yes, I know we are allowed to be selfish, but not to the point of harming others and that's where Gideon is at. It's where he's always been. I bet he assumes his namesakes did fine, even killing Maryanne, because it was his family who wanted and needed the riches too. There didn't seem to be any sense of sharing in the HJS who came over here first. And as we all know problems like this within families usually cause great trouble."

"Yes, that sounds right to me, Sam. How do you feel about it HJS?"

"We've all been there in one way or another, I guess. But by not having siblings, I've missed out on the worse parts of family problems I guess. But there were many such problems among the kids at boarding school and most of them, including me, felt we were shipped off there so our parents didn't have to deal with them, and in my case it was due to Gideon."

"Have you ever tried to talk to him?" I asked.

"No, and I really don't want to."

Sam got up and went over to Harry. "Listen old friend, there are a lot of things we don't want to do in our lives but really should, because they have an effect on those we like or love, and whether you know it or not, you are still in love with Terry. And since you are, you should do everything you can do to protect her. Therefore, I strongly suggest that before we leave for the city we drive up to his place. It will only take another day to get home and we can overnight it somewhere, because you need to speak to him." He had placed his hands on Harry's shoulders while he said this so he was turned away from me.

"That's a lovely thought, Sam, but I feel it's not the best idea in the world. I don't trust Gideon either, but I think he must have some time to work things out for himself and besides, I'll still be here for another three to four weeks and I really believe George should be consulted. After all, Gideon is part of his family and you just can't go barging in and slam someone on the head and hope they get it."

"Yeah, you're right, Em. Besides I don't know him and Harry really hates him."

"No, I don't hate him, Sam! I just don't trust him. There is a difference. Now let's go and pack. I want to stop and see if George is around, if not, I'll call him later when I get home." Harry had no sooner said this then the doorbell rang. Sam, already standing, went to get it. "Wonder who that could be, Emma. You know 'The Postman Always Rings Twice'," he said laughing nervously. "I wonder what's going on," he said, getting up and heading for the doorway. He reached it just as Sam came in steadying George who had tears running down his face.

Harry grabbed George's other arm and shoulder and they guided him to the divan where I had been sitting. "George, dear George, what is it? I asked softly thinking something terrible had happened to Maude for without her, he really couldn't exist, not as the George we knew.

They were truly a couple—the unique kind where one really could not live without the other.

"It's Gideon," George sobbed.

"Is he . . . " I couldn't finish the sentence. Horrible pictures crowded my mind; everything from a car crash to suicide to murder.

"He's gone! He left a note to be delivered to me by his neighbor's son Toby. He never said good-bye!" he sobbed. "And Maudie doesn't even know. Today is her day in town!" His sob turned into a wail.

"Do you have the note?" I asked quietly. He reached into his shirt pocket and handed it to me."

"Dear George,

"I have to leave here. After yesterday I cannot stay. Too much has happened. Sent a notice about the tours too, but asked Toby to bring this to you first even though things were sort of out of the way for him. Cannot look anyone in the face any more. Love Terry. Always have. But I really also want to get my hands around her neck and shake her until . . . no, that's not right. Will send you a post when I arrive wherever I decide to alight.

"You and me, we grew up together. We knows one another. I do love you and I know you will be okay. Maude is right for you. Harry and I cannot get along. Never was able to get along with each other.

"This is the right thing to do. Might even understand yesterday. If so, I may come back. Do not worry about me. Going north and west. Far north and west.

"Gideon"

"George, I bet you know now he'll be ok," I said. "Sometimes after we are faced with so much we need time and space away from the family and all involved in order to sort it out."

"Tell you what," Harry chimed in, "I agree completely. And what is more, I know he will be back. You see, George, we cannot stay away from this land forever. It calls us back. Haven't you realized that? Even me! I have to come up at least once a year and now that things have been cleaned up, I can come up more often and I will not be sleeping my time here away as I used to do. This I can promise you." He came over and helped George to stand and then gave him a big hug. "I know how close you two are and you cannot be separated forever. This I can tell you."

George took a very deep breath, pulled out his kerchief and wiped his eyes, blew his nose and closed his eyes. "I'm so sorry you had to see this Doctor Emma. I just didn't know . . . "

"Nothing to be embarrassed about, George," I interrupted him gently. People cry. Men and women alike. Just ask these two! I have seen them both cry before, and probably will again. It is natural. It is a release.

"Yesterday was very heavy as the kids say, and I know none of us has let it seep in yet, although Harry and I can testify that the mirror is clear and the Widow's Walk looks as though it had been whitewashed it's so pristine. All that matters, dear George is that we do not allow anything to deter us from what we have to do now with our lives, and it doesn't even have to be anything big. All that's required of us is just to be and do as we've always done, but the Light that is shining through us will reach all we come in contact with, including the animals and plants. Do you understand? I think Gideon is searching for his true self. It will take some time, but he will find himself and understand it all. His mind is sharp, you know; as sharp as yours, and I bet you two will be in touch with each other very soon. He's just been terribly upset, probably because no one taught him how to work with himself before. Your aunt and uncle never gave him any self-esteem. They probably never even complimented him on any work he did either at home or at school. Am I right?" George nodded vigorously.

"Well then, let him find himself. All that matters is that we do find ourselves; that we find out who we are and what we can do. By doing this, we find our connection to the entire universe as well as this planet and what we do here and what we are going to do here. That really is all that matters.

George turned and gave me a great big hug and a kiss on my cheek. Harry and Sam walked him out, returned and packed their bags and were gone all within half an hour with many promises to call as soon as they arrived home and to stay in touch while I was still at the French Blue House with the White Trim. I knew they meant what they said, but I knew better than to hold my breath until they did call. I waved them off and returned to the kitchen for another cup of my favorite brew. After all, I had two friends waiting for me, and that too, was all that mattered.